Fifth Column

David R Ewens

Grosvenor House
Publishing Limited

This book is published by
Grosvenor House Publishing Ltd
28-30 High Street, Guildford, Surrey, GU1 3EL.
www.grosvenorhousepublishing.co.uk

A CIP record for this book
is available from the British Library

ISBN 978-1-78623-027-0

About the author

David R Ewens worked for many years in the further and adult education sector. He lives and writes in Kent.

Also by David R Ewens in the 'Frank Sterling' series

The Flanders Case
Under the Radar
Rotten

Prologue

The compactly built man in the checked shirt approached the large, dark man at an inner table for two in the first floor café at Waterloo station, and they shook hands. The time on the departure boards said 9.30am. It had been a very early start.

'Long time, Mohamed,' he said.

'Yes, Mike. Too long. Thanks for coming up. I didn't really want to involve you, not after Dubai, but I think my section has been compromised. So you're the only person I can trust. And it's a national emergency.'

'OK,' said the man called Mike. 'Let me get some coffee. Then you'd better put me in the picture.'

When he'd settled down, the big man began his story. 'Seven months ago I penetrated a cell, here in London. I've been in the game for a long time, as you know, but I've not come across anything quite like this before. It's what would popularly be termed a terrorist group, but it has no religious or ideological affiliations, and it seems to be for hire. Its members are diverse. The overall leader is a Bosnian Serb and the number two is an Iraqi – a marsh Arab. There are two other Ma'dan, a couple from the Balkans, and some British men – mainly from up north. One of them I'm pretty sure got mixed up in it by mistake. I haven't had time to find out any more about the parent structure or other cells. You know how it works – one bit of the organisation has no knowledge of any other.

'I do know this: there's an event planned on the south coast, what the media would call a terrorist attack. From the little I've gathered, my cell is meant to be supporting the one actually carrying out the attack. The details are on these memory sticks – I think.' The man called Mohamed showed the small rectangular blocks as if they were a poker hand and handed one over. 'I don't know for sure because I didn't have time to do more than copy them. I've password-protected them but it's nothing you haven't the capability to crack. I've added a rendezvous to yours – disguised, but not difficult for you to work out. The codebook for the main details is Muhsin Mahdi's 1984 edition of *One Thousand and One Nights*. I think at least two of us are needed to thwart the attack, but if I don't make it to the rendezvous at least you have the chance to take things forward,' – he paused for a moment, and shifted uncomfortably in his seat – 'or the other way round,' he said softly. 'You can't let this fall into the wrong hands.'

'So we rendezvous somewhere on the south coast, but if one of us doesn't make it, the other can carry on. It's all a bit muddled, Mohamed.'

'I know. It's a mess. I've been under pressure. This is the best I can come up with. If you don't want to carry on, now's the time to go.'

'No, I'm in. You wouldn't have contacted me if it wasn't really serious, and I wouldn't have come up in the first place.'

The briefing, including questions and answers, continued. The men's heads grew closer together to reflect the intensity and urgency of the conversation.

Then the man called Mohamed stopped. His neck stiffened as he looked out over the concourse.

'It's worse than I thought, Mike. We're out of time. My cover's blown.'

Mike followed the big man's gaze. At the entrance to the station, a group of about twelve men appeared and fanned out.

'I've left this life behind, Mohamed,' Mike said. 'I'm out of practice. So nothing's guaranteed.' He paused. He'd thought of something. 'If I don't meet you, I might arrange a replacement.'

'Becky?' said Mohamed.

'No, not her. Let's keep my wife out of it. Frank Sterling. Remember the name. Frank Sterling.'

Mohamed nodded. 'We must go, Mike. See you soon, my friend, inshaa'Allah.'

He left the table and disappeared down the stairs, reappearing a short while later on the concourse. Mike moved to the window and watched. Mohamed seemed to approach two young men in jeans and anoraks, and Mike saw a wad of money being flashed, and a short, intense conversation. The young men exchanged nods and shrugs. Then they grabbed Mohamed's arms and frogmarched him towards the Waterloo Road exit and out of sight. To an untrained observer it would have looked as though the young men had made all the running in the brief incident.

Mike watched three men, who had been converging on Mohamed from the open doorway of a newsagent's on the concourse, hold back, in a state of confusion. One listened intently to the mobile at his ear as he looked up to the balcony. He placed a restraining hand on the arm of the man next to him. Then the whole group stopped and withdrew. From above, a tall man with long dark hair looked down like a prophet surveying the multitudes beneath him, one hand on the railing, the other also holding a mobile to his ear.

Mike got up, strode swiftly to the back of the café and pressed on through the emergency exit, ignoring the baristas' startled glances. He scurried down the dirty, narrow stairs, onto the concourse and out of an obscure back entrance of the station. At Waterloo East station, reached by a circuitous route of little-used stairs, tunnels and covered walkways, he timed his arrival on Platform C just as the Sandley train, via Ashtonleigh and Dovethorpe, pulled in. But boarding the train at the first carriage right at the far end of the platform, his rusty field craft let him down. At the other end, a young, wiry man in jeans and bomber jacket slipped on unseen just as the doors were closing.

Chapter 1

'Hell's bells, Mike, where did you come from?' said Sterling.

Mike Strange put a slender forefinger to his thin lips and edged over to the window behind Sterling's desk. Flattened hard against the wall, he peered sideways down into Sandley's narrow main square. 'We've got about two minutes,' he said softly, 'perhaps less. You're going to have two principal advantages. You're resourceful, and you know the terrain. They don't.'

'What on earth…?'

Strange put his hand up. 'You need to be quiet and listen, Frank. There are some people after me – determined people – and they've caught up with me. They think I've gone in the library downstairs. There'll be blokes out the back in case I try the fire door. When I don't come out, never mind the fuss, never mind Angela objecting, they're going to come in for me. Can you get out other than by your stairs?'

'Through the window at the back of the landing, across the gap between the roofs and down a hooped ladder thing at the back of the Thai restaurant. You could do that yourself. We could go together.'

Sterling looked at his friend, the landlord at his local, backup in a couple of his cases, the man with a shadowy security service past. Normally, Mike Strange was neatly

1

and precisely turned out in a checked shirt, pressed jeans and desert boots kind of way. Now, the signs of distress were plain – the scuffs on his shoes, the shirt front half-hanging over his trousers, but most starkly of all, the unkempt hair and hunted look in his eyes.

'Won't work, Frank. There are about twelve of them after me. I'm your decoy. I can stall them for a short while until you can get away.' He looked at Sterling – a calculating, appraising look – and Sterling saw something like reassurance flit over his friend's features.

'So, I'm your decoy,' Strange said again. 'And you've got the baton.' He slipped a small white envelope onto Sterling's desk. 'There's a memory stick in there, password-protected but accessible for someone of your… resourcefulness. Where's your bag?' He nodded when Sterling produced his small emergency backpack from under the desk and held it up. 'I don't know much about this, Frank. There's been no time to get in and work out what's on it. But something bad's going to happen. And now, you're the only person who can stop it.'

'Whoa, Mike, this is mad. I'm not ready…'

'From what I can gather, you need to head south and maybe west. Definitely south and west. Got it? There'll be a rendezvous, details on the stick, and then something else, something much bigger. The man you'll meet is good, but sometimes… untrustworthy, so watch it. If you miss him, the codebook is Mahdi's *One Thousand and One Nights*. Right, time for us to go.'

Sterling looked at the proffered hand. 'Things must be bad,' he said.

The last Frank Sterling, private investigator, saw of his friend was his head and back, as Strange padded off down the rickety stairs to his fate in and beyond the library.

Sterling took a deep breath. Just then, nothing made sense, but he was savvy enough to realise already that this wasn't a game.

After what Strange had said, there was no point in looking out of the office window into the square, and it was probably too dangerous anyway. Sterling closed and locked the door, hooked his bag onto his back and stepped across the bare landing to the sash window at the rear. The catch squeaked as he eased it around, and the lower panel inched upwards only through firm pressure. He had to keep the panel vertically lined up or it snagged lopsidedly in the grooves on either side. His beating heart had added a tremor to his hands that made him clumsy. Adrenaline was for flight, not fiddly small tasks. He bumped the top of the sash with his head and then the bag as he ducked through and onto the channel between the roofs. Although he closed the window, a sharp-eyed pursuer might notice the opened catch on the inside, but Sterling couldn't do anything about that. He edged along the channel to the end and then at right angles onto a narrow ledge with guttering that led to the Thai restaurant next to the library. This was his designated fire escape route, but he'd never needed it before. Moss, mould and slime underfoot made him cautious. He wasn't too bad with heights – enclosed spaces spooked him more – but he didn't want to let Mike down by falling off and breaking a leg only a few seconds into his commission.

The hooped ladder clanged as Sterling slipped into the small courtyard of the restaurant. It was eleven o'clock – a quiet time before the lunchtime rush, but anyway, Priawh and her family knew him well enough, and what he did, so they'd have been ready to accept an explanation

– an emergency, a small fire… The door into a small covered passageway was unlocked and he slipped through unaccosted. He paused in the gloom. The bricks on either side were damp, and a strange aromatic blend of exotic cooking and mouldiness infiltrated his nostrils. Everything had happened so quickly and it felt far-fetched. He needed to think. He leant against the cool wall.

Mike Strange wasn't the type to mess about, so it certainly wasn't a hoax. He didn't really do humour. His wife, Becky, also an ex-member of a never-disclosed branch of the British security services, balanced things out in that department. Mike was more of a literalist. He was an action man too. When Sterling had been in trouble in Flanders, it was Mike who had done the rescue and got him back in good order to England, and likewise provided key help and support both in the Bawdsey radar case and the viper's nest of Earlsey Tech. He was loyal and straight, and if he said something was so, it was so.

But there was something else – something much less comforting – the fact that Mike, coolness and competence personified, was clearly rattled and dishevelled. It meant that the people after him were skilled, and if they had hunted down the resourceful and expert Mike Strange, what chance did Sterling have? He would have liked to consult his friend Angela Wilson, who ran the library beneath his office. She'd talk sense, but he knew that was out of the question. He tightened the grip on his backpack and edged to the end of the passageway. There was no choice – it was south and west for him, as directed.

Strange had given Sterling a bit of time. He'd slip out of Market Street past his office, down No Name Street and across the road to the Guildhall, where the buses left from, and get one south to Deeping. He'd find out about the 'baton' on the way. But before that, some reconnaissance. As he peered left out of the passageway, his heart lurched. Although he expected to see something, it was still a shock to find two men stationed on one of the forks out of Market Street, and two on the other. Glancing right, he made out another at the other end, and, most morale-sapping of all, one at the bottom of Milk Alley, almost opposite his office and next to Freddie Henderson's greengrocers. Every exit from the little square was covered. Well, perhaps not every exit...

He'd stick to his original plan. With luck, the people after Strange had not yet picked him up from the library, or they'd taken him but knew nothing of his meeting with Sterling. Sterling adjusted the bag on his shoulder and set off past his office. He was just someone finished with a bit of business in Sandley and strolling out of the commercial centre of town – maybe to go back home on the outskirts, maybe to go to the old cattle market car park beyond the Guildhall to get his car, or maybe to catch a bus in front of the Tourist Information office. He tried to adopt a nonchalant manner, but felt wooden and awkward as if he was in front of a camera.

The wiry young man in jeans and bomber jacket at the link between Market Street and No Name Street had a mobile phone glued to his ear. He was pacing back and forth on the pavement in a short two-metre pattern, and getting increasingly agitated. When Sterling was five metres away on the same pavement, the man looked up, straight at him. In his small, sharp eyes something flickered.

The bus stop at the Guildhall was instantly out of the question. So was Milk Alley. So were all the other exits.

Sterling stopped, checked the road and plunged over it and off into the churchyard. It wasn't even a change of plan – just a visceral reaction to what he knew was imminent danger. Who dares wins – he had his first slice of luck when he heard the squeal of brakes and furious beeping of a horn and glanced back as the young man with sharp eyes leapt back from in front of a large white Range Rover. With a few seconds' start, Sterling scuttled around the path by the side of the church and up to the gap between the ancient flint walls at the St Peter's Street end. The young man would be close behind, perhaps at the point of the path just around the corner of the church, only marginally held up by phoning his associates to alert them to Sterling's escape.

There was an odd hissing sound and then a puff. Just by Sterling's hand, dust rose into the clear, bright, April air and a piece of flint from the wall spun jerkily away. *Christ*. He was closer than Sterling imagined. And wasn't that a gun with a silencer? Sweat pricked up all over Sterling's frame as he ducked to the right of the wall and momentarily out of sight.

You know the terrain. They don't. Sterling needed to use that now. Almost opposite was Holy Ghost Alley, one of the narrow passages that led through to the High Street near the barbican on the quay. He slipped into that and walked briskly down the narrow twists and turns. His pursuer would surely not be far behind. The young man with sharp eyes would reach St Peter's Street, find no sign of Sterling in either direction, see the entrance to the alleyway and conclude that it was as likely an escape route as any other.

The young man's associates would be monitoring all traffic, foot and vehicle, around the centre of the town.

Sterling knew he couldn't just walk out of here. He had to find another way of slipping the net. As he burst out of Holy Ghost Alley just by the Masonic Lodge, it came to him. The river. But first he had to get away. He turned left towards the barbican, the old toll bridge and the river. Escape from here was too obvious. Instead, a few metres along he turned left again up Seven Post Alley, doubling back up to St Peter's Street. He felt himself getting more assured and confident after the initial shocks, and the fact that the entrance to this second alley was barely visible even from the other side of the road gave him heart.

At the mouth of the alley, a slit in the middle of St Peter's Street, Sterling again stopped and peered out, and, as he did, listened for footsteps behind him, which would be amplified by the narrow brick walls. Just at that moment, it was all clear. He turned right for a few metres down St Peter's Street and then turned right again into Three Kings Yard. This was the trickiest bit. He felt a nag of doubt overlaying his fear. Although the end of this alley went into a sharp bend and ended up in the Strand and not the High Street, perhaps he was being too clever. Winding back and forth and doubling back twice might just lead him into the arms of the people after him. But he needed to get to the river further down from the quay and this was the best option.

In the Strand there were thirty risky metres before he could get into the bend that hid the pavement from people looking down it from the town. He scurried past the Beach Hut Café, a favourite lunchtime destination, waving distractedly as Cherry Smith, the owner, looked out and recognised him. Twenty metres, ten metres... at every moment he expected a shout, a flurry of running feet, perhaps even another silenced gunshot. He felt his sphincter relaxing. 'Not now,' he muttered as he strove to get a grip, and succeeded... for the moment. Then he was around the bend and out of sight. He passed a few Georgian town houses, and on the opposite side of the road St Mary's Church, adapted now for concerts and other community events. He contemplated ducking in there to draw breath and look at the envelope Mike Strange had passed onto him. There'd be a bit of peace and quiet, but on the other hand he'd lose time and was scared he might be cornered. He plunged on and then stumbled right into the car park at Bazen Salts, abutting the river half a mile upstream from Sandley's main quay.

The warren of Sandley's central medieval grid would have left the pursuing strangers completely confused. Although for the moment he was out in the open, Sterling felt safer than he had since the adventure started.

Some of the riverbank on the Sandley side was partitioned off by temporary metal fencing panels with stabilisers. Behind it, workmen in hi-vis jackets and safety helmets moved around on the nearly completed flood defences. A JCB mini-digger with tracks jerked busily about, as if in an old 16mm film, shifting soil towards the new barriers. In the distance upriver, Sterling could see the pharma company complex on which Sandley depended for its economic good health. Next to the car park a man in white overalls on a ladder was painting the eaves of the cricket pavilion, and beyond that Sterling could hear the chirrup of an unidentified bird in the nature reserve. A seagull rested stock-still and hunched up, its beak in its wing feathers, on one leg like a flamingo, in the roped-off cricket square that glinted emerald-green in the sunshine.

Workaday Sandley – but of course it wasn't, not for Mike Strange and not for Sterling. He couldn't waste time on ridiculous contrasts – the ordinariness here and the silent menace behind him. Moving beyond the fencing, he cast his eyes over the river. That's where his salvation lay.

Chapter 2

Sterling would have recognised the irony. Four hundred metres downriver, the Bell and Tower Hotel looked over the Sandley's quayside, and in the balcony suite a man sat on a sofa peeling an apple. His dark-blue suit looked freshly pressed and immaculately cut, and his black shoes shone in the soft hotel light. His manicured hands managed the knife and apple deftly. A napkin rested next to the plate onto which the peel unfurled in one unbroken roll. Although he was elegant, his jowls and neck were thick and his frame stocky.

Another man, tall, thin and fierce, with a long Middle Eastern face and bright, dark eyes, stood with his hands behind his back, his back to the window. His black hair fell over his collar, and his dark beard covered his neck. A suit hung loosely from his narrow body and his shoes were worn and scuffed.

'Go on, Irfan,' said the seated man.

'We've picked up the man Strange,' said Irfan Zahra. 'We had to… subdue him on the way to the van until we could get him to the secure base. We've found nothing on him so far. But…'.

The senior man, Kurjak, paused from peeling his apple and looked up.

'… We thought he went into the town library. Now we think he went upstairs – there's a small office up there

– to a private detective. Strange may have known this man.' Zahra blinked and coughed. Behind his back his hands twisted. 'Strange could have passed the package on.'

The senior man tossed the apple and knife onto the plate. The peel broke. 'But you don't know,' he said.

'The detective was not there when we went up,' said Zahra. 'Rashad thinks he went out by a window at the back. By the time he phoned the others in the street, the man was getting away. Nevin spotted him.' Zahra found something on the ceiling that required his attention. 'You know that Nevin can be a bit of a hothead. He fired his gun in the churchyard.'

'Spotted him. Fired his gun,' sighed the senior man. 'Speak to Nevin. We can't afford an incident.'

'This town is like a souk. All the alleys and small streets.' Now there was something interesting in the carpet.

'So he got away. What's his name, this man?'

'Frank Sterling. We don't know anything about him.'

'Have Asif find out. Put a cordon around the town. Find a picture and circulate his details to all the followers. When Strange is ready, begin the interrogation.'

'All these things are in hand, Excellency.'

'Good. We don't have long, Irfan. There can be no mistakes.' Kurjak picked up the apple and knife and resumed his peeling. Zahra withdrew from the suite, went down the corridor and then unlocked and entered a more modest room towards the back of the building.

A slight young man wearing an outsized pair of black-framed spectacles and headphones was hunched over a laptop open on the small desk at the window. Instead of the river, the view was of the brick wall of the house next to the hotel. Electrical equipment lay in various states of assembly and use around the room, which, together with the figure at the laptop, gave an impression of a teenager's set-up without the pop-star wall posters.

'Anything?' said Zahra.

The young man took a headphone from one of his ears and propped it on the scalp above. 'He's disappeared. No one has seen him. He might have ducked into one of the houses near the square, but Nevin didn't think he'd have time to knock and get in.'

'Who is he, Asif?'

'Well it's weird,' said the young man. 'He's a private investigator, but he hasn't got a website. You'd think, in this day and age…'.

'What else, Asif?'

The young man refocused on the screen. 'We know where his office is. I've found out where he lives, which is close by, but he couldn't get to that because we'd blocked the roads off – unless there's a back way, which I don't think there is.' Pictures flashed up, as if to demonstrate the hermetic nature of Market Street. 'He's had one or two high-profile cases.' Pictures of Sandley were replaced by newspaper reports, some local, one or two national. 'He helped a girl in a wheelchair to find her grandmother's killer and ruined a small electronic communications company in the process. He smashed a kind of criminal gang operating in a college about twelve miles from here. It looks like someone has ghosted a story of his cases.'

'Credit cards? Facebook? Mobile number? Car? Car especially. We can't let him get out of here.'

'It doesn't look like he's got a car.' Asif looked at the tall, fierce, scruffy man. 'This is one odd bloke, brother.

Lives and works locally, no web presence to speak of. No car. How can he run a detective business?'

The tall man Zahra frowned. 'Maybe that's how. Keep looking, and update me regularly.'

The young man readjusted his headphones and turned back to the laptop.

Zahra eased softly from the room, padded along the corridor and slipped down the stairs to the car park at the back of the hotel. He got in his car and headed out to the bridge over the river to Earlsey, nodding to his men stationed on the quay, who formed part of the cordon around the town.

Beyond former RAF married quarters, a sign on the right indicated half a mile to Stonham quay and Stonham café further down on the river. Zahra kept going, driving sedately past Averton Generator Hire, and then Stonham Garage, with its eclectic collection of aging cars in front of the servicing shop, optimistically priced even to Zahra, who took no interest in such things. Pride of place was taken by a top-of-the-range yellow Saab coupé whose dilapidation even a wax and clean could not disguise. Just after a printworks and a shed construction business, Eagle Sheds, and before the pharma plant and offices began, he turned right into a compound once designed for making fireworks. He pulled the silver Mercedes around the front administration block, where the 'Cosmo Pyrotechnics Limited' sign was still faintly legible above the warped, decaying fascia, and parked in a space hidden from the road, next to a large black Ford van with tinted windows at the front and no windows at all at the back.

It hadn't been difficult to 'hire' one of the brick blockhouses in the compound for the few days it was required. There had been no talk of contracts in the telephone conversation with the letting agent. Zahra had sent a British subordinate with the cash, and the young man had come back with the key to the gates and the blockhouse. If he'd given it any thought, Zahra would have concluded that the hefty roll of money, an eyebrow-raising amount for such a short time, would stay in the agent's pocket and go nowhere near the site owner. Cash, a lot but not too much, eroded curiosity. No paper trail meant that if anything went wrong, the agent could deny all knowledge and responsibility. It was the same the world over, in the developed world or in any failed state. There were rules, and the rules were circumvented by money and negotiation.

As he reclosed the galvanised steel gate, Zahra looked calmly over to the road. Three hikers in sturdy boots, one with a hiking stick, marched resolutely past in broken step towards Sandley, hunched over under the weight of their rucksacks. At the generator hire outfit, a forklift truck darted busily back and forth in front of the plant entrance, shifting materials in a pattern that was hard to fathom.

Zahra walked around the corner to one of the blockhouses at the back. That each was separate, so accidental explosions during firework making would be isolated and contained, was useful to him. He rapped softly on the solid wooden door, waiting and watching as the sun glinted on Stonham lake, an expanse of water between the industrial-pharma complex and the river, and a ruffled-looking black bird with a wide wing span and a long neck drifted down and splash-landed. It was good that it was a weekday, and therefore there was no activity at the sailing club over the fence and on the far shore.

A burly, pale-skinned man with a long beard like

Zahra's and a slight cast to his small eyes opened up and peered out through the sliver between door and jamb, recognising Zahra and stepping aside so he could enter.

When Cosmo Pyrotechnics moved their manufacturing to the Philippines, they stripped their premises of everything. The blockhouse, about the size of an average sitting room but with a higher ceiling, was completely windowless. The concrete floor, a dull grey-white, was empty apart from a solid wooden chair with arms like a primitive throne against a wall, a structure in the shape of an operating table in the middle of the room, and various pieces of equipment clustered in one of the far corners – plastic jerrycans of water; some groceries; cushions and mattresses; a couple of folding chairs. Light in the dark, musty, damp room came from a mixture of cargo and trawler lamps dotted around the room in each corner, the electric power supply having long gone. There was an atmosphere of hurry and improvisation.

Zahra approached the hooded man slumped in the chair, bound to it by his arms and legs. 'When will he come round?' he said, turning his head. A fourth man approached from the other corner of the room, his shadows from each of the lamps long and short, sharp and blurred, and all overlapping.

'Soon,' said the man. He was as tall as Zahra and had the same build. His face had a hangdog air, and his eyes were expressionless.

'We don't have much time. Speed it up. I don't care how.'

The man went over to the chair, removed the hood, pulled Strange's hair back and slapped him hard on each cheek. Strange's head lolled and his eyes fluttered as he came to.

'He's ready,' said the hangdog man twenty minutes later.

Zahra took the dusty folding chair he'd been sitting on and carried it over in front of the tied-up man.

'You know what we want, Mr Strange.'

Strange turned towards him with a faraway look in his still-glazed eyes. A snail's trail of spittle, tinged pink with blood, crawled down the side of his mouth.

'Don't make us go onto the next stage, Mr Strange. We know all about CIA methods – from personal experience – and how effective they are. Two simple questions to begin: Where are the instructions that were stolen from us? And of course, closely linked to that, where is the renegade Mohamed Husain?'

'I… I don't have a clue what you're talking about. I just run a pub.'

'Don't insult us, Mr Strange. We know your background in British Intelligence. We know about your service here in Europe and in the Middle East. We even know about your previous… encounter… with interrogation. They say you can only go through it once, twice at most. Any more, and, well, things fall apart. The trembling, the nightmares, the bouts of sweating, the fear of enclosed spaces. Every kind of fear that never goes away.'

'I'm just a publican.'

'Enough,' said Zahra. 'We suspected Mohamed Husain. We watched him meet you at Waterloo station. We even know what you ordered in the coffee shop. It was clever of Husain to lose his brothers, but we did not lose you – all the way back to this insignificant little town. I could show you the footage. Be sensible, Mr Strange.' Zahra got up from the folding chair, leaned against the wall next to the tied-up man and clasped his hands. 'I could go over the river and fetch your wife,' he said softly. 'OK, the pub is shut up right at this moment, but we could just wait. You'd not be the only one who would suffer.'

Strange tipped his head forward. A very astute observer might have seen the downturn of lips and flicker of eyes – the very briefest of tells, immediately hidden.

Zahra sighed. 'We have no more time, Mr Strange.' He nodded to the jailer-torturers. Roughly, the two of them undid the bindings and dragged Strange, writhing and struggling, to the table-board in the middle of the room, onto which they re-strapped him on his back. Zahra's lip curled as he found himself compelled to assist in subduing the prisoner.

Hangdog man tilted the table-board about twenty degrees using a ratchet device under the board at Strange's feet so that his face dropped down. Strange emitted a loud, low moan – memory-laden and full of dread – which was immediately absorbed by the thick brick walls.

Squint-eyed man took a cloth like a tea towel, thoroughly steeped it in water and laid it over Strange's face. The moan turned into a kind of whimper. Strange's body convulsed as he wrestled with the binding on his arms and legs.

Hangdog man acknowledged Zahra's nod and started pouring water from a jerrycan over the cloth on Strange's face. The water saturated the cloth and almost immediately, Strange gagged and jerked on the board. The torturer's lips moved as he counted the seconds. After twenty, he stopped pouring and removed the cloth. The other torturer checked Strange's mouth for signs of vomit from stomach into lungs, whilst Strange continued to jerk and convulse, his eyes staring wildly.

Zahra loomed over him and spoke softly. 'No more "I just run a pub", Mr Strange. Answer the questions and it all stops. Where is the memory stick? Did you give it to the private detective Frank Sterling?'

Strange nodded vigorously.

'Did you open it?'

'I tried to – on the train back to Sandley,' said Strange hoarsely. 'But it was password-protected. I didn't have time or tools to get in... I swear.'

'What did you tell the man Sterling?'

'Get out of Sandley and sort it out.'

'Where did you tell him to go?'

'North. London. That's where Mohamed Husain still is.'

'Ah. Mohamed Husain. Yes, I was coming back to him. London is a big place, Mr Strange.'

'I don't know any more than that. I knew him from... before. He found out where I was and contacted me. I agreed to meet him in Waterloo. I didn't want to know where he was staying. It was safe that way... safer for me.' Strange was speaking quickly now. His voice had acquired a quaver and its pitch was higher.

In the background, hangdog man let drips from the jerrycan splash on the hard, cold floor.

Zahra asked a few more questions, and Strange replied in the same half-panicky way, and then the interrogator motioned to squint-eyed man to join him at the door. 'For the moment, keep him tied up and conscious,' Zahra said under his breath. 'Take no chances. We'll need to ask him more questions. What happens after that... well, we'll see. I'm going to check on progress in the town.'

Squint-eyed man nodded and unbolted the heavy door, and Zahra stepped out into the spring air, narrowing his eyes to the brightness after the gloom within. Over on Stonham Lake, the black-feathered bird had gone. So had the man Sterling and the renegade Mohamed Husain – for the moment. Zahra scowled and walked to his car.

Chapter 3

Along the riverbank there seemed few possibilities. Perhaps a river-borne escape was not such a good idea after all. Sterling cast his eye over the motley collection of yachts, cruisers, barges and tubs moored on his side. It wasn't those that piqued his interest so much as any tenders that might be attached to them. What he was looking for had to be something sturdy, and not in bad nick, preferably a rubber dinghy with an outboard. He spotted something, attached to a fifteen-metre-long boat apparently designed to look like a miniature steamship, or even a small ironclad. He stole a glance right and left. It was lunchtime on Friday, and there was no one in the car park behind him or on the boats in the river below. The workmen on the flood barriers were busy on their duties. Sterling hopped over the new red-brick flood defence wall and approached the ironclad. The tender wasn't a rubber dinghy, but otherwise met his criteria, and there was a bonus – as well as an outboard, rowlocks were fitted and oars lined the gunwales. He stepped from bank to boat and wobbled as it bobbed underneath him.

He'd noticed before that the tide was going out, and that would suit him very well. Sandley quay and the town behind it were situated at the base of a watery horseshoe. The river came down from Cantcester in the northwest and then looped back on itself and into the North Sea at Pegsill Bay four miles up to the northeast. It was better for him to go with the current four miles north and east to the sea rather than north and west up to the old power station and Roman fort the same distance the other way. Then, if he chose, he could hug the coast and go south to Deeping and beyond. He freed the painter and used an oar to poke the boat away from the bank. It was best – quieter and less conspicuous – to start the outboard when he was out of sight of Sandley around the bend, using the oars first. Clumsily, he fumbled them into the rowlocks and paddled the left one to turn the boat in the right direction. He felt a surge of optimism. He knew the terrain and was thinking creatively. If he kept calm, this could go well – this bit anyway. He couldn't remember the last time he'd rowed, but the knack came back easily. The danger point was coming up as he approached the bridge that joined Sandley and the barbican at the end to the Isle of Earlsey. If the men hunting him decided to look outward from their cordon, and not into the town…

The combination of oars and current made progress downriver satisfyingly quick. As he hunched over, facing in the opposite direction and glancing occasionally to the bow to avoid collisions, he caught sight of a silver Mercedes coming over the bridge from Earlsey. In the damp, dark arch he heard the car above him. On the other side, by the barbican, two men loitered casually, looking along the quay to the east and down the High Street to the south. If they turned to the river and spotted him, there wasn't much they could do – except shoot him of course – but even then it was broad daylight, there was a tidy bustle of people about and he had something they probably needed. He looked down into the bottom of the boat where a small puddle vibrated above the current. The ostrich act – avoidance of eye contact as the boat made its way into the strangers' line of vision below the quayside – was strangely comforting.

Just before the bend took him out of sight, he couldn't resist looking up to Sandley. There was no one running along the path extending from the quayside before it veered off inland. No one was frantically jabbering into a mobile and looking downriver. There were no shouts and gesticulations – only the gentle slapping of the water on the hull, the dull methodical splash of the oars, and the tinkling Greensleeves tune of an ice cream van, getting fainter by the minute as the van came onto the quay from Knightrider Street and parked by the jetty.

Then Sterling could no longer see the town at all. On his left, the land stretched off towards the sea coast beyond the northernmost jut of the golf course. On his right, in the river's horseshoe, a series of ramshackle boatyards, jetties and ramps, complete with another gallimaufry of vessels, clung untidily to the river between the mudflats emerging as the tide continued to edge out. Sterling had to work hard to keep the boat on course through the kinks and bends that would finally end at the North Sea three and a half miles ahead.

Now it was time to take stock and get the outboard working. He aimed for the jetty that he was next approaching, and the boat bumped awkwardly against the old tyres suspended over the side. He only just managed to stow the right oar in time before impact, which bounced him out of his seat and almost caused him to lose the other oar. 'Jesus Christ,' he said, but then, realising what he'd managed, a wave of euphoria swept over him. Mike Strange had made the right choice for handing over the baton. Sterling had been resourceful, and self-congratulation blended with exhilaration. But as the boat bumped and chafed against the jetty, other thoughts and questions began to jostle, principally, 'What next?'

Through a gap between a dilapidated boatshed and a rusting hulk supported on a crisscross of boat stands he could see the old Cosmo Pyrotechnics sign high at the back of the compound, and beyond it the pharma company. He knew that Stonham Lake was between the boatyard and the industrial park beyond.

He weighed the options. He could abandon the tender here, and with it the idea of a sea trip south, but then he could only make his way back to Sandley by road through Stonham, coming out at the junction just before the bridge back into the town. What was the point of that? It was just back towards the lion's den. On the east side of the river, opposite the jetty, there was no mooring and no easy climb up the bank. From memory, the country that side was difficult, full of ditches, dykes and scree until up to the golf course – and it was still pretty close to the town.

It looked as if his original plan was still the best – into the sea at Pegsill Bay and then south, hugging the coastline. The outboard looked old but in pristine condition. He hadn't used one before, but helpfully the starting instructions were on a plate on the casing. 'Shift lever to neutral,' he muttered as he searched. 'Engine probably cold, so choke out a bit... Turn hand grip on throttle to start setting...'. He was flummoxed for a moment and then found it. 'Find resistance on start rope... and then PULL.' The motor turned over and did not catch, but on the third jerk, it whined into life. 'Houston, we're go.' Sterling experimented with the hand throttle and then eased the boat back into the river. As he slipped the shift lever to 'Forward' the dinghy picked up speed and his euphoria returned.

The boat glided serenely along while Sterling experimented with the throttle and the steering. He calculated that it was about three miles into the bay. The fumes from the pharma plant came down on the wind – sulphurous and irritating on the back of his throat. Then the plant itself hove into view on the north bank, a vast proliferation of silvery pipes and scaffold and tanks and chimneys glinting and glittering in the sunshine, emitting an enormous belch of chemicals from behind the dark-green metal fencing that was topped with barbed wire and encroached right up to the waterside. On the other side, nature held full sway as an egret flew languidly from a reed bed and Sterling saw other birds amongst the mudflats – cormorants and waders – that he had not seen for years.

Up ahead and around a bend, he could hear the regular ticking-over of an approaching boat engine and then the boat itself appeared. He recognised it straight away – the Orca – run by Captain Barry Cavendish, the Sandley harbour-master, who ran tourists from the quay to see the grey seal colony up at Pegsill. Captain Cavendish, usually known as CC or Cap, was an occasional drinking companion in Mike Strange's pub, the Cinque Port Arms – a cheerful, witty, profane man with a fund of stories about Sandley quay, the river and the startling things tourists got up to. It didn't seem to matter if some of them were apocryphal, and were changed or exaggerated in the telling and retelling.

Sterling hadn't realised how large the Orca was when it was moored at Sandley quay. Now he did, as it bore down on him. He swung the outboard handle violently to the left and the dinghy sheered dutifully to the right.

'What the f...' shouted Captain Cavendish as he saw the obstacle in the middle of the river as he rounded the bend. 'Strewth.' His head, and the yachting cap with Sandley's coat of arms above the peak, ducked out of sight below the Orca's garish blue and white striped canopy and a moment afterwards the engine went into a reverse whine, churning up turbid, grey, muddy water underneath it. The bump of the collision, the bow of the Orca against the middle of the dinghy, was enough to send Sterling sprawling, but enough momentum had been lost by both boats that there was little obvious damage.

'You bloody idiot,' bellowed Cavendish, 'why weren't you on the starboard side? Don't you know the rules of the sea? Jesus.' He shook his head. 'Unbelievable.'

Sterling picked himself up from the bottom of the dinghy. 'Oops,' he said. He smiled slyly. 'Sorry, Cap.'

'Frank,' said Cavendish. 'Frank bloody Sterling. I might have guessed.' But the smile hadn't mollified him yet. 'What the fucking hell are you doing on the wrong side of the fucking river in Jimmy Heselthwaite's dinghy, heading out to sea?'

Sterling weighed his choices. He could be vague and come up with a cock and bull story about a short expedition to practise his boat craft, with Jimmy's blessing of course. Or something. Or he could tell the truth, or an abridgement of it, and hope that he could rely on Cavendish's discretion. There was no choice really. The man wasn't stupid.

'I'm kind of on the lam, Cap. I had to get out of Sandley, and this was the only way available at the time.'

'Does Jimmy know you've got his boat?'

Sterling made a face. 'No. I'm looking after it though. It's not nicking, it's borrowing.'

'Without him knowing,' stated Cavendish.

'Emergency,' countered Sterling.

'Well, I suppose I know all about your emergencies, Frank. Your various cases have put Sandley on the map.'

'And this is another one, Cap. Look, if you could tell Jimmy Heselthwaite I've got his boat and it's OK, that would be great. If there's any damage, I'll pay for it. I'm not going far, just away from Sandley by unexpected means, as it were.' Talk of the boat and damage triggered a thought. Who was going to pay for his time and effort on this little jaunt – and danger money for that matter? He remembered the puff of flint in St Peter's churchyard. A gunshot and a chase in sleepy Sandley.

Something changed in Captain Cavendish's sceptical face. 'Well, you're an honest enough bloke…'. He seemed to be getting in the spirit of it. 'All right, I'll tell Jimmy. The weather's going to continue like this, Frank, so it won't be rough, but there'll be a bit more wind from the northeast when you get out in the bay. Where are you heading for?'

'South', blurted Sterling, 'towards Deeping.' He should have said north to Ramston, and kicked himself inwardly. A little white lie, a little misinformation would have offered a larger sliver of protection, covering his tracks for longer and ensuring that Cavendish wasn't put in danger by knowing too much.

'Deeping, then,' said the other man. 'Well, with the

wind and tide where they are, it will be a bit choppy out of the bay. You're competent with the boat?'

'Sure,' lied Sterling. *Christ*, he thought, *I don't even know the right side of the channel to keep to.*

Cavendish raised his eyebrows. He seemed to have the same view. 'Don't go too far from shore. As much as possible, don't go side-on to the waves – zigzagging might be best. You'll be all right when you get in the downs. Here.' He rummaged in his boat and came up with a life jacket. 'Just in case.'

'Cheers, Cap,' said Sterling. 'Keep mum and when it's over I'll tell you all about it over a pint.'

'Deal. Right, cast off. Good luck. And Frank… keep to the right side of the fucking channel. Got it? Right. That's starboard.'

Sterling raised his arm and puttered away.

Chapter 4

'Anything?'

'No, brother, nothing.'

Zahra had been around the whole cordon and though some of his men had been talkative, some optimistic, some pessimistic, some engaged, that was the basic message from all of them. He'd still barely got used to the medieval centre with its alleyways and crooked streets – the benefits of and rationale for the old layout forgotten centuries ago. He was reminded again of a souk. In addition to the inner cordon, he'd stationed the rest of his group at all the roads out of the town – to Deeping and Dovethorpe to the south, to Earlsey across the bridge, to Cantcester to the west, to Woodnesbrook to the southwest, to Sandley Bay to the east.

Asif had been busy. Each watcher had the most recent available picture of Sterling, high-quality colour prints, and press cuttings of his previous exploits for context. Zahra looked at his own copy, as if there was a clue in the determined, sardonic face. He and his group had caught the professional, Mike Strange – not easily, not that quickly, but they'd got him. Why was Frank Sterling becoming more of a challenge?

One of the men on the quay beside him was saying something. 'Maybe he's managed to get into one of the houses – a friend's. And Asif says he hasn't got a car. We just need to stay patient.'

Zahra nodded. Patience. That's what they were good at, and operating calmly, quietly and legally – just a group of tourists in Sandley for the afternoon. He lingered, not ready to go to the hotel suite to report something that his boss already knew, not ready for the silent recriminations. He listened half-heartedly to the desultory conversation of the other men. Then he felt a kind of energy in the space on the quay by the barbican where his little group was standing. A small, wiry man emerged from the Strand, walking purposefully toward the quay swinging a small jerrycan. Behind him, an even smaller woman of the same age, perhaps early fifties, in a dark quilted jacket, followed on a step or two behind, slightly out of breath, struggling to keep up.

Attuned to nuance, to observation, to the accents, pitch and timbre of voices, to all the subtleties of verbal and non-verbal communication, Zahra became alert.

'It's bloody well not on. If you can't leave your boat out for half an hour in Sandley – *Sandley*,' repeated the man, '– where can you leave it?'

'It can't have gone far, Jimmy. Are you sure you tied it up properly when you finished rowing? Maybe it drifted with the tide. It could be downriver a bit.'

'Of course I bloody tied it up properly. We've been keeping boats on this river for twenty years. I know how to tie up a boat.'

'Well, Cap will know. If it's been nicked, he'll put feelers out. Talk of the devil. What a bit of luck.' As she spoke, a boat with a blue-and-white canopy pulled up to the quay in an eddy of turbid water and with a dirty, acrid puff of diesel.

She's spent half a lifetime placating and smoothing things over, thought Zahra. He concentrated, filtering everything out – the idle chat of his men, the drone of cars as they crossed the bridge, the regular green, amber, red, red and amber, green of the traffic lights, and the waft of coffee from the café next to the hotel. If his hunch was right, the next exchange was important.

The man Jimmy loomed over the newly arrived boat.

'Oi, Cap, someone nicked my tender while we went to get some petrol for the outboard.' He held up and waggled the jerrycan. 'You're the so-called harbour master. What are you going to do about it?'

'Ahoy to you too, Jimmy. And I am the harbour master, not the so-called harbour master – appointed fair and square by Sandley Town Council. Give us a bleeding chance. I'm not even moored yet.'

Zahra watched as Captain Cavendish peered around the quayside, taking in the tourists, a couple of children who looked as though they should have been in school, and Zahra himself and his little group. Zahra avoided the captain's gaze – but sensed that he knew something.

'Right,' said the captain to Jimmy. 'You and Debbie had better come aboard.'

Zahra signalled to his companions and withdrew casually to just beyond the barbican and out of sight. He knew he couldn't get close enough to eavesdrop the conversation taking place in the boat without being spotted on the quayside above it. He did what he was good at – waiting.

A few minutes later, the man and his wife appeared and started back along the Strand.

'At least we know who's got it,' said the woman.

'Frank Sterling's all right.' She brightened as a memory struck her. 'He's livened things up around here.'

'Hmph,' said Jimmy. 'What he told Cap had better be true. And he'd better make all this hassle worth my while.'

Zahra turned to his men. 'You stay here, just in case. Things might not have changed,' he said to one. 'You,' he said to the other, 'go and see Asif. Tell him I need detailed maps of this town and the surrounding area within,' he paused and calculated, 'a radius of fifteen kilometres from here. Quickly. Go.'

Zahra paced back to the quay. He sometimes wondered if he still had the finesse and flexibility for situations like this, and even the vaunted patience for that matter, when the prize was so close. He wouldn't know until he engaged.

'Captain Cavendish?' he called down. He'd seen the notice – 'Captain Cavendish's Sandley Riverboat Cruises'.

The grizzled face and yachting cap appeared from under the canopy. 'Obviously,' he said, 'since the notice is over the boat. Weren't you and a couple of other blokes mooching about on the quay?'

Zahra smiled, though the smile did not reach his eyes. 'May I,' he faltered, unsure of the correct phrase, 'come on board?'

Captain Cavendish made a little flourish and retreated to make room by the ladder. Zahra came down and looked around. The little tour boat was old – no amount of paint or polish could disguise that – but it was clean and extremely orderly.

Zahra tried to gauge his approach and decided quickly. He produced the colour print of Frank Sterling and thrust it in front of the captain's face. 'I'm looking for this man.'

Captain Cavendish's eyes flickered. 'I know him. Frank Sterling. Works in the town. I drink with him sometimes.'

'You've seen him recently,' stated Zahra. 'In a boat. A boat with an engine.'

'What is this? Quiz night? Who wants to know about Frank Sterling?'

Zahra got out his credentials. 'It's a security matter. Mr Sterling is not in danger,' he lied, 'at least, not from me and my agency. We need to trace him to help him.'

Captain Cavendish took hold of the laminated card with its elaborate patterns and watermarking, like a bank note, and the picture of Irfan Zahra, and held it to his face, pushing back his cap, flipping up his spectacles and perching them in the frizzled, wiry grey hair over his forehead, squinting as he read.

'Irfan Zahra. Funny name,' he said, handing back the validation, 'for military intelligence. Dark skin too.'

'It takes a thief, Captain,' said Zahra. 'It's not the Cold War any longer. The threats have changed. So, Frank Sterling.'

'Well, you were on the quay with your mates when Jimmy and Debs came by about their missing little bumboat, so I expect you already know some of it. I was coming back up the river and he went past. We had a little chat. I wasn't sure if he knew entirely what he was doing. Messing about in a boat is dangerous if you're an amateur.'

'Where was he going, Captain?'

'North. Out of the river mouth, across Pegsill Bay and into Ramston Harbour. I told him he'd need to be careful and do it in zigzags because of the wind and the waves. It will take a couple of hours.'

'Zigzags,' mused Zahra. He'd barely ever been at sea, or on any large expanse of water. He hadn't a clue what Captain Cavendish was talking about. He hoped someone in the group knew something about boats. 'Thank you for this information, Captain. Very helpful.' He was grateful too – grateful that he hadn't needed threats, hadn't needed to draw unwanted attention to himself and his group's activities. Sometimes it was easy. This time it was very easy. 'I wonder… would it be possible to hire you and your boat to follow Sterling?'

'It would, certainly, but it wouldn't do you much good. The tide is going out quickly now, so even if we got to Pegsill Bay we wouldn't be able to get back for twelve hours.'

'Ah. Well, perhaps you will at least accept a small token of my appreciation for your cooperation… and,' he paused, 'for your silence – all on behalf of the nation of course. He peeled off some notes from a bundle he took out of his pocket.

'Don't mind if I do. Thanks,' said the captain, as the notes slipped from one pocket to another.

Zahra climbed up the ladder and back onto the quayside and disappeared without looking back. Cavendish sank down onto a bench under the canopy. It was still a bright spring day but in the mid-afternoon a chill had penetrated the clear air. That didn't stop the outbreak of sweat that ran in a little rivulet down his back. The man had been polite enough but those dead eyes suggested that he was capable of anything. The ID had been good too, but Cavendish didn't believe it for a moment. It had been better to cooperate though. It made the misdirection more plausible, gave Sterling some more time, and saved Cavendish from, well, something. He'd chosen not to mention the lack of fuel for the outboard.

Just in case, he thought it might be a good time to pop down to Hastings to visit his brother. 'Bloody hell, Frank,' he muttered. 'What have you got yourself mixed up in this time?'

Chapter 5

Upriver, nature and humanity were in a tussle along each bank from the town, from the marine settlement to the pharma works. Nearer the sea, nature held full sway, with occasional rotting hulks, jetties or breakwaters clear evidence of her victory. Here was the realm of mudflats and reed beds, swans and cygnets, geese and goslings, and other birds and creatures few townies would recognise. None of that mattered to Sterling, who had got the hang of the outboard, and increasingly the little boat itself.

But then everything changed. Just as he reached the final bend and could see the river widening into Pegsill Bay, the outboard's steady note stuttered. The motor almost stalled three times and then finally died away. Sterling did what he might better have done at the riverside in Sandley, and checked the fuel gauge. Unequivocally, the tank was empty, and all he could do for the moment was drift on the current to the scrubby, sandy spit on the wrong side of the channel.

As the boat beached lightly on the mud and sand, the colony of grey seals basking there in the afternoon sun looked curiously on, one or two of the younger ones laboriously working their short flippers to manoeuvre themselves to get a clearer look. Close up, some seals were very large and weathered, and although Sterling knew that humans and seals were generally not enemies, he wasn't going to disturb them more than necessary. Wavelets bumped at the side of the boat and rocked it gently as it rested sideways onto the shore.

Sterling continued to sit at the back of the boat next to the outboard. It was peaceful and isolated here. A colony of seals meant there were no humans nearby. About half a mile inland, behind the scraggly woodland of the nature park straddling a long ridge rising from the riverbank, was the main road between Sandley and Ramston. It would be chancy to abandon the boat and trail over to the road. He needed more distance between himself and his pursuers, and he certainly didn't want to be found out in the open. In the hazy sunshine, he could see the blurred outline of the two small tower blocks on the edge of Ramston, perhaps four miles away. Any useful destination in the sea was too far for rowing.

He stirred himself and examined the boat again. Like the outboard, it was in pristine and well-kept condition. If he was lucky there might be a jerrycan of fuel. He shuffled up to the forward compartment at the front end, where there were two little cupboard-like spaces with knob handles. There was no jerrycan inside either, but two duffel bags carefully stowed. One contained a small sail and fittings, and the other miscellaneous nautical trappings that Sterling barely recognised. He began to see the boat with new eyes, noting clips for the oars, which could be stowed neatly on each side, and other paraphernalia, for sailing rather than rowing, also neatly housed. Cut neatly into the forward compartment was a kind of insert or step, and what was clearly a mast wrapped in a long waterproof sleeve protruded horizontally from the insert to the back of the boat, and parallel to that a shorter beam.

Sterling's new idea seemed plausible.

He had had a peripatetic upbringing in various east Kent coastal towns by his lone parent, customs officer father. It had been a loving childhood and adolescence, but a constant struggle of wills, between a father who wanted a highly educated, high-achieving, left-leaning, multi-skilled son, and a son who had always known best without knowing best, and who treated his opportunities carelessly. So while one of his opportunities had been dinghy sailing with his father, learned principally off the coast at Deeping, and while he had become quite proficient, he had never persevered. There had been distractions in his middle and late teens, he remembered. A pretty, kind girl called Stacey had been the main one.

But surely dinghy sailing was like riding a bike. You learnt it and never forgot. It wouldn't be difficult to get out into the bay, around the shallow point and then south a few miles towards Deeping. The boat was in good nick. The wind was gentle. There was still plenty of sunshine and daylight. He'd be all right.

Warming to his plan, Sterling set to work under the alert, dark eyes of his new acquaintances. He unhooked the outboard from its housing on the left hand side at the stern and grunted as he heaved it aboard and lugged it to the top end of the boat. No matter how small and compact, it was heavy. He identified the combined rudder and tiller unit towards the front of the boat and retrieved it, hooking it into place at the stern and locking it with the key-type device attached. A cord allowed him to pull up the rudder while he was in shallow water, and he could release that when he set out.

He went back to the duffels and looked at the sail again. What was this small one called? The jib. He stuffed it back. He had enough to remember without having to manage two sails. He turned to the mast. Removing the sleeve, he found the mainsail already rigged – a stroke of luck. In his sailing days, the mainsail threaded into a groove in the mast and you hauled it up with a rope and then fixed it at the top. Trying not to overbalance, he pushed up the mast, with the sail still furled, so it went to the vertical, the base anchored and hinged in the insert. A circular device on the insert, like a collar, slipped around to fix it firmly.

A couple of wires dangled loosely from the top of the mast. Sterling fumbled around the bow looking for hooks, attached the wires with the fasteners and then tightened them. He noticed how he was remembering the drill but that most of the vocabulary was gone. With the mast in place, he unfurled the sail and let it flap listlessly in the breeze. He fumbled for the boom, on which was a device like Captain Hook's claw that clicked into a groove at the bottom of the mast. A cord threaded through holes along the bottom of the sail attached sail to boom. Sometimes memory and sometimes logic guided Sterling to sort out various ropes and blocks, and when they were in place he recalled or realised their function. Fixing the rope to the end of the boom and sorting out the pulley was the most important thing. He'd almost forgotten. What if he'd set out without the means to control the sail? Rigging the kicker was also important – to stop the boom riding up if the wind freshened.

He rehearsed what he needed to do. The sail was flapping and the boat was pointing northeast towards

Ramston so at the moment the wind was northeasterly. He needed to get into Pegsill Bay from the river mouth, out around the shallow point, and then, surely, it would be a straightforward run south down the coast. He had to zigzag up against the wind and then, judging the moment, turn and let himself be swept before it. If he didn't know exactly where he'd end up, then his pursuers would have no idea at all. He did a final check with the nagging feeling that it was pointless. If something wasn't right, he'd find out soon enough when he was on the water. A song came into his head that he struggled to identify, but after a few bars it came to him. 'Wanted Man', he muttered. 'Very apt,' and he began humming it under his breath.

Still humming, he hopped out onto the grey, tar-pocked beach, squelching on fronds of stringy black seaweed, pointed the boat out into the river and dived back in just before it pulled away. The drama whipped up excitement among the seals. A posse barked and flip-flopped down to the water's edge. Instantly, ten hopeless clumsy animals changed into sleek and glossy Olympic swimmers. Then Sterling could see eyes and whiskers as they circled the boat. Straight away he knew that something was wrong. Easing the rudder down didn't cure the helpless sideways drift to the river's other bank. The daggerboard! Remembering to stay pointed into the wind so that nothing unexpected happened, he stumbled up to the front to get the device and inserted it halfway into its slot in the middle. Straight away the boat's drift abated.

Sterling had managed, after a fashion, to rig the boat. Now it was time to see if he could sail it. He took up station next to the tiller and found the rope attached to the mainsail block. Pointing just right of northeast, he pulled the sail in towards him. Immediately, the flapping ceased, and along with it the boat's bobbing and floundering in the river mouth. There was a lurch and list as the wind filled the bulging sail and the dinghy began to make way. Sterling, recovering from almost being pitched into the well of the boat and leaning out to keep it on an even keel, felt butterflies in the pit of his stomach. Exhilaration was there, and vindication for a bold decision, and defiance – no one could possibly know where he was heading now. He smiled as the nautical terms came back to him. The rope he was holding was the mainsheet. The dinghy was close-hauled and on its first tack, and all was hunky dory. He stretched forward and pushed the daggerboard further down in its slot. He was in the middle of the channel now, flanked by a small escort of seals, and there would be enough depth.

Now was the time to practise some boat-handling. He pushed the tiller away from him and as the boat turned across the wind, stumbled over to the other side, almost losing hold of the tiller. The sail flapped momentarily, and then filled on the other side. He pulled further on the mainsheet and managed to get a little closer to the wind. Memory and long-forgotten reflexes were again coming to his aid. If he tried to go too directly into the wind, the sail began to flap and he lost momentum. If he went too far off the wind he began to go too far east from northeast and drifted too far back to the southerly shore. Gradually, he made the zigs and zags into the wind longer and continued to get the feel of the boat, which bumped and smacked on the short waves in the shelter of the bay. As it rocked and wobbled, Sterling had to concentrate on the tiller to maintain his course, assisted, he noticed, by the fact that the tide was going out and carrying him with it. He reckoned the choppiness must be the wind and tide in opposition. With a wide, 360° sweep of his eyes, he calculated he'd need a good few more close-hauled tacks to get him out of the bay and beyond the shallow point to the south.

His movement from side to side on the point of each tack was getting smoother, his body hunching, twisting and rolling under the sail, with right hand lightly on the tiller and left grasping and adjusting the mainsheet. In this mode of sailing, the movement of the boom was across a short arc, and the control he was mustering reassured him. He bobbed forward or leant back over the side in tune with the wallow or heel of the small craft. What made a significant difference was the cleat device he stumbled on by his feet. Threading the mainsheet into it enabled him to make it fast between turns and relieve the strain and chafing to his hands.

He was getting the hang of things. But when the changes came, not one, not two, but many at the same time, Sterling could not have been less prepared. In an instant, the breeze that had been gentle freshened sharply and gustily, and the dinghy heeled dangerously. No longer were there choppy wavelets. A much larger wave, in a new, more open stretch of water, thumped against the raised side that Sterling was desperately leaning out of, drenching his bottom half. The shock and impact made him lose hold of the tiller and sheet. Fear and disorientation, visceral and immediate, assailed him as he was tipped into the well of the boat. More large waves came battering in, and the sail smacked full onto the wire supporting the mast. Sterling's disorientation worsened.

Amidst the sudden roaring noise, the press of the breeze and the waves hitting relentlessly, a small corner of Sterling's brain continued to function. It was something the sailing instructor had said two decades ago. 'In a crisis on the water, don't think about your own safety; think about the boat's safety.' Skulking by the daggerboard, his body gripped with terror, Sterling realised he was doing things the wrong way round. He could be safe only when the boat was safe. He dredged his memory for more. What do you do in a sailing boat when you lose control? He fumbled for the tiller. Get the boat into the wind and let the sail flap. It yawed around, and that might have given some respite, but the waves were coming in the same direction as the wind. Sterling was in open sea and now the dinghy was bucking like a bronco from the watery assault. It wasn't going to be long before something happened, something bad.

'Jesus, get a grip,' muttered Sterling. From the well, barely comforted by Captain Cavendish's buoyancy jacket, he did another quick 360° sweep. Out here, the Ramston towers seemed only marginally closer, while the river mouth was a long way behind him. The tossing and buffeting distracted him, but he realised that he was beyond the point to the south. What he wanted to do and what he had to do came together in a happy collision. Any further close-hauling against wind and waves was dangerously out of the question. Now there was an alternative.

He grabbed the tiller and scrabbled for the mainsheet, which was whipping and cracking in the stiff breeze. He needed to turn to the south. Instinct told him there would be a moment of maximum danger when he was broadside to the waves, a crisis worse than the current pitching and bucking, and he had to be ready.

He pulled the tiller towards him and reeled in the mainsheet. Immediately, the dinghy veered rapidly from northeast to east. With the wind blasting into the sail, instinct and dredged-up learning kicked in again and he eased out the sheet to release some tension. Just as the boat turned further to the southeast a wave struck from the side and back. The spray, the wind, the turbulence and now the beginnings of what Sterling thought was seasickness were becoming overwhelming. This moment could not end well.

But it did. Seconds later, the roaring and buffeting eased. Instead of a conspiracy of elements, Sterling was working with them. Now he was on a course south and a touch to the east, with the wind not immediately behind him but coming from the right-hand side and back. He knew there were technical terms for the set of the sail, the course and the wind direction – there always were – but they were long forgotten or never taken on board in the first place. Who cared? He was back in control. It was still turbulent and noisy, he was regularly spattered with spray from all directions and his hands, along with the rest of him, were so cold that he could barely grip tiller and sheet. But the dinghy was rolling and pitching with and not against the waves and he knew that his apparently slow pace was illusory. On this slow-motion watery roller coaster, he was travelling far faster and more comfortably than he ever could close-hauled. He concentrated on steering an even course. The rolling and pitching meant constant adjustment of the tiller. Behind and to the right, the sun was making its slow progress to the horizon, tingeing the sky and thin clouds with pink. He shivered.

Of all the things he hadn't planned for, being drenched and cold were the most unexpected. He eased up the daggerboard a few notches. Another memory had come back. If the wind was behind, a fully inserted daggerboard could slow a boat down.

The shallow point was far back in the distance, but Sterling noticed that the current course was taking him gradually further from the shore. He edged the tiller towards himself, letting out the sail to match the adjustment, and aimed to run parallel to the coastline. It was choppier progress as the waves were coming not quite from behind, but he reckoned he could manage. He'd been intending to sail all the way down to Deeping, by his reckoning about five miles, but he remembered another thing – at sea, everything took much longer – and now his little micro world was being bathed in an eerie, dusky half-light. He didn't want to be out on the water in the dark.

Peering under the sail, he saw a settlement on the coast framed against the evening sky. It couldn't be Deeping, so it had to be Sandley Bay. The decision wasn't hard. There was a shingle beach there. He'd land on that and make it the rest of the way to Deeping on foot. Again he adjusted his course, heading southwest for the bay, with the wind almost completely behind him. The breeze and the water were exhilarating now, and Sterling almost forgot about his cold hands and shivering. But after all that had happened, it would be still be good to be back on dry land.

He set a diagonal course, still southwest, towards the cluster of houses abutting the links golf course he knew was behind. Sitting on the seaward side, with the sail on the other, he noticed flapping from the back of the boom.

At the same time, the momentum of the dinghy was falling away. Increasingly sensitive to the nuances of boat craft, he tried to make connections. If the sail flapped at the mast when the boat was close-hauled, it was too close to the wind. What did this mean?

'Whoa. Damn.' Sterling just had time to duck before the boom, jutting out beyond the opposite side of the boat, swooped in a wide and quickening arc across and over to the other side, luckily halted by the kicker before it hit one of the mast support wires by the mainsail. Hand on tiller, Sterling recovered relatively quickly, shifting to the opposite side to the sail. He remembered the manoeuvre but not its name. He remembered another thing. You could control it or it could be done to you. He'd want to do it differently next time.

At last, the jagged silhouettes of the Sandley Bay settlement morphed into houses. Sterling was just a few hundred yards from the shore when he spotted the wooden slipway stretching out from the shingle beach into the water. He hadn't thought about it before because he hadn't needed to, but now the next predicament popped up. He was going at quite a lick. How did he stop? There wasn't time to take down the sail, even if he could fathom how, but then it came to him. So easy. He bore down on the end of the slipway, the wind almost completely at his back, and then three metres from head-on collision pushed the tiller sharply away. The dinghy lost way immediately in the face of the wind, the sheet in his hand went slack and the sail flapped limply. A kind of residual momentum carried the back of the boat into the jetty with a little bump. Sterling's hands scrabbled at the slats and brought the boat parallel. He fumbled at the cord attaching sail to boom and allowed the wind to separate them. Painters at the front and back he hooked onto stakes on the jetty. Then he half-crawled, half-stumbled from the boat. As the pink-golden light leached from the silent evening sky and darkness took over, he sat still. Never mind about the men after him. Never mind why. Never mind what next. He'd done something impulsive and foolhardy, but he'd got away with it. Relief washed over him in huge waves. He savoured his luck for a long moment.

Chapter 6

'Well?' said Zahra, as the two men, Hamid and Rashad, came into the room occupied by the young computer geek.

'Nothing,' said Hamid, the older man. 'Like I said on the phone. There's a café on the harbour wall where you can see everything and there was no sign of a small boat or outboard coming in or tied up. We walked up and down all the duckboards where the yachts and cruisers are moored and there was nothing there either. We asked someone about a boat with a small outboard and he said there had been nothing. We checked the village before Ramston but it's on the cliff top and there's no way up from the bottom, and there was no sign of a boat. Either he sank or he went a different way.'

Zahra nodded. He trusted Hamid absolutely. They went back a long way, to the marsh village and then the refugee camp where they grew up as Ma'dan between the Tigris and Euphrates river basins in southern Iraq. Rashad too was Ma'dan, but younger and less experienced. Of the present cell, only Zahra, Hamid and Rashad were not European. Hamid was loyal, thorough and committed. It was sensible to put the young hotheads with the old hands.

'What about the drone?' said Asif.

'No,' said Zahra. The young man and the others

4 7

waited. Zahra at first saw no reason to explain but then thought better of it. 'Just to be clear to you all. We keep it lo-tech and low key. It's difficult enough that there are a good number of us strangers in this town, and that a few of us have a skin colour that stands out. So we mainly do this the old-fashioned way. No drone. No upsetting the townsfolk. Make sure that message gets passed on.' He turned to Hamid. 'If this man didn't go to Ramston, and he hasn't sunk, he will have gone the opposite way down the coast. Do a trawl in that direction. You,' (he motioned to Asif at the computer) 'do some calculations of speed and time. Look at the map. Work out possible destinations down the coast to the south. Liaise with Hamid by phone.' If he'd had the resources, he'd have done the searches, north and south, at the same time. In due course, he'd have to report back to Kurjak – another tiresome duty. He pressed his fingers and thumbs to his temples. Sometimes that staved off a migraine. It shouldn't have been like this – missing information, broken-down network communications, civilians involved, and worse than that, civilians who were surprisingly elusive. He'd cut corners. There was still time, but it was more complicated than it should have been.

'We need more than maps and calculations, more than what you've found out so far,' he said to Asif. 'Step it up a level. I want to know everything about this man Sterling, his background, his friends and associates, where he grew up, schools, where he's lived before. Everything. Get under his skin. When we pick up his trail again, we need to be ready for the next stage. Do it quickly.' If the man Sterling could go to ground, he'd have time to examine the instructions Strange had passed to him. They would be in code, but Strange had not passed the memory stick on randomly.

Asif turned back to the screen. 'Bastard,' he muttered. This wasn't what he had signed up for, skivvying for someone who demanded so much and thanked so little. The whole thing had been a mistake – wrong choice, wrong group. His fingers flicked over the keyboard in an anxious quest. He wasn't only resentful. He was scared.

Zahra looked out of the window. Unlike his boss's, there was no gracious river view, just the red brick and newly applied repointing of the old house next to the back of the hotel. The thought, discordant and uncomfortable, nagging away at him was that after all this time, and with all his experience, he'd been complacent. He should have wrapped this affair up in Sandley. For an ex-agent, the man Strange had been relatively easy to track down and abduct. The man Sterling was unexpectedly the elusive one.

He opened his telephone and went to speed-dial. Other men in his group were monitoring the activities of Jimmy and Debbie Heselthwaite. It was possible they might be contacted to be told the whereabouts of their boat. Sandley seemed a tight community, and Zahra had never been able to understand that kind of eccentric act ('Jimmy, I borrowed your boat. I've left it… somewhere or other. Sorry'). There would always be a 'sorry' in there somewhere though.

'Any movement? Any calls?'

'Not so far. We're in a pub at the moment.'

'Stay close. But be discreet. You know what to do if you hear.'

Even if Sterling did not make the call, but someone in

Zahra's group found the boat, a picture of it could be shown to the Heselthwaites.

'Of course, brother.'

With Asif hunched over his computer, Zahra slipped away. As he made his way downstairs, he reviewed how he'd deployed the group. Men were monitoring the Heselthwaite couple. Hamid and another were checking landing spots to the east and south of Sandley, down towards the town of Deeping. The man Strange was being held at the industrial estate. Everyone was on high alert. Later on, if it was necessary, he'd arrange for Sterling's house to be broken into. There might be helpful indications there. He paused and rolled his shoulders at the discreet back entrance of the hotel and felt the tension dissipate from the muscles in his neck and upper back. He and the group were doing all they could after the initial failure. The momentum would return, they'd get Sterling sooner rather than later, and they'd retrieve the information he carried with him. Then the plan would be back on track. The main worry was liaison with the other cell, and whether they'd be in time.

It wasn't just the current crisis. The English had an expression, he remembered, for his own predicament – 'Always the bridesmaid…'. That poser Kurjak on the third floor peeling his fruit and playing God was not even at the top of the pyramid – just a building block himself. But Zahra was aiming to be more than him. He was going to get to the top once the local difficulty was resolved and the mission completed.

His own contribution, and a way to keep himself occupied as things played out, lay back in Market Street. He looked for the gap in the wall just up the High Street from the hotel where one of the alleys started. He could understand, even if he could not forgive, how his men had failed to track Sterling down in this town centre warren. He allowed the alley to funnel him into St Peter's Street where he saw the church a few metres down on the right. Another alley beyond the graveyard joined St Peter's Street to Market Street, and Zahra strode down it.

Trigger-happy Nevin was loitering outside the library. Spotting the tall, fierce, dark dervish, jacket panels flapping from the centre vent, Nevin's back stiffened and he clasped and twisted his hands. 'Sorry, Zahra...' he started.

Zahra raised his own hand, as if he was stopping traffic. 'Anything of interest?'

'No. Just the usual coming and going from the library.'

Zahra nodded. 'Come.'

They clattered up the narrow staircase to Sterling's office. Since his last case, where he'd been attacked and almost stabbed, Sterling had replaced the old, thin, rickety door with something more solid, with a Yale lock and a dead bolt. Zahra stood aside and tipped his head towards it.

Nevin stepped forward, wiping his hands on his jeans. 'If he's put the deadbolt on, we'll have to do a wee bit of damage.'

'Try it,' said Zahra.

The younger man got out a small wallet of equipment, from where Zahra couldn't work out. But he wasn't interested in the small matters. Only the big picture was important, and to help him he used only people with the right set of skills. Nevin inserted the shorter end of an L-shaped instrument into the lock and selected a pick from an array in the wallet. Zahra could see the pink tip of Nevin's tongue as he went to work, and could feel himself becoming mesmerised as the younger man's slim, nimble fingers gripped the tools and started the manipulation. No more than a minute later, Nevin gently pushed at the door.

'No deadbolt. He must have been in too much of a hurry.' There was pride in Nevin's Scottish-accented voice, and an almost canine wish to please.

Zahra grunted. If the group had been more competent, he would not have been in this position. He gave no thanks because none was deserved, and because anyway it wasn't in his nature. 'Close the door. Stand in front of it,' he said from the middle of Sterling's office. He looked around. The office told him about the man. For one thing, it was tidy. For another, it was spartanly furnished and organised to maximise space. The desk opposite the door was old and cheap, but large, with a telephone on the right and a late specification computer in the middle. Between the desk and the sash window which overlooked the square was a modern office chair. Next to the desk squatted a two-drawer prison-green filing cabinet and at right angles to that a sofa, which was neat enough but had seen better days. An editor's lamp on the desk, with its green shade and faux-gold stem, together with landscapes, rural and riverain, containing buildings that Zahra didn't recognise – Kentish oast houses – gave the room a comfortable, almost intimate air.

None of that interested Zahra. 'Look at the computer,' he said to Nevin, whilst he walked around to the filing cabinet. The contents confirmed the view he was developing about their owner. There weren't many files, but they were meticulously organised and in complete, logical order. He riffled through the invoices, the details of past cases, lease and contracts information about the office and all insurance and other details about office and home. He picked out and pocketed one or two utility bills and debit and credit card statements, which might be of some use to Asif. But on the face of it, there was little clue here at all to indicate where Sterling might have gone. He had no time, thought Zahra, and there was no personal stuff here.

Nevin looked up from the computer. His eyes avoided contact. 'It's password-protected. Only Asif has a chance of getting into this.' Zahra eased closed the top drawer of the filing cabinet and moved to the desk to look at the computer screen. He sensed Nevin shift away, and it pleased him. People were more compliant when they were scared.

He went through the drawers of the desk desultorily. An envelope caught his attention, with a Belgian postmark and Sterling's address in that common European writing style. The letter inside, presumably from the young woman in an attached photo, and whose contents were cheerful and affectionate, with a hint of nostalgia, held little interest for him. But there was also a separate folded sheet with a seemingly random list of numbers and letters.

'Nevin, what could this be?' said Zahra, holding the sheet up. If it was to do with IT, he had little knowledge or interest, and was content to rely on his associates.

'You've found a password list, brother. Asif will find that very useful, if Sterling uses the cloud.'

'The cloud? Explain.'

Nevin was eager to please. 'We can't take Sterling's computer. It's too big. But he might keep backups of his computer files in a data storage bank – electronically. So they are not in his computer but in a secure place somewhere else. Not really a physical place.' He fluttered his hands, as if to demonstrate something ethereal, and tailed off. His nervousness made him less coherent.

Zahra nodded. Every time something was explained, by Nevin or Asif or one of the others, he understood the whole a little better. He folded the sheet and put it in his pocket. 'Turn the computer off. We'll get nothing more here. We leave everything as we found it. Come.'

Zahra had already clattered down half of the rickety staircase when Nevin clicked the door shut. As he turned to follow his boss, he heard a strong, clear, assertive feminine voice reverberate upwards from the tiny lobby at the bottom, a voice that even from the landing Nevin knew was direct and uncompromising. What would Mr Unpredictable Hard Man Zahra make of that? Nevin smirked, but even though the landing was gloomy, he was careful to turn his face to the door.

Chapter 7

'What's going on? There's a lot of sudden activity around here.' The voice belonged to a striking, slender black woman in her thirties, with the high cheekbones, flawless skin and deep, intelligent eyes of ancient West African royalty.

Zahra continued unhurriedly to the bottom of the stairs. He was taller than the woman, but not as tall by comparison to other women he occasionally had dealings with.

'Good afternoon. We are looking for Mr Frank Sterling, but he doesn't appear to be in.'

'You're in the right place. Obviously. I thought I heard rummaging around up there. More than usual.'

Zahra smiled. White teeth. Dead eyes. He said nothing.

'Well, if he's not in, he's not in. Communication isn't always his strong point. Did you leave a message and contact details under his door? Or I expect you could write an e-mail. He even carries a mobile.'

'It's a little more urgent than that, I'm afraid. And you are…?'

'I'm the librarian downstairs, and in the interests of safety and security I take an interest in all these premises, including Fr… Mr Sterling's.'

'Ah,' said Zahra, whether to acknowledge her role or because the woman's intimacy with Sterling hadn't escaped him. 'And you don't know where he might be, Miss...?'

The woman ignored the fishing. If this man wanted to know who she was, let him find out by himself. 'I have no idea. As I said, I am the librarian here, not a private investigator's keeper.'

'Of course, of course,' said Zahra. He motioned to Nevin, who was almost at the bottom. 'Come, brother. We must be on our way. Thank you,' he said to the librarian with a slight incline of his head. He watched her as she walked back into the library, and then set off back to the hotel. As he went, he felt the weight of a community against him. His headache was worse than ever and the familiar surge of paranoia further soured his bitter mood.

*

'Kerry,' said the librarian, Angela Wilson, to her main assistant, 'I'm going into my office to make a phone call. Can you carry on holding the fort?'

'Sure,' said the girl.

Angela closed the door. Something was very wrong. She hadn't even bothered to ask the man if he had a problem and wanted to engage Sterling. 'Frank, Frank,' she muttered under her breath, 'what now?' Her best friend and near neighbour in Sandley wouldn't be meeting her tonight in the snug of the Cinque Port Arms to do the crossword over a pint and a gin and tonic, she was sure of that. She had been involved in more than one of Sterling's scrapes and escapades over the couple of years she'd known him, but this episode, and that man, had real menace. She sat at her desk and drummed her fingers. Then she pulled the phone towards her.

'Becky? It's Angela… yeah, hi… have you seen Frank Sterling?' She listened and then spoke again. 'The pub? Jack's café? OK… OK… see you shortly.'

There was a corner table in the Secret Garden Tea Room away from all the windows and obscured from the front entrance by the cake counter. When Angela arrived, her friend Becky, Mike Strange's wife, was already waiting there.

'Any signs that you were followed, Angie?'

'No. I came through the alleys as far as possible, and then down Strand Street. What's going on? There were a couple of very dodgy blokes hanging around Frank's office. I'm almost certain they broke in, and Frank was nowhere to be seen.'

'I don't exactly know. It's good that they were obviously looking for him, because it implies that he's on the loose – or anyway out on a case or something. I'll tell you what I do know, and maybe we can take it from there. Mike got a call late last night from an ex-colleague of ours – Mohamed Husain. He's in an intelligence section that deals with terrorism and the stuff that goes with it. We hadn't heard from him for, what, eighteen months?'

Angela nodded. She knew about Becky's and Mike's intelligence background, and the botched operation that caused them to leave the service and take over the Cinque Port Arms, where they applied the same pragmatic efficiency to running a pub as they had to espionage. Becky was blonde and pretty, but only if you looked closely. No one was more adept at merging so successfully into the background, and only after long acquaintance could you be aware of her loyalty and dry wit.

'So Mike agreed to go up to Waterloo to meet

Mohamed early this morning. Only Mike would do because Mohamed reckoned the section had been compromised. On the way back he called me on his burner phone. He couldn't talk openly, but I got the drift. Something big and bad is going to be happening soon, somewhere on the south coast. Mike had details on a memory stick. The problem is that he became aware that he'd been followed on the train back. When he got back to Sandley... he was taken.'

'What, kidnapped?'

'Yep.'

'You seem quite sanguine about it, Becky. Your husband kidnapped in Sandley, presumably in broad daylight. And I thought this was about Frank Sterling.'

'It is, Angie. Just before Mike was spirited away, knowing that he couldn't elude about twelve people after him, all having motored down from London, he passed the memory stick on to Frank. Frank's not field-trained, obviously, but he's pretty savvy in his own way.'

'But why didn't you help Mike out?'

Becky looked around the café. The tables nearby were occupied by elderly couples and a noisy party of tourists. The young waitress who took their order for tea had a harassed look and a shiny forehead.

'We couldn't plan it in time. Frank was the only option in the circumstances. While Frank applies his usual creativity to looking after himself, and hopefully to what Mike gave him, I rescue Mike...'. Becky stopped and put her hand up to pre-empt her friend's protest. 'And before you put in an objection on Frank's behalf, this is national security we're talking about here. As I said, we had to do things on the hoof. We'll be looking after Frank, don't worry.'

'But Mike?'

'His transmitter is on, so I know where he is.'

'His transmitter?'

'He's got a microchip embedded in him. I have too – just in case of situations like this. Like a dog.' Becky smiled. 'He's my bitch, I suppose, this time around. I'm waiting for it to get dark, and then I'm going to get him.'

'I can help,' said Angela.

Becky weighed her up and smiled again. 'Well, you won't need blacking up, and I heard a few things, after Frank's case at Earlsey Tech.'

Angela smiled back. 'Anything you heard wouldn't have been from Frank. He knows how to keep his mouth shut. I bet it was Jack, wasn't it?' Jack Cook was Sandley's café-owning king of gossip, who, together with Angela, had got mixed up in Sterling's business.'

'I did hear something the other evening, after his fourth pint. I made sure no one else did, though, Angie. You know what he's like – all nudges and winks. The hint was that you used to run a gang in London in your teenage days, and that you can handle yourself. There was the broken window of Frank's office too. And the body.'

'All accurate, I'm afraid. I'll have to go and see Jack and put him straight. But Mike…'.

'Well, I could do with some help, certainly.'

'I have the perfect skill set.'

'Clincher. OK, meet me at eight at the bench on the Town Walk behind the Bowling Club. I'll park the van nearby. Check no one is following. Dark kit…'. There was another tiny smile. 'Sensible shoes.'

The waitress brought the tea. Angela ordered a dough-nut – for fortification, as she put it – and the two women discussed rescue strategy and tactics, and speculated on the wider picture involving what information might be on the memory stick Mike had given to Sterling, and the nature of the people after it.

'I'd better get back to the library,' Angela said finally. 'I can't leave Kerry any longer. I wonder where Frank is now. I think you and Mike took a bit of a liberty involving him, Becky, if I'm honest.'

'He'll be all right. Look at his track record. Amazingly good, if you think about it. He might not always go about it in the right way. He might be a bit ramshackle. But he gets results. We felt bad about landing him in it, but at the time we didn't have much in the way of alternatives. Anyway, we've helped him out a lot in the past, so we had a favour to call in.'

Angela shrugged. It was still cavalier. 'We are where we are, but you and Mike volunteered,' she said. 'Poor old Frank got conscripted.'

Chapter 8

Sterling remembered a football match he'd played in when he was about twelve or thirteen, at his school in Deeping. It had been December, in a gale that became a blizzard in the second half. The supervising teacher, a stubborn old time-server by the name of Mornard, had made them carry on even though they could barely see the goalposts from the halfway line. Sterling had wept with cold in the changing room afterwards, and he couldn't seem to thaw his frozen hands. Even though it was now April and not December, that's how his hands, and the rest of him, felt now, and there was no hot radiator within reach to get him gradually back into the land of the living. He left the boat and shambled along the jetty until he could jump down onto the shingle beach. Stiffly he began to run up and down, the pebbles shifting and leaving indentations under his feet. Although he quickly became breathless, the stiffness from hunching in the boat gradually dissipated and his sluggish circulation began to improve. The transition from frozen hands and feet to warmth through exertion began after about eight or nine minutes, with an almost unbearable short period of pins and needles in his extremities.

He'd only stayed because he felt a nagging guilt about the boat. Temporarily recovered, he turned his attention to his new surroundings. This part of Sandley Bay was remote. The shingle beach formed a natural barrier between sea and low-lying land. Sterling could see the top half of a large Lutyens house beyond the shingle and the dunes – all faux-Tudor beams and latticed windows. The jetty continued back up to a padlocked double gate and beyond that into a compound surrounded by metal fencing. Above the gate was a faded sign, battered by wind and spray – 'Sandley Bay Sailing Club and Social Club – New Members Welcome'. Now he knew exactly where he was and memories of the whole area came back to him from his teenage years in Deeping.

Most boats and dinghies were inside the compound, their masts thin pencils in the dark blue evening sky. But there were others, mostly old and battered, and therefore hardly worth stealing, beyond the fencing. They lay at strange and random angles on the shingle, lopsided and sometimes turned upside down. Sterling walked back down the jetty to the Heselthwaites's dinghy. He hadn't made nearly the progress he should have in his escape from Sandley. At this moment, he was only three miles from his office, six hours after Mike Strange had come visiting. All he'd done, for all that effort and in reality's harsh light, was escape his pursuers' initial cordon. It reminded him of a previous case, where he'd escaped with a girl in a wheelchair at an average speed of six miles an hour. Looking on the bright side, though, there was hardly a better place to leave the dinghy than camouflaged near a sailing club compound.

It was still lapping and bumping against the jetty when Sterling returned. He slipped down into it and started the process of unrigging, stowing sail, mast, boom and everything else as tidily as he could, though he realised that that would not make Jimmy Heselthwaite any less aggrieved. Then he untied it and pulled it back towards the shingle. When it was three quarters beached, he hopped down and started hauling it up further, his heels scrabbling and sliding on the slippery pebbles. At least he had thoroughly warmed up now. When he judged that the boat was beyond the high water mark and further up to the dunes than the others, he paused again to rest.

Up to this point, he'd been so pleased to have escaped and reached land undrowned and unscathed that he hadn't had time to consider anything else. Now the question appeared and immediately became urgent. What next? The destination was clear – Deeping – and the mode of travel – Shanks's pony. But there were more fundamental issues – like whether his trail had been picked up, where he was meant to be going and why, and how, without a laptop or equivalent, he'd be able to gain access to the contents of the memory stick.

Just as he was casting a final look around the landing place and checking the position of his escape-vessel in relation to the other boats dotted around outside the compound, he thought he heard something above the gentle, rhythmic sighing of the wavelets on the shingle and the more constant sough of the breeze coming off the sea. The light changed imperceptibly, and something rumbled in Sterling's gut.

Around the jetty it was very open, and there was still enough lingering sunlight in the gloaming for Sterling to be very visible. It was risky but he had no choice. Taking his bag, he scrambled over to one of the upturned hulls and slipped underneath. His gut was right. He could hear the deep growl of a car engine – possibly an SUV – and see the beam as it feebly and obliquely penetrated under the hull. At eye level, he could see all the indentations his shoes had made, including close to his current hiding place. He reached out and smoothed over the nearest shingle as best he could. Then all he could do was wait. The light intensified. Sterling's heartbeat became more rapid, and a surge of adrenaline started the butterflies. He heard the creak and clunk of heavy car doors opening and closing, and soon after the crunch of shoes on shingle. He concentrated on his breathing, keeping it shallow and quiet.

The crunching continued. From his ground-level vantage point, he could see two pairs of black shoes shuffling and clumping around the area of the jetty. It seemed darker now, even with the headlights, and it buoyed Sterling to realise that some of his tracks were being erased by the new visitors, especially by the shoes that were a foot from his nose.

'There's no one here, brother,' said a young voice. Sterling detected a querulous note, and an accent he'd need to hear more of before he could identify it.

'Wait, Rashad,' said an older voice. 'You're too impatient. Too careless. Look, by the jetty. Footprints. Leading where?'

There was a pause. Agonising. The shingle had begun to dig into various parts of Sterling's prone body and the underside of the boat carried the tang of seaweed and the earthy smell of damp wood.

'Here, brother.' Not querulous now but excited. A discovery seemed to focus the two men, and Sterling hoped that the crunching and scrabbling would cover his other tracks. He shut his eyes, as if it might help him to disappear.

'Take photos of this boat. Send them to Asif. Zahra can show them to its owners.'

There was a flash and a click, and then two more.

Sterling wondered if these men would ever go away. If he started to get cramp, he'd be finished.

'The message is sent, brother.'

'There's no fuel in the outboard,' said the older voice. Sterling could hear doubt amid faint rummaging sounds. 'If this isn't the boat... But it must be... None of these other tubs even look seaworthy. Did he run out of petrol at the end? Did he row all the way? Never mind. We'll know soon if it's the right one.'

'What now, brother?'

'Sandley is that way. There is only one other way out of here. To the town down the coast – Deeping.'

'There are no tracks from the boat except ours, Hamid.'

'He is sly, this Sterling,' said Hamid. 'Here's how he did it.'

Sterling saw shoes going backwards up the shingle, and then dark-skinned hands flattening over the indentations. Hmm, he reflected. Perhaps he was sly, but doing that hadn't occurred to him. Along with 'lo-tech', he added it to his growing list of dubious character traits and non-accomplishments.

Chapter 9

As Angela left the Secret Garden Tea Room, a few metres away in the Bell and Tower Hotel, Zahra lay on the bed as Asif hunched over the computer. Zahra's migraine was in full oppressive flow, fuelled by paranoia and, up to this point, his group's failure to catch up with Frank Sterling. Sandley, and its souk-like qualities, symbolised the obstacles he thought he faced. He lay and stared up at the ceiling – not asleep, not awake, but in a kind of aching stupor.

The sun was just disappearing as he came to a couple of hours later, its rays slanting into the room from the back window for the few moments before they were shut out by the brick wall opposite.

Asif hovered by the bed. 'His Excellency wants to see you, brother, to know what's happening.'

Zahra swung his legs off the bed and sat up. The pills seemed to be working, though the throbbing hadn't completely gone. He massaged his temples again, willing the grogginess to go away. Without a word, he got up, left the room and walked down the corridor to the luxury bedroom overlooking the window. He knocked and entered without waiting.

Kurjak was at the window, looking down at the river. The light was going quickly, and the delicate china-blue of the afternoon sky was rapidly becoming a much darker hue. 'Should I not have had an update much earlier, Zahra?'

'If I had had anything to report, Excellency, you would immediately have been informed.'

'You forget who you are talking to,' said the other man, turning sharply from the window.

Zahra was silent. *No I don't, you dog*, he thought. His resources were slender, relatively speaking, he had a community against him, and was powerless, in this rule-of-law country, to use all the methods he would otherwise have chosen to meet his objectives. Everything was against him, and this conceited idiot was simply adding to his difficulties. His phone chirruped in his pocket. Without any acknowledgement to his boss, Zahra took the call. It was Asif from the room along the corridor, too nervous to interrupt the meeting by appearing in person.

'I've just had a message from Hamid and Rashad, brother. They have found what they think is the boat Sterling took, at a place called Sandley Bay, about three miles from the hotel. They sent photos.'

'Have one of the others find the man Heselthwaite in the pub and get him to confirm that it's his boat.'

Because it was Hamid, Zahra knew that the information was correct. He ended the call with Asif and phoned Hamid direct. 'You've found the boat,' he stated.

'I'm pretty sure of it,' said Hamid. 'There's a little...' – he struggled with unfamiliar vocabulary – 'pier with a compound for boats on the land behind it.'

'And Sterling?'

'He's gone, Irfan. But not long ago, I think.'

'You're sure he's not still close by?' Zahra thought he heard Hamid sigh. Of all the people he commanded,

Hamid was the least cowed by his presence, voice or reputation. In fact, he showed no fear at all. But then, they had been associates for a long time.

'No, Irfan, he's not here,' said Hamid. Not many in the cell used Zahra's first name, either.

'Check that he hasn't started walking back to Sandley – or that he hasn't found some other type of transport.' It wasn't likely, but nothing seemed likely in this stage of the operation. 'I'll send someone reliable from this end. He visualised the map in Asif's command centre along the corridor. 'We'll concentrate now on the next town down the coast – Deeping. Go there once you have checked.'

'Is it worth backtracking to Sandley, brother? Surely we should go straight to Deeping'

'Doing the least obvious thing is exactly what Sterling might be thinking. He seems to have done it before,' said Zahra. He was angry; angry that his brothers asked too many questions or were incompetent, and angry with himself for lapsing into explanations. 'Do as I say.' He ended the call and put the phone back in his pocket.

'News?' said his boss.

'We have found the man Sterling's boat about three miles from here. We're going to check the road back here and then concentrate on the next town down the coast. It won't be long now before we get him, Excellency.'

'It had better not be,' said Kurjak, turning back to the view of the river.

'Idiot,' muttered Zahra. He hurried along the corridor to the back room to instruct Asif and deploy his forces in the new location. His migraine had gone.

Chapter 10

A new set of creaks and clunks by the boatyard at Sandley Bay indicated that the men had returned to their vehicle, and immediately Sterling felt more comfortable in his hiding place. Just as he was beginning to get cold again, the breeze becoming stiffer in the wind tunnel created by the upturned hull, the engine growled into life, there was a last sweep of headlights in an arc around the beach as the vehicle reversed, and then desolation returned to the area. Sterling slipped out from under the hull and onto his feet too quickly. The cramp that had been threatening in his upper thigh and the large muscle at the back of his lower leg erupted and he quickly fell back onto the beach, straightening both legs out and pulling his feet back from the toes. He grunted and grumbled from the pain and effort, but gradually the discomfort subsided. More gingerly, he got up for a second time and retrieved his bag. He'd already made the decision about his next destination – Sandley was tempting, and going there would be counter-intuitive, but ultimately out of the question. So it had to be Deeping – even if his pursuers would also be switching their focus there. But when he arrived he couldn't risk a hotel or bed and breakfast. These people knew what they were doing.

There was a levee from this point down to Deeping, keeping the sea from a second, more southerly golf course on this shallow headland. Sterling scrabbled up to the chalky path at the top and set off. Who were these men? Of the ones he'd seen briefly in Sandley, some had dark colouring, black hair and brown eyes, indicating that they came from the Middle East or the Indian sub-continent, but there were Europeans as well, and they all seemed to speak English.

As the moon rose, the temperature dropped. Sterling slipped his hands in his pockets and hunched himself up in his coat, following the luminous white of the uneven track, a golf course's width away from the road running parallel. He started a spontaneous whistling, and the thin high notes of 'Wanted Man' vanished into the air almost as soon as they emerged from his mouth.

Forty minutes later he had reached Downley Castle. In fact, to call it a castle was a stretch. It was never more than a small artillery fort, linked with larger, proper castles up and down the coast as an integral part of a coastal defensive chain commissioned by Henry VIII. Sterling approached the ruin beyond the southernmost tip of the golf course. Its keep and bastions were long gone. Now, after centuries of official modifications and unofficial pilfering, it was little more than a few stones, with an equally faded, weathered and forlorn display panel explaining its history.

His memories of it had nothing to do with history and plenty to do with Stacey Sunnington, the first girl he had been really serious about, and, as far as he remembered, the first who had been serious about him. They'd come up here from Stacey's busy, noisy, crowded family council house home at the north end of Deeping for what had become known between them as 'peace and quiet'. 'Fancy a bit of peace and quiet?' 'Let's get out of here for a bit of peace and quiet', one or other of them would say.

She'd been a kind girl, Stacey – pretty, good fun and, crucially for a hormone-driven seventeen-year-old boy, up for it. How had he let her slip away, the first of the procession?

He didn't remember a terrible falling-out. They were just kids. But whereas there had just been him and his father, Stacey came from a large family and was about the third of five. Not only that, but her extended family had colonised the social housing up this end of the town. Downley Close contained Stacey's parents, aunts, uncles and cousins, all entwined in the working fabric of the town as fishermen, shop assistants and schoolchildren. No, it wasn't a falling-out, but after all this time he couldn't work out just what had happened.

Right now though none of that mattered. His priority was some kind of refuge for the night that was rapidly approaching. As Mike Strange would say, he needed to go to ground, and Stacey and the Sunningtons were his best option. He'd avoid pursuers inevitably swarming after him, having found the boat, and he might even get access to a computer, essential if he was going to find out what he needed to do next.

Alert at all times to danger, but even more so as the lights of long, thin Deeping, clinging to the coast from north to south, stretched out before him, Sterling moved south along the very beginning of the promenade. Crossing over to Downley Road, which ran parallel, he slipped into the alleyway that linked Downley Road to Downley Close. More reminiscences of the 'peace and quiet' missions flooded into his consciousness, but then came doubts. He hadn't been up here for twenty-odd years. Perhaps Stacey and her family had moved away. If they had, he'd be stumped.

Downley Close hadn't changed much. He'd start with the parents, who, if anyone, would still be in the same house. He checked the time – just after seven o'clock – so not too late to be ringing on the doorbell at number eight. There was a metal rail by the side of the path leading to the front door. That hadn't been there before, and in the orange gloom of the street lamps the garden was no longer immaculate. Having rung the bell, Sterling stepped back so that Mr or Mrs Sunnington would have a clear sight of him if one of them opened the front door.

He was about to ring the bell again when he heard a shuffling and movement from inside. A slight, stooped, white-haired man with a stick opened up.

'Mr Sunnington? It's Frank Sterling.'

The old man peered into Sterling's face. 'Who did you say?'

'Sterling, Mr Sunnington. Frank Sterling.'

After a long moment there was a flicker in the old man's face, adding to the hundreds of creases already on the leathery, sun-beaten skin, and then a wide smile.

'Frank Sterling. Son of a gun. I haven't seen you for what, twenty years?'

Sterling shuffled his feet on the path. He'd been Stacey's boyfriend, but the whole family had adopted him as an honorary Sunnington, and then he'd pretty much moved on without looking back.

'How are you, Mr Sunnington?' Sterling projected his voice. He'd noticed the hearing aids on each ear and remembered a deaf client from an earlier case.

'All right, Frank. Better for seeing you. But I lost Rachel a few years back,' He looked over the expanse of scrabbly front grass, 'and as you know, she was the gardener. Come in, boy. I'll put the kettle on.'

'I'm sorry about Mrs Sunnington. She was really kind to me. Her scones… But actually, Mr Sunnington, I can't really stop. I'm trying to contact Stacey.'

The old man's eyes glinted, from anger or mischief Sterling couldn't tell. 'Stacey,' he said. 'Well, what makes you think she'd want to see you? You were a real heartbreaker in those days.'

'I'm hoping time will have made it all right.'

The old man shrugged. 'Maybe. We all liked you, Frank. It wasn't just her loss. Anyway, she's still here in the close. Different house now. Number twenty-three. If it's her you must see, she's not had an easy time of it, but she can bring you up to speed about that and all the rest of us.'

'Right,' said Sterling. 'It's a bit of an emergency, so I'd better get on.'

The old man smiled. 'We read the papers up in this corner, you know. We know what you've been up to these last few years. Don't leave it another twenty before you do come visiting again.'

'I won't, Mr S. Nice to see you. I'll be back when this latest thing is over. I'll go over to Stacey now.' As he walked down the road counting the odd numbers to twenty-three, Sterling could sense the clan chief's eyes on his back, and when he looked back from Stacey's front door, the old man raised his stick in salute before shuffling back indoors.

Sterling had known from mutual friends afterwards how Stacey had felt about their break-up, but the rest of the family… Surely boys would just come and go. Standing at her front door, he ran his fingers through his hair, wiped his palms on his coat and brushed himself down. His body and clothes felt gritty from the sailing

and the sea-spray, and he probably looked equally dishevelled. A strange emotion washed over him, a mixture of
yearning, loss, nostalgia, expectancy and hope – the hope
aspect to do with his current predicament and how he
needed refuge. This was not how he imagined it would
be, the sense of being a suitor as well as a supplicant.

Again he rang the doorbell and stepped back into the
orange glow. A light came on in the hallway, the door
opened fractionally on a chain and two pretty dark eyes
looked him up and down.

'Stacey? It's Frank. Frank Sterling.' He was beginning
to sound like a broken record.

'Who? It's late for callers, and I don't buy on the
doorstep.'

'I'm not selling, Stacey.' Using her name again ought
to be reassuring. 'It's Frank Sterling,' he repeated.

Recognition dawned in the small face. The chain
rattled and then the door swung open. The woman's
pleasure was as evident as her father's. 'Sorry, Frank, but
you can't be too careful these days. What a lovely surprise.
How did you find me?'

'I didn't think you'd be far away. I've just spoken to
your dad and he pointed me over here.'

'Well, come in. Take off your coat and jacket, and
make yourself comfortable.'

The clear, light, welcoming voice triggered relief, and
Sterling almost stumbled, not realising how tense he'd
been. Supposing she'd been unfriendly and kept the
chain on – he'd have been stumped. He stepped through
the small hallway beyond the front door and directly into
the living room, a cheerful, comfortable, immaculate
space whose walls smelt slightly of new paint. In the bay
window looking out into the close was a full array of

family photos. Of course, things were not frozen in time – what had he been thinking? – and Stacey had moved on just as he had. A small terrier-type dog continued the yapping that had started when the bell had chimed but gradually it fell off as the dog sniffed around Sterling's ankles.

'Cooper,' said Stacey, 'here,' and the dog reluctantly withdrew from its investigations. 'So, Frank Sterling, after all this time. Let me look at you.' She held him at the tops of his arms and examined him thoroughly, lingering on his face. 'You seem a bit messed up, but otherwise pretty good.'

'You too, Stacey.' Sterling could see the faint beginnings of crow's feet around her dark-brown eyes as her face crinkled into an amused, appraising smile, but he wasn't fibbing. She might have been wearing mascara but otherwise there seemed to be no make-up, unlike in her younger, more experimental days of foundation and lipstick. She still favoured the similar style of spangly, sleeveless T-shirts of her teenage years. Sterling was surprised he remembered – in those days he'd been more interested in what was underneath. Skinny blue jeans hugged her still-slim figure. Pink slippers adorned her feet in a clash with the rest of her outfit. Gone was the unsophisticated perfume. Something like Miss Dior had replaced Zoella, or whatever it had been back in the day. In her almost-black straight hair, plaited as it was when she was a girl, but shorter now, he saw no grey, unlike the flecks in his own. He was thirty-eight now, so she must be thirty-seven. That was the comfort of getting older. No one escaped – not even, in the end, the Botox crowd.

'Sit down.' Stacey muted the television and swept

aside some sewing from the sofa. 'Tea? Coffee? Beer? Maybe something a bit stronger?'

'Coffee, please, Stacey. I'm still on the cold side.'

'Coming up. This is such a surprise. I'm looking forward to catching up.'

Sterling leant back in the sofa and closed his eyes. It had been an exhausting day, with more to come. He was probably safe for now, but specialising in slow, short-distance escapes was turning out to be not that helpful. Luckily, Stacey was as cheerful and generous as he always remembered her, and there was clearly no bitterness on either side in this reunion. That wasn't always the way of it. Already he felt confident about what he could ask of her.

Chapter 11

'I'm in a fix,' said Sterling. 'A friend came up to my office in Sandley and gave me something. A large gang of blokes took him from the library. I just managed to get away through a window at the back when they came for me. I lost them in the back streets and alleys but I reckoned they were watching all the roads out of town. So I took a boat on the river and rowed out on the tide. When I was around the bend of the river, I started the outboard, but I ran out of petrol just as the river got to Pegsill Bay. So then I sailed down as far as the Sandley Bay Estate. I'd just moored up when a couple of men turned up in an SUV looking for me. They'd have got me, too, if they'd bothered to look under a boat on the shingle. When they'd gone, I walked down by the side of the golf course till I got to Downley Castle. That's when I thought of you. Obviously. So here I am, and that's why I'm a bit dishevelled.'

'God, it sounds like something out of a Bond film,' said Stacey. 'The baddies chasing the goodies.'

Sterling nodded, not smiling. 'You could say.'

'Wow.' Then something made her smile, which she tried to conceal by breaking her gaze and looking down into her coffee cup. Sterling saw the flush on her slender neck, under the plait. 'Downley Castle. Peace and quiet,' she murmured.

Sterling shuffled on the sofa and twisted his fingers. He felt a flush in his own face and neck, not an unpleasant sensation. 'Yeah, well…'.

'Never mind that for now. So some people are after you and you're in danger. Do you think they followed you here?'

'No, I was careful, and I've stayed on paths and then the promenade and alley. I reckon I'm pretty safe, and I certainly don't want to get you mixed up in this business.'

Stacey waved her hand, as if batting away an insect. Like many people, she seemed to relish being able to help in a crisis. Sterling had noticed that before, in other cases. 'Never mind about that, Frank. What do you need?'

'Well, I could do with a bed for the night, or this sofa – whatever is possible and convenient. A computer and an Internet connection would be really good. I need to look at what's on this memory stick, but without prying eyes.' He put the small device on the coffee table. 'I'm hoping it will be able to tell me where I should go and what I should be doing.'

'Staying is no problem. You can have Michael's room – he's my son – he's not around for a few days. The computer stuff isn't a problem either. Liv – Olivia, my daughter – has got a laptop. She's a wizard on it. If you need some help, I'm sure she could give it.' As she spoke, Stacey moved to the bottom of the stairs, which were part of the open-plan ground floor layout. 'Liv,' she called up.

'What?' came a young voice from an open door near the top of the stairs.

'Can you come down for a minute? There's someone I'd like you to meet.' She looked at Sterling, rolled her eyes and whispered, 'She's all right, Liv, but she's a teenager and everything's got to be a performance.'

A girl appeared at the bottom of the stairs. At first sight, Sterling found it difficult to believe that she was Stacey's daughter. It was much easier to see her father's genetic influence in the large-boned frame, the wideness about her chest, the long, shiny, curly, dark-auburn hair, the freckles over her nose and spilling across her cheeks, and her pale skin. She was a couple of inches taller than her mother, and in the transition from girl to young woman. A sensuous quality, along with delicate, clever facial features, was perhaps Stacey's contribution.

'Liv, this is Frank, Frank Sterling, a friend of mine when we were kids.'

Sterling creaked up from the sofa. 'Hi, Liv. Nice to meet you.'

The girl looked at him. Her eyes were clear and blue. 'A friend of Mum's...' she said, letting the words hang. There was a silence.

Stacey hadn't mentioned a husband or a partner. Perhaps that had something to do with it.

Stacey stepped in. 'Frank is facing a bit of an emergency. We thought you might be able to help.'

The girl shrugged, noncommittal, in full teenager mode.

'I'll probably be stuck otherwise,' offered Sterling. He didn't really have time for an uncommunicative teenager, but he needed computer access. 'I need to get information from this memory stick, but I don't want to be monitored.'

'OK. But everything is set up in my room, so it would be better if we went up there.'

'You go up, then,' said Stacey to them both. 'I'll make some more coffee. Are you hungry, Frank?'

'God, yes, now you mention it. I haven't had anything since breakfast.'

'An omelette or something?'

'Perfect.'

'While I'm sorting that out, Frank, why don't you get out of those clothes? You're about the same size as Michael, so I'll look out jeans and sweatshirt. I'll wash, dry and iron yours and they'll be ready for tomorrow.'

Memories had been bubbling up since Sterling came through the front door and stepped into the spotless living room. Now they came cascading back. It wasn't just the sexual initiation. Stacey seemed virtually to have emerged from the womb as a homemaker. Housework, cooking, cleaning, washing and ironing were her enthusiasms to the point of obsession. In his time in the bosom of the Sunnington family, he'd never lifted a finger, not even to put the kettle on. Now the pattern was repeating itself.

Upstairs, there were no surprises in Liv's bedroom. It smelt of pomegranate shampoo and teenager. A battered grey toy rabbit with missing patches of fur lay spread-eagled on the pillow, as if utterly exhausted. There were pictures of young men – pop stars Sterling did not recognise and would never remember – on the walls. Squeezed between the bed and the side wall was a small desk with a laptop. Schoolbooks and folders were piled neatly on the duvet. It seemed that teenagers could go two ways at that age – to excessive untidiness or the complete opposite, with nothing in between. Liv was clearly in the tidy camp, like her mother.

She cleared the books and folders, invited Sterling to sit and put out her hand for the memory stick. 'I'll just set things up. Then tell me how you want to do this. Do you want to sit at my desk with the laptop and do it yourself? You mentioned you didn't want to be monitored.

Do you know how to do that – you know – make sure you aren't? If the memory stick is password-protected, have you got the password? If it is, and you haven't, do you know how to crack it and get in?'

Sterling blew out his cheeks. 'Whoa,' he said. 'You know a lot. I tell you what – let me sit there and put the stick in and take it from there. If I can't do something, I'll turn it over to you.'

'OK.'

Sterling and the girl swapped places and he settled himself on the small folding chair in front of the screen. He plugged in the stick, and a message came up straight away – 'New device found' – and soon – inevitably, he decided – he was asked for a password.

'Back to you, Liv. It's already beyond my pay grade.' He was noticing a change in the girl. There was a glint in her eyes and she was flexing her fingers, rising to the challenge.

'Oooookaaaay,' she said again. 'First thing to do is download and install a password-cracking program.' Her fingers danced over the keyboard.

'Wait, wait,' said Sterling. 'We don't know who might be monitoring this machine and finding out about this program.'

Liv sighed and gave him a pitying look. 'Well, first off there are loads of these types of programs and anyone trying to find you would be hard pushed to link this machine to you.'

'Unless they were focussing on Deeping...' said Sterling.

'... And secondly I use Hideaway.'

'Hideaway,' said Sterling.

'Hideaway is a Virtual Privacy Network which I guess

is like…' Liv thought for a moment, 'like a letter box you keep but not at your own house, so you keep your own address private.'

'A PO Box,' said Sterling.

'Yeah, for, like, wrinklies who still use snail mail.' Liv kept her eyes on the screen but a small smile spread from her lips to her eyes.

'I'm not that old,' said Sterling. 'Only a year older than your mother.'

'Yeah, well…' as if that proved the point. 'Anyway, what we do here can't be traced back, that's what I'm saying. By the way,' Liv turned her head to Sterling while keeping her eyes on the computer, 'don't mention Hideaway to Mum. She doesn't know she's paying the subscription.'

'Cheeky,' said Sterling. He was warming to this girl, so physically different from her mother and so like her in character. 'Why do you need Hideaway?'

Liv ignored the question. Her fingers continued to range busily over the keyboard, whilst the screen filled up with different tabs and windows, packed tightly with columns of letters, numbers and symbols. As she typed and frowned, she kept up a small commentary under her breath. 'Copy this and this to desktop… Load from desktop… Search… Get to breakpoint… Debug… Put in fake password… Retrieve password… and… we're in.' She sat back and clapped her hands once, one palm sliding off the other.

Even if Sterling had got to a computer in a public space – a library or somewhere – he would have fallen at the first hurdle. Ever since he'd got out of Sandley at midday, he'd been lucky. Meeting this girl was the luckiest thing yet.

'There are only two documents on this. What shall I do?'

'Open them, of course.'

When she did, the password problem was replaced by others. In the first document were numbers sandwiching a script that Sterling did not recognise. In the second was just a series of numbers in blocks. He pointed to the script, little more than a squiggle. 'Could that be Arabic?' he said.

'Search me,' said the girl, shrugging again. She took her eyes from the screen and looked up at Sterling. 'What's this about, Mr Sterling?'

Shrugging and keeping her distance, thought Sterling, noting the formality. Just what teenagers do. 'Dunno,' he said. 'Not yet. Let's concentrate on the first document. Can you go to Google Translate? Right, copy the script from the first document into the box. Paste it into that box. Now click on "Detect language". Arabic,' he muttered to himself. 'I was right. Where is this going?'

Liv had moved on straight away, translating the script into English. Borrowing a pen and sticky pad, Sterling wrote the combination of numbers and letters down.

514813971so614061

'Just two letters with the numbers. None of that is ringing any bells at the moment. What about the numbers in the second document, Liv? Got any wizardry to apply to them?'

'Sorry, Mr Sterling. Even my genius can't help here. What you need for this, I reckon, is a codebook.'

Everything was starting to make sense. Mike Strange had told him what it was already – *One Thousand and One Nights*. Sterling was familiar with the technique from his case at Earlsey Tech, but how did the girl know so much?

'It's one of my school projects – history. Bletchley Park and that.'

'School sounds much more interesting than when I went,' said Sterling.

'Frank,' called Stacey from the foot of the stairs. 'There's some food down here for you.'

'Thanks, Stacey,' Sterling called back. 'I'll be down in a minute.' He turned to the girl. 'Liv,' he said more softly, 'can we keep this to ourselves? I'm going to sort it out, but you need to stay out of it.'

'Not old enough, I suppose. Too dangerous. And I'm not a bloke.'

'None of those – really – more a question of security. Thanks for what you've done. We'll talk about it later.'

'Can't wait,' said the girl, poker-faced. She turned back to her computer, already returning to her own on-screen preoccupations. Sterling had been dismissed.

Chapter 12

The street lamp, a faux-antique design like a large shepherd's crook with a lantern hanging from a hook and looking as if it should be powered by gas rather than electricity, cast an eerie yellow glow on Angela Wilson's dark features. She had come up the steps adjacent to the bowling green and reached the bench on the Town Walk, a semi-circular bank around the back of Sandley that divided the town from its marshy hinterland, just before eight o'clock. At that time of day there was no one about. People would be resting after their dinner and catching up on the soaps.

Shortly afterwards, Becky appeared, similarly dressed in black jeans and jacket, her blonde hair completely covered by a matching black woollen hat. She looked Angela up and down and nodded her approval. They walked swiftly along the embankment, down another set of steps, through St Clement's churchyard and up to the van in the small church car park. Becky paused and listened before she unlocked the doors, scanning the silent graves and gently swaying trees for signs that anyone might have followed. Satisfied, she and Angela slipped into their seats.

'Mike's just on the other side of the river on the way to Earlsey. It looks like somewhere within the pharma plant or nearby. We'll do a drive-past, see how everything looks and take it from there.'

'You're the boss,' said Angela.

Soon they had left Sandley's one-way system behind and were easing through the barbican and across the bridge that took them onto the Isle of Earsley.

'It's not Paxton,' said Becky. 'It's one of the businesses before the pharma complex.' The van slowed down. 'Cosmo Pyrotechnics. Not unexpected. It's been closed down for years.' She carried on driving through the complex on either side and up to the roundabout at the top, came right around and pulled into a bus stop. 'Although it's closed down, there'll be fencing all around it, to stop vandalism and the like. There's a printing works and a sheds construction business next door, one in front of the other. We'll park the van in the entrance-way to those and slip around the side. It's a bright night so we'll have to take care.'

At the identified point, Becky turned left up a potholed driveway that bounced the van gently in every direction. Fortunately, there was a patch of leafy, tatty vegetation just inside, behind which Becky parked, screening the van from the main road in the Earlsey direction, whilst a wide assortment of garden sheds did the same job on the Sandley side. Anyway, the two women agreed, what could be more natural than a van of nondescript colour parked in a light industrial compound?

Becky opened the back of the van and rummaged around in a large tool bag.

'Forgotten the Uzi?' said Angela softly as she loitered nearby.

'Curses,' said Becky. 'Yes. We'll have to improvise.'

She hefted a monkey wrench and handed it over. 'All right?'

'Fine. Reassuring too.'

Becky picked out a lug wrench, and what Angela assumed were wire cutters, and then from a custom-made compartment cut neatly into the floor of the van extracted a small canvas shoulder bag. 'Most of what's in here is what you'd expect from a work person's van, but this is strictly off limits and not what you'd want the local police to be coming across in any stop and search.'

Angela raised an eyebrow.

'Stun grenades,' said Becky. 'Come on.'

The two women made their way further down the potholed entranceway, the squat buildings of Cosmo Pyrotechnics' premises to their left, dark blobs under the starry sky. When they couldn't get any further, they crouched next to the fencing and Becky got the cutters ready.

'When we're inside,' she whispered, 'we'll locate which building and have a little chat. They made fireworks here, so they had to have lots of little buildings to minimise the risk of one explosion triggering other, bigger ones. It's a perfect place to keep someone. Right.' She began snipping, and when she had judged that the hole was big enough, turned back to Angela. 'Ready?' On seeing Angela's nod, Becky ducked through the wire and into Cosmo Pyrotechnics, followed closely by her friend. 'There are a couple of acres between here and Paxton – about two football pitches. The buildings will be set out in a grid, apart from the admin building, which is, if I remember rightly, at the front. Let's start out at the top nearest the road. I reckon abductors are as lazy and unimaginative as anybody else.'

They crept on cautiously, alert to every sound and movement, Becky glancing at her phone to monitor her husband's location. After a few minutes, they were near enough to the main road to hear the occasional hiss of a vehicle going from Sandley to somewhere in Earlsey or the other way round. The fencing at the front was solid and screened everything within from casual eyes – everything except the large 'Cosmo Pyrotechnics' sign atop the main administrative building, whose latticed support structure at the back was clearly visible in the moonlight.

'It's not this side,' said Becky. 'We'll go back a bit, behind the big building, and across.'

Angela grasped her arm. In front of the blockhouse immediately in view was a large black van, all tinted glass and, at the back, blocked-out windows. 'Surely...' she started.

'Yes,' said Becky, looking down at her phone. As if to confirm, they could see a tiny sliver of light at the bottom of the blockhouse door. 'Come around the back, Ange.'

The two women squatted down with their backs to the blockhouse. 'The walls are double-bricked,' said Becky, 'but don't speak too loud. Right, well, we've not brought a door ram and I haven't got one in the van – it would be at least as difficult to explain as these,' she said, holding up the canvas bag. 'A crowbar or whatever, which I have got, would be too slow, and probably not even successful.'

'Which means that...'.

'We knock, and pray like madwomen that there is no stupid code. Hopefully a couple of firm masculine knocks will do the trick. Here's what I propose: you knock, and when someone opens the door, I'll put my foot to it, force it open and toss in one of the stun grenades. As soon as it goes off we both burst in and deal with what we find. We'll have about five seconds.'

'The stun grenade: sorry, Becks, I just ran a gang. It was knives, and towards the end, guns. We hadn't got onto anything more sophisticated. What does it do?'

Becky sighed. 'This is turning out to be a very Heath Robinson operation. Not your fault of course. Circumstances. Let's go through it properly, or Mike is going to cop it. And us too, if we don't get it right... This grenade isn't meant to kill or injure. It'll produce a flash of blinding light and a really loud bang – enough to confuse and disorientate anyone in the blockhouse, including Mike. We of course will still be outside so it will affect us only minimally. When I've tossed it, close your eyes tight and put your hands over your ears. Even then it'll be brighter and louder than you'll ever imagine. They're not call flash-bangs for nothing. I'll go in first and deal with the man who opens the door. You follow me in and go for the next one. If there are two, well and good. If there are more, we'll have to improvise a bit, but we'll still have plenty of advantage. If all goes well, I'll plasticuff the targets so that we've got time to get Mike to the van. The objective is rescue and escape, disabling the kidnappers long enough to achieve that. OK? Ready?'

The two women moved around to the front and braced themselves.

'Right, Ange, knock twice, nice and masculine,' whispered Becky.

For a few moments afterwards, they heard nothing. 'Knock again?' mouthed Angela.

Becky raised her hand and shook her head, staring intently at the door. Another few seconds passed and then there was a muffled scraping noise, and the tiny sliver of light at the bottom of the door became a narrow triangle. Instantly Becky rammed the door with a sharp karate kick and in the same movement tossed the stun grenade firm and low into the interior. She stepped back and to the side and mirrored Angela's hunched hands-over-ears posture. Angela recoiled as the blinding light and bang assailed her eyes and ears exactly as Becky had predicted. Disoriented herself, she still had wits enough to plunge in after Becky. She could see her friend swing the lug wrench backhandedly upwards, catch a large man on the side of his head and leap on his chest as he crumpled untidily to the floor.

Fascinated and distracted by her friend's energy and focus, Angela was slower into action. She spotted a man in the corner and hurried over, her grip on the monkey wrench white with tension and intent. Just as she was about to strike, something in the shape and impression of the prone form held her back. 'Mike,' she muttered. 'God, I could have bashed him.' Something else, in the smallest part of a second, made an impression in the corner of her eye, and she wheeled around and recoiled just in time to avoid taking a huge blow square in her face. As it was, she felt a harsh, searing jolt in her shoulder as a stun stick thudded in. Streetwise rage, pain, survival instincts and adrenaline forced her response. Screaming like a berserker, she jumped forward, swinging the wrench in small arcs against the body of her attacker, driving him back to the wall next to the door. Had it not been for the man's initial flash-bang disorientation, the fight might have been more even, but soon Angela's stocky opponent had dropped the stick and had his arms across his chest and face like a defeated boxer.

'Ange. Angie. Enough,' said Becky, pulling her back from the figure cowering against the wall. The monkey wrench was flecked with blood and Angela was panting and weeping. 'I've disabled the other man. Let me sort this one out. At least you didn't go for his head. His arm's broken, though.' She did a thorough check, put the arm in a sling-type posture and got busy with the plasticuffs.

Recovering herself Angela looked around the gloomy room, taking in the chair against the wall where Mike was slumped, the operating table contraption in the middle and the various bits of equipment and gear strewn untidily around the room. 'What's been going on here, Becky? What have they been doing to Mike?'

'Waterboarding by the look of it,' said Becky. Her lips formed a thin white line in a grim, angry face. She and Mike hadn't planned for this. She moved swiftly across to her husband. 'Mike, Mike,' she said softly and firmly, her finger on his pulse and her arm cradling his head. 'Can you get me some water, Angie?'

She cleaned his face. 'His pulse is strong. He's probably been drugged. He should be OK when we get him to come round.'

Mike's eyes fluttered and came into focus. 'You're late, Becky.'

His wife buried her face in his neck. When she looked at him again, tears were creeping down her cheeks.

'What about a glass of water?'

Angela rushed to comply and Mike drank greedily. 'I'm pretty peckish,' he said.

'Don't push your luck,' said Becky. Her face admitted a tiny smile. 'Come on. We'd better get out of here.'

Outside, she slashed a tyre of the vehicle outside the blockhouse with a Stanley knife from her bag. Then together, the women helped Mike up, draped his arms around their shoulders and walked him out of the blockhouse, shutting the door behind them, calculating that once the abductors had recovered, they'd be able to free themselves and get help – but not for a good half hour. Those bastards deserve a lot less was Angela's verdict. Mike and Becky seemed more sanguine. In a dirty war, everyone did dodgy things.

Mike was still groggy, and Angela's other shoulder was throbbing and sore from the stun stick, but the priority was to get through the fence and back to the van. 'Where now?' she said, when they were all settled, Mike lying on a makeshift bed of blankets in the back. 'The pub? My house?'

'Neither,' said Becky. 'Those men and their associates will know exactly where Mike and I live, and as they've been to the library, some of them, they'll probably know about you and how you're connected to Frank. No, it's Ramston for us – to our very own little safe house.'

The house turned out to be a well-proportioned 1950s semi down the road and around the corner from Ramston's Victorian station. Mike was made comfortable and warm in the front room, whilst Becky and Angela aired the musty rooms and prepared some food.

'You're dark horses,' said Angela, when they were all settled, injuries soothed and dressed, with sandwiches and stiff drinks. 'We knew a bit about you, Frank and I, after those other cases, but this is a cosy little hidey-hole. What else have you got up your sleeves?'

Becky tapped her nose. 'That would be telling.' She turned to her husband. 'But now we're onto telling, why don't you give us an update, sweetheart?'

Mike took a long pull of his Scotch, put his head back and shuddered. 'OK. First off, I wouldn't want to go through any of that again.'

Chapter 13

'Any luck, Frank?' Stacey was sitting at the small table at the far end of the downstairs living space with her chin cupped over her clasped hands, watching as Sterling devoured his omelette and chips. He could hear the washing machine in the scullery beyond the kitchen. An ironing board had been unfolded and was standing in front of the window in the living room area.

He took a long sip of coffee. He'd been light-headed in the girl's bedroom, and realised how thirsty he was. 'She's a bright kid, that girl of yours, Stacey. And pretty.'

'Yes, bright and pretty, but that age as well, you know – not far off sixteen. I shudder to think what she gets up to if she's anything like I was at her age.' Stacey remembered who she was talking to and her neck flushed again.

Sterling concentrated on his knife and fork, as if he hadn't noticed, and took another mouthful of omelette. 'Yeah, we did have some luck, actually. Liv cracked the password – don't tell me how – and we opened one of the two documents on the stick.' He showed Stacey the sticky note with the numbers and the translation. She was trustworthy and straight as a die all those years ago, and nothing that he'd seen and heard since suggested that she'd changed in those respects. 'We can't do anything with the second document because it's just numbers and we need a codebook.'

Stacey looked at the sticky. 'I'm hopeless with anything like this. Liv might be having a few ideas. She's quick with everything.'

'I said I'd have another chat with her later.'

'So what sort of things are you looking for?'

'There's often a date in sets of numbers like these but I can't see anything. The letters – "so" – could be anything. I need to worry at it. This is the key to what I do next. Right now I don't really know what I'm meant to be doing or where I'm meant to be going.'

'Well, you're welcome to stay here, Frank, while you do your worrying. But don't you think we should contact the police or something?'

'And tell them what? The powers-that-be get threats like this every day. I've been at one or two police station front desks in my time, and at the end of CID phones when crank calls come in. I can tell you, none of this is weirder than some of the things I've heard. There's something else too, Stacey. Mike, the mate who gave me the memory stick, was relying on me to sort this out. I might have to contact the police or someone down the line, but I'm not at that stage yet. About staying... I don't want to get you and Liv into trouble...'.

'We'll be all right, Frank, if no one saw you arrive.'

'Thanks again, Stacey. Tell your dad to keep quiet as well, if anyone comes snooping. Not that it's likely.'

'I'll ring him straight away.'

Later on, towards ten o'clock, coffee had given way to beer. Sterling had got little further with the line of numbers and text, and he knew himself well enough now that having a rest from it might get the breakthrough he needed.

It was relaxing in the armchair, and Stacey was curled on the sofa with her legs underneath her.

'So, Stacey,' said Sterling, 'what have you been up to…?'

'… these last twenty years.'

'Sense of humour's intact, then.'

Stacey tipped her head. 'I suppose. Do you remember Jason Eliot?'

'Jace,' said Sterling. 'His parents ran that pub in Middle Street. What was it, The Albert? Good bloke. Liked to have a laugh. Cheerful.'

'That's him. Well, I married him. Had the two kids early on – Michael and of course Liv. Michael – the oldest – works with his dad on his boat – fishing, and Liv – Olivia – you've met. You know that jewellers in the middle of town – next to Savers – I manage that now. We got this house as soon as it came up. You know me, Frank. I like to be with my family.'

'But you're an Eliot now, Stacey.'

'Not really – or only by name. Once a Sunnington, always a Sunnington, I suppose.'

'So where are Jace and Michael now? Fishing?'

Stacey's face fell. Sterling saw a frown as she looked back down into her cup. 'Maybe fishing. I don't know. Jason and I separated about six months ago. He moved out to some flat between here and Dovethorpe. Michael still lives here, but I don't see much of him. Jason *was* cheerful – when we first got married, and for a few years after that. Then things changed. Got… darker. It's hard to make a living from fishing these days, and he always liked a drink. When the kids were young, we really struggled.'

Sterling brought up a memory of the occasional drinking session with Jace and their mates. He had been a big, chirpy, wholehearted, pale-skinned, good-looking young man with a shock of true auburn, curly hair and a witty line in chat. But things did change, and so did people, sometimes from choice, sometimes circumstance. 'I'm sorry.'

Stacey shrugged. 'We're all getting over it. What's happened has happened. There's no point in getting bitter. What about you, Frank? You got married, didn't you?'

Now Sterling looked down. 'Yeah. Not to someone from around here. Someone I met in Fenningstone, when I was in the police. Nurse. I broke my nose in a ruck at the dog stadium. Or more accurately, someone broke it for me. I met her on the ward. It didn't work out. The shift work. She wanted kids. I wasn't sure. We divorced. I don't even know where she is now.'

'I'm sorry too, Frank. You can't tell what's going to happen. You've done well as a private detective though. Dad comes around with the paper when your cases come up.'

Sterling tilted his head from side to side and pushed out his lower lip, as if weighing things up. 'Well, one or two things worked out. There was that rescue case that Nicky Moran wrote up.'

'Nicky Moran... who'd have thought he'd be a journalist. He was such a joker at school as I remember. Never took anything seriously. And that girl in the wheelchair...'.

'Emma Jameson.' Sterling smiled at the memory. 'She

looked as though butter wouldn't melt in her mouth, but she swore like the proverbial.'

They were quiet for a few minutes, on different memories.

'Why didn't you come back before, Frank? Why didn't you visit? You and your dad weren't that far away down in Middle Deeping. It wasn't just me. We all loved you up here, you know that.'

Sterling shrugged. 'I thought I'd burned my boats. If we weren't together...'.

'Well, I was gutted, no doubt about that, but that didn't mean I was going to be awkward or unpleasant – not after a bit of time had passed, anyway.'

'And there were your brothers...'.

Stacey laughed. 'Jack and Billy. They called me a silly bint for letting you go. Couldn't get their heads around it. They were on your side. "He's all right, that Frank Sterling," they used to say.' Then she was suddenly serious. 'Anyway, why did you let me go?'

'We were young, Stace. That's what happens. I regretted it afterwards, but by then I was too proud and it was too late.'

'Isn't that a bit, you know, flip, Frank?'

Sterling squirmed. She was right. That wasn't it.

There was a clump down the stairs. Liv appeared halfway down and looked into the sitting room area. *This is cosy*, said her face. The excitement of working with Sterling was offset by suspicion and disapproval. 'Have you got anywhere with those numbers, Mr Sterling?'

'Not yet, Liv. I've been having a bit of a break and chatting to your Mum.'

'Right, well, I've been doing a bit more research,' she said. 'Arabic writing is funny.'

'Yeah?' said Sterling. There was so much he didn't know.

'Yeah. It goes from right to left.'

'So those numbers and letters might make more sense the other way round.'

'Einstein,' murmured the girl with a slight roll of eyes.

'Liv,' chided her mother.

'Except that, wouldn't Google Translate automatically put it all the right way round?' said Sterling.

'I thought that,' said the girl, 'but I tried it the Arabic way.'

'OK, said Sterling. He looked again at the sticky note. 'So, 514813971so01614061 becomes 16041610os179318415. Is that what you got, Liv?' The girl nodded. 'Interesting. Remember what I was saying about a date, Stacey? Look – the first six numbers – 16 04 16 – 16th April, which is…'.

'Tomorrow,' said Stacey and Liv.

'So if that's the date, maybe the 10 after it is the time – morning rather than evening, which would be 22 to avoid confusion. So far so good. But what about the rest of it?'

'I bet "os" is "Ordnance Survey",' said the girl. 'You've got the date and time maybe. Now it's moving onto place.'

'You know a lot, Liv.'

'Geography is one of your GCSEs, isn't it Liv? She's doing ten, Frank,' said Stacey. The pride shone in her eyes.

'Map-reading is part of it,' said Liv. 'Hang on a sec.' She clattered back up the stairs and came down with a battered map. 'Like I thought – o/s 179 – Deeping and Dovethorpe.' She spread the map on the coffee table.

'318…'. The index finger of her left hand swept from right to left and stopped. '415…'. Now her right hand index finger moved down and then her fingers touched as the lines came together. She looked up triumphantly. 'Right in the middle of Dovethorpe.'

'So, I know where I'm going. The snag is how I'm going to get down to Dovethorpe tomorrow morning.'

'Bus from South Street. Simples,' said Liv.

'No, it isn't, actually.' Sterling paused for a long moment. Liv had helped him crack the files on the memory stick, and she'd said she'd keep quiet about things, but she didn't know why he'd come calling in the first place, including the protracted escape from Sandley. He looked at Stacey, and she gave the slightest of nods.

'I told your mum before you came downstairs… There's a gang of blokes after me who want the memory stick. It's a bit of a story, but it's pretty certain they know I'm in Deeping. They'll have tried all the hotels and B & Bs, and they're probably investigating where else I might have gone. The point is, if I'm anywhere in public, even in a car going through the town, they could well spot me because right now, I reckon they're swarming everywhere around here.'

'Why not go to the police?' said Liv. 'Witness protection and all that.'

'We've already talked about that,' said Stacey. 'Not the witness protection, though, love. You've been watching too many films.'

'Like I said to your mum, there's not much I can say to them at the moment – not much sensible anyway. "Excuse me, but there's a bunch of blokes after me in Deeping, and this vague terrorist threat." I can tell you,

I wouldn't get far with that.' Sterling turned to Stacey. 'I'm still sorry I've had to involve the two of you.'

'Don't be daft, Frank. I'm glad we can help.' Her hand patted his, and lingered a fraction.

'Uncle Billy,' said Liv. She had switched off during the speechifying.

'What about him, Liv?' said her mother.

'He's been keeping his fishing gear and moped in our shed.'

'So?'

'Mr Sterling could use them to get through Deeping and down to Dovethorpe. No one would recognise him with the crash helmet on.'

'The moped's been in there for months. It's about thirty years old. We don't even know if it's still working,' said Stacey.

'If it is, Stace,' said Sterling, 'it sounds like a plan.'

In the shed, Liv was as adept at making sure the moped was serviceable as she had been with the computer work. Sterling watched her fill the tank from a jerrycan, put air in the tyres, make the appropriate adjustments when the engine initially wouldn't fire and finally, by a methodical process of trial and error, get it going. It was so ancient it had pedals, and Liv had started it on its stand, the dense smell of petrol and blue exhaust filling the shed, even with the door wide open. 'Uncle Billy showed me,' she had said simply. 'Any stuff like this interests me.'

Back in the house, the only evidence that the washing machine and tumble dryer had been on and the ironing board out were the perfectly clean, dry and creased trousers, shirt and jacket on the arm of the sofa. Now everything was set. Sterling would leave at 9am for

Dovethorpe by moped in Billy's gear. Liv would be having her Saturday morning lie-in if she didn't manage to wake up beforehand, and Stacey would have left at 8am for work. 'What else can you do?' asked Sterling when she had lamented her other commitments.

At one o'clock, Sterling was in Michael's bed between crisp white cotton sheets in a room that had been dusted, vacuumed and aired. He should have been exhausted, but then there was something else, the culmination of an undercurrent growing throughout the evening. His door opened and he heard Stacey's soft whisper.

'Frank, do you fancy some… peace and quiet?'

'What about Liv, Stacey?' His voice was hoarse and he couldn't stop a gulp.

'I've checked. She's asleep, and that girl sleeps the sleep of the dead.'

Sterling hadn't been with a woman for a long time. This was his childhood sweetheart, the one it had all started with – his first time – their first time. He'd lost her too casually and for no good reason. But he'd been suppressing his feelings and trying to ignore hers all evening. Now was not the time for rekindling an old romance, not while he was running from a gang of thugs and grappling with some big emergency. He felt a double guilt – abandoning Stacey all those years ago and using her now. It was all wrong.

'Frank?' she whispered.

He was wide awake and completely aroused.

'Certainly,' he whispered. He pulled back the covers. There was a rustle as a dressing gown slipped to the floor and he welcomed the cool, fragrant, naked figure into the bed. Stacey pressed her breasts and hips against him and sighed.

Chapter 14

Zahra had had a bad day, and now he was having a bad night. He sat in the room's only easy chair and stared at the brick wall. Hamid and the others had found no trace of Sterling on the back road from Sandley Bay back to Sandley, or on the path across the golf course. The odds were much stronger that he had struck out to Deeping, which was closer. He would not know that his boat had been found. Zahra had deployed his men to Deeping en masse and instructed them to check all the hotels, pubs, café-bars and bed and breakfasts. They loitered on street corners, at the railway station and the bus station. They checked the taxi ranks and taxi cubbyholes masquerading as offices, and roved ghost-like through the town, to the point of complete infiltration.

At the desk, Asif's fingers continued to dance over the keyboard of the laptop, the screen reflected in his glasses. Even Zahra, to whom others' tiredness and discomfort were entirely immaterial, noticed the frown in Asif's forehead, the red-rimmed eyes and the occasional typing error. Still, mused Zahra, he was useful, and so, particularly at the moment, was the profile he had built up of Sterling as a local person seemingly unwilling to leave the immediate vicinity and not even owning a car. The password list Zahra had found in the private investigator's office had proved useful.

On the run since midday, Sterling would not have had access to technology to look at the memory stick. He'd have known it was too risky to use his mobile, even if he had taken it. So there would be no specific destination to aim for. The challenge for Zahra and his cell was that Sterling would hole up with a friend. As Zahra mused and calculated, Asif pressed on with his hacking, his maps, the information supply to and liaison with the men in the field, the monitoring and analysis of communications traffic, and all the associated activity of a skilful and inspired cyber expert.

Everything was being done that could be done, but Zahra still had to swallow a bitter pill: Sterling continued to be on the loose, and the trail had gone cold. His phone chimed. 'Yes.' He listened and then spoke tersely. 'Wait there.' The pill had just become even more bitter. Saying nothing to Asif, he left the hotel, took out the Mercedes and headed over the bridge to Cosmo Pyrotechnics. Hangdog man had jacked up the other vehicle and was in the process of changing a tyre. Squint-eyed man was watching from the door of the blockhouse. Zahra got out of the Mercedes and stood in the moonlight, his arms akimbo. Neither of the other men could look at him. They shuffled around, busy on their tasks.

'Well?' said Zahra. 'What happened?'

'There were four men, brother,' lied hangdog man, 'wearing balaclavas. They knocked on the door and we thought it was you. They threw this in.' He held up the spent stun grenade, finally making eye contact. 'We thought it was you,' he repeated. 'We were due a visit. No one else knew we were here.' A whine had crept into his voice. Now, it seemed, the ambush was Zahra's fault. 'The men took Strange away and slashed the tyre. We have not long managed to get out of the restraints.'

Zahra was incandescent, and the effort of will to keep himself calm was fully noticed by the two erstwhile torturers. Whilst Zahra trembled and his eyes bulged, they shifted from foot to foot and stared at the ground. Zahra's hand twitched by the gun in his waistband. Someone, sometime, would pay for all the frustration and incompetence, but these men could still play a part, their fear making them zealous. Now was not the time for extreme measures. 'Pack up here. Leave nothing. No evidence. Nothing. Join the others in Deeping. Asif will tell you where and give you details. Hamid will deploy you when you are there.'

The men hurried to complete their tasks. Zahra stood watching for a few moments, a malign and oppressive presence. He should have pressed the man Strange harder while he had the chance. He should have broken him. On the way back to the hotel, he wondered if he was losing his grip, making mistakes where before he made none. He and Hamid had been globetrotting as terrorists-for-hire for so long, perhaps too long. When he let himself into the room, stealthy as an assassin, Asif looked up briefly from his screen and then resumed what he was doing. Questions and comments were pointless. Only when he had something to report would Zahra show even a shred of interest.

The moment came later in the night. Zahra wasn't even lying on the sofa. His tall frame was upright and there was a pillow to support his head. His hands were clasped in his lap, and his legs, bent at the knee, perfectly parallel down to his feet. His breathing was calm and measured.

'Brother,' whispered Asif. 'Brother,' he repeated, more loudly and firmly.

Zahra opened his eyes and they came into focus. For the briefest of moments, he looked disoriented, and then he registered Asif. 'Well?'

'I've found a Facebook posting which mentions Frank Sterling. Some traffic analysis. Open source, pretty much.'

Zahra blinked. For him, there was only one important rule about technology – not how it worked, not what it could do, not even what it might be able to do in the future – just what results it achieved. He filtered out Asif's geeky jargon and concentrated only on what was useful to him. 'And?' he said.

'It's on a girl's page – Liv Eliot. It looks like somewhere in Deeping. There are a lot of references to her family on the mother's side – the family name is Sunnington. I'll be able to get something a bit more specific in a few moments. She's talking about Sterling visiting last night and helping him to solve a computer problem – no other details. But she also mentions a rendezvous in the centre of Dovethorpe at ten o'clock this morning.' Asif chuckled. '"How cool is that?" she says. Cool for us, I'd say.'

Zahra's deadpan expression didn't change. 'What's the time now?'

'Six thirty, sir.'

'Where is Dovethorpe? Show me on the map.'

Asif pointed out another town further down the coast to the south. 'It's about seven miles from Deeping, fourteen from here.'

'Find out exactly where the girl lives.'

'That might be tricky,' said Asif.

Zahra looked at him. Asif returned to the keyboard.

'There are so many Eliots – literally dozens,' he complained 'and she might be in a set-up where the address and phone number are ex-directory. But there aren't so many Sunningtons, and most of them are bunched in Downley Close, Deeping. Look.' Asif pinpointed the road on Google maps. 'That is right at the north end of Deeping, only a couple of miles from where Hamid found the boat.' He did something to the screen to produce a street view. 'If the girl is not there, then someone in Downley Close will surely know where she is.'

'That's the best you can do?' asked Zahra.

'For the moment, brother. I will keep trying of course.'

'Phone Hamid and tell him that I'll meet him at the entrance of Downley Close. How long will it take me to get there?'

'About half an hour.'

'In half an hour, then.'

Zahra went to his car and programmed his satnav. Maybe his luck had turned much earlier than he would have guessed. The odds were great that Sterling was somewhere at the top end of Deeping.

In the hotel room, after he had given Hamid his instructions, Asif was carrying out a dialogue with himself. 'Thank you for staying up all night to find me this vital information, Asif.' 'It was my pleasure, brother.' 'Your work is always of the highest standard. You will be well rewarded.' 'Arsehole,' he concluded.

Chapter 15

The bedroom window faced east, and when Sterling woke up, there were the faintest glints of sunlight from the direction of the sea. His watch said 7am. He'd sensed Stacey steal away not long before. He had at least an hour before he needed to move. He turned over and buried his face in the pillow. The stiffness of the sailing adventure had been offset by last night's passion, but he still needed that hour.

A moment later, he heard the door open, and Stacey slipped in with a mug of tea. 'Plenty of milk, no sugar,' she said softly, 'unless it's changed.'

'No, spot on. Thanks, Stace.'

She sat on the bed and beamed, to Sterling's thinking as much from the pleasure of remembering accurately about the tea as all the early hours' excitement. 'You've got plenty of time, but I haven't, and I wanted to enjoy a bit more time together.'

'Right,' said Sterling. He sipped his tea. New stirrings of guilt tied his tongue.

'Hang on a second. I thought I heard something outside.' Stacey got up and Sterling could hear her pad across the landing and into the main bedroom, whose window overlooked the close. She returned quickly. 'There's a big car outside Dad's house, and two men are talking to him on the doorstep – at seven in the morning.

Something's up.' Sterling followed her and glanced cautiously to his left. The taller of the two men, who had jet-black hair and was wearing an expensive suit which hung badly on his lean frame, was clearly in charge even though Sterling could only see his back. The other man stood behind him, his posture showing a curious mixture of deference and menace.

'How the f...?' Sterling muttered.

'Never mind that. Dad will be as stroppy as he can be with strangers, and he'll have twigged that he needs to stall, but you've got to get out of here. Go and get ready. I'll wake Liv and she'll help you get the moped into the alley and out into Downley Road. As soon as you're out the back, I'll go and help Dad. Take care, Frank. Stay safe.' She kissed him hard and hugged him tightly so he could feel every contour under the thin dressing gown. 'Come back.'

The last Sterling saw of Stacey, after she had roused Liv, was hurrying downstairs with her mobile pressed against her ear and the small dog yapping by her feet.

In her own dressing gown and slippers, hair tousled and bleary-eyed, Liv eased the moped out of the shed while Sterling pulled back the bolt of the garden gate that opened into the alley. He was already hot with waterproof fishing gear squeaking and crackling over his everyday clothes, despite the early morning nip in the spring air. The fishing rod, strapped to his back like an ammunition belt, caught at each end on the door posts and almost provided a comedy moment when his legs kept walking as his body was held back. Liv giggled and grimaced. They stole down the alley and into the road, checking beforehand that there were no unpleasant surprises beyond the alley.

'Here, let me,' said Liv, as Sterling's efforts on the pedals resulted in nothing more than a feeble, short-lived putter. After a moment astride the moped, she powered the motor into life.

'Thanks, Liv. Thank your Mum again – for everything.'

'For everything,' echoed Liv, knowingly. 'Right.'

Sterling plunged on. 'One thing I didn't have a chance to tell her… Before, I said the police would be no good. Now I think things have changed. You need protection. Get your mum to contact Detective Chief Inspector Andy Nolan. He should be based at Cantcester Police Station. Tell her to mention my name. He'll take what she's got to say seriously. Got it?'

'Yep. DCI Andy Nolan, Cantcester.'

'Good. I'm off. I'll leave all this in the central car park in Dovethorpe like we agreed, and your uncle Billy can collect it.'

He put on the old helmet, which smelt of Billy, he assumed, and felt gritty, and slipped the visor down. As he revved up, he caught her look, no longer cocky and knowing. 'I'll make it up to you, Mr Sterling.' Then she was gone, back down the alley, her dressing gown flapping as she went.

Downley Road was the beginning of Deeping's promenade, which stretched beyond the centre of town and as far as Walbrook Castle to the south, but for Sterling, College Road leading into Middle Street, exactly parallel, was much less conspicuous. Checking everything carefully, he turned right and then left and was properly on his way, noting as he went the knot of activity just beyond the entrance to Downley Close. A swirl of questions and speculations should have been shaping up in his head, along urgent, serious lines, to do with how he'd been found and where he was going next.

Instead, he thought about Stacey and Downley Close. This woman, and this life, could have been his. Perhaps they still could be. The spark was still there, and the passion, and the affection – no doubt about it. But the downside was still there too, the reason he'd left all that time ago. His lonely father had described him then as 'proper looked after', all that time up in the north of the town getting 'meals and pampering and whatnot', not without envy. But his father hadn't felt the suffocation, the sense of life going on without you having any choice in the matter, and the… yes, the dullness. Stacey was a homemaker then – all those domestic skills willingly learnt from her mother and practised on him. She was just as much one now, and still with all her family around her. Odds were that she'd slipped a lunch box in his bag as she'd said goodbye.

He revved the moped. He wasn't being ungrateful, he told himself – just realistic – that life might not be for him, and to be fair to Stacey, why would she want someone like him – intent on going his own solitary way whatever the consequences? Still, nothing was going to happen till he got out of his current fix.

Now, he forced himself to concentrate on getting used to the machine under him. He could think things through later. He kept to 20 mph in this built-up area. There was no need to hurry, and it was sensible to keep the whine of the engine as quiet as possible since most people would still be asleep or just waking up.

Gradually, the social housing at Deeping's north end gave way to Victorian terracing on one side, and even older town cottages, built in the Napoleonic era, on the other, with more modern infill inserted higgledy-piggledy in gaps. Outside Jason's parents' pub in Adelaide Square a dustbin spewing its rubbish lay knocked over in the gutter after a raucous Friday evening. As Sterling got closer to the town centre, small Georgian squares and town houses began to prevail, and then the pedestrianised shopping district. He followed the road to the left along the one-way system, back up to the promenade, Deeping pier and the sea. In the corner of his eye, he saw two gang members stationed at the front of the pier where a seagull perched on the sou'wester of the fisherman sculpture. They had a perfect view along each side of the promenade and down into the town, but Sterling was just a bloke with a rod on his moped, off on some quirky quest to catch a tide somewhere down the coast. Fishermen started early, or late, or at any time the elements dictated. They dressed entirely pragmatically, and carried outlandish equipment no one else would ever recognise. Gliding past with his helmet on and his outfit crackling, he knew he had the perfect disguise.

Soon, Deeping had become Walbrook. The moped carried Sterling past the lifeboat station and the green, and then he was going up Dovethorpe Hill and leaving the built-up area behind. The main road was usually busy, but at seven thirty on a Saturday morning the rush hadn't yet started. Now Sterling was fully attuned to his current situation, and he found the rhythmic drone of the engine at 30 mph calming.

Had he been lucky or hadn't he? The people tracking him were effective. They'd had the resources to trace him to Sandley Bay, and there they were at Stacey's father's place in Downley Close. He'd only just got away out the back. Why would it be any different at the grid reference spot in the middle of Dovethorpe? What had Liv said when she'd left him? Something wasn't adding up. Then his mind drifted back to last night with Stacey.

A horn blared and a car, black or dark-blue, flashed by. He'd wandered almost onto the other side of the road. The moped wobbled as he tried to recover. He'd been dreaming, not thinking. The moped puttered on along the low hills and dales of east Kent until he reached the roundabout on the far outskirts of Dovethorpe. Right would take him up to Cantcester and beyond that, London, left down the wide sweep direct to the ferry terminal on the eastern side of Dovethorpe, avoiding the town altogether. He went straight on – the most direct route into the centre of town but via a violent series of twists and bends, steep, short hills and sudden plunges. It was a challenge enough on four wheels, and he had to concentrate on the moped, whose engine whined in sharper than ever protest at the steepness of some of the inclines, and even once or twice threatened to give up. Here, after the independent military school on the right, was a landscape of rolling pastures dotted with sheep and patches of scree, skeletal steel communications towers studded with satellite dishes and other, stranger signal paraphernalia. Only coastguard cottages clinging to the hillsides indicated human habitation in this windswept area.

In the distance, Dovethorpe Castle was a stony sprawl at the highest point, brooding over the town kowtowing underneath, and, by some quirk of the light or angles, it appeared to loom larger and then recede during the early part of Sterling's approach. After a few minutes, the road rounded the side of the huge Norman outpost and dropped sharply into the heart of the town. The car park where Stacey had told him to leave the moped was to the right of Castle Street. He parked it in the motorcycle section and unstrapped his bag from the rack. Having taken off Billy's helmet, he had a last wrestle with the fishing rod. Then he took off all the waterproof fishing equipment and stuffed it into one of the panniers. From the other, he took out the long cable lock and strapped moped, helmet and panniers to one of the bars provided. He couldn't secure the rod, so he laid it lengthways along the side of the moped. If it was nicked, or anything else happened to Billy's moped and equipment, or even if it didn't for that matter, Sterling had racked up another debt.

His pursuers had found his boat at Sandley Bay. Then somehow, more worryingly, they had made a connection to Downley Close and the Sunnington family. So he looked ultra-cautiously around the car park from under the discreet shade of a leafy young ash tree. Stacey and Liv both knew where he was going. Supposing they had been forced to spill the beans? Not only was he in danger – pretty much all the time since Friday lunchtime – but he'd landed them in it as well. He remembered that, amidst her gentle-natured qualities, Stacey had a rarely revealed layer of toughness, and she could shout like a fishwife when her dander was up. From the little he'd experienced of Liv, she was no pushover either. All the Sunningtons were cheerful, welcoming and easy-going – until you got on the wrong side of them. Then it was all for one and one for all. But still, for Sterling, twinges of conscience mingled with unease.

For the moment, though, as the springtime sunshine strengthened and cast long shadows to the west, everything seemed quiet. The car park was relatively empty, and at 8am there only seemed to be shop workers gravitating singly or in desultory dribs and drabs towards the centre from a range of different directions. A flock of sparrows fluttered busily down to a tired-looking flower bed close by, and their foraging made Sterling realise he needed waking up. He edged across to a supermarket whose frontage lined the road opposite. The cafeteria would be the perfect obscure place to charge up with caffeine, have breakfast, take stock and wait for his ten o'clock rendezvous. His mind went through possible scenarios. He wondered what would happen next. The answer was easy. He didn't have a single clue.

Chapter 16

Zahra and Hamid were exactly where Frank Sterling was about ten hours before – standing at the door of the head of clan Sunnington. Their knocking was urgent and persistent, with the assumption that older people went to bed early, slept fewer hours and rose at dawn. After two minutes they could hear movement behind the front door, just as Sterling had. 'Sorry to trouble you, Mr Sunnington.' Zahra's face and eyes said different. 'We're looking urgently for Frank Sterling. He is wanted for questioning in connection with a recent incident in Sandley.'

The Sunningtons had a default position for outsiders – the very opposite from their warm embrace of family, friends and local community. 'Who wants to know – at seven o'clock in the morning?'

Zahra flashed his credentials. This time there was no fear, no overawed effect and no obvious respect for authority.

'There's no Frank Sterling around here. I haven't seen Frank for years,' lied the old man.

He and Zahra stared at each other. Normally, a staring match with Zahra ended when the other person broke gaze. Not this time. There was some movement from a house a few doors up. A slender, pretty woman appeared in tan boots and a dressing gown, wrapped close, her hands gripping the lapels.

'What's going on, Dad? These blokes bothering you?'

'They're just going, Stacey, love.'

Hamid's phone pinged, just as a girl with red hair came into view. 'Irfan,' he hissed urgently, showing Zahra the phone. Zahra looked from the picture on the phone to the dishevelled girl in front of him. His eyes flicked to the open front door in the nearby house. Abruptly, he turned on his heel and walked off, drawing Stacey and Liv with him.

'You can't…'.

'Shut up,' said Zahra, as he and Hamid went into the house.

'I'll call the police,' said Stacey. 'My dad probably already has.' Unlikely, she thought. More likely he'd phone her brothers.

Hamid returned to the front room from the search he'd been conducting. 'No one down here. No one upstairs. Two beds slept in, but not the main bedroom. He was here.'

'Try the shed, why don't you?' said Liv. 'Bastards.'

Zahra nodded to Hamid. He and Hamid were not British. Both were literalists with no ear for irony.

Hamid came back again. His shoes made watery prints on the carpet. 'No one in the garden or the shed. But there's a back gate into an alley. The alley leads up to the road by the sea.'

'Tell the others to keep alert around there and in the town.'

Immediately after Zahra's instruction, there was a loud thumping at the door, the kind made by a dawn raid, just prior to application of a battering ram. Zahra nodded to Hamid, thankful that he had his most competent lieutenant with him. Hamid flicked back his jacket to show a shoulder holster and gun, and opened the door.

Two tall men in their early forties stood in the path – wiry and solid at the same time. Their dark hair and handsome faces, even if they were weathered from fishing, made it obvious that they were Sunningtons, and Stacey's brothers.

'What's up, Stace? Dad phoned,' said the taller one slightly in front, peering past Hamid at his sister, who looked suddenly small and vulnerable in her own front room.

Zahra did rapid calculations, as he had before on Sandley waterfront. The man Sterling had been here but he had gone. It was likely he was still in Deeping, where Zahra's men were out in force. If he wasn't in Deeping, Asif had found details of a rendezvous in the next town. It went against the grain in this stupid rule-of-law country, but there was nothing to be gained here from violence and retribution, and it would just make an escalating situation worse. 'This is about national security,' he smiled – except for his cold eyes. It was true, though not in the way these idiots might understand it. 'We are sorry for the intrusion, but speed and...' – he searched for a word – '... disruption were unavoidable, and we had no time to go through the usual channels. The man we seek is dangerous.'

'My arse,' said the taller of the two men. 'You come up here, bullying my dad, trespassing in my sister's house... Let's see some ID.'

Stacey spoke, her face peeping out from behind the two interlopers. She'd seen Hamid's hardware. 'Leave it,

Jack. It's disgusting, but it's sorted now. Billy?' She appealed to her shorter brother, who put a restraining hand on Jack's forearm.

Zahra and Hamid walked past the brothers, the four men locked in customary macho eye contact until the strangers reached the front gate.

'Get the car number, Billy,' hissed Liv.

'When you've done that,' said Stacey, 'and they've properly gone, come in for a cup of tea, and get Dad. There's a lot to tell you.'

As Stacey filled the kettle, her daughter sidled up to her. 'Only two beds slept in, Mum?' she smiled. 'Better leave that bit out.'

'You cheeky minx,' said her mother. She stared at the work surface and blushed.

Chapter 17

The pasty girl in the poorly fitting supermarket livery and matching sun-visor-style cap banged trays and clattered around the tables at which Sterling, and a tall man with shiny, coal-black skin, thin to the point of emaciation, whiled away their time. The man had the air of a refugee from a failed sub-Saharan state, a mixture of aimlessness and insecurity. The girl was full of angry resentment, fuelled, Sterling was sure, by fear of strangers.

Having had breakfast and three cups of tea, Sterling was ready to go. He caught the stranger's eye and nodded, slipping a high-denomination note across the tables. The man looked back, his face sad and unsmiling, but bowed his head and put his hands together as if starting to pray. Then he slipped the note into the pocket of a tatty, too-small bomber jacket, its Formula One branding at odds with the status of its wearer.

'Too noisy for this time of day,' said Sterling to the girl, who tossed her head and flounced off.

Two minutes later, at ten to ten, under a brisk, sunny sky, with clouds scudding swiftly from west to east, creating bursts of bright but not very warm spring sunshine, he was slouching on the corner of Market Square. He'd taken up station against one of the thin pillars holding up the overhang of a large block of flats, under which an equally large charity shop sprawled along its whole length. 'Furniture and Electrical' proclaimed its business boldly. To an observer, Sterling might have seemed casual – a husband waiting for his wife to come off an early shift, or to come out of a shop in which he had no interest. He shifted his weight to the other leg. His palms felt sweaty, and the perspiration on his back, combined with the moments when cloud obscured the sun and the temperature dropped, made him shiver.

The square was getting busier as it was Saturday. It was largely pedestrianised except for the road that curved around the edge. Next to the fountain, whose fine spray created a sphere of misty, shimmering water, two plump girls in tops and leggings gossiped as they sat on the stone edge and shared a cigarette. A couple of boys about the same age wheeled languidly around on skateboards. A young father struggled to keep up with his toddler daughter as he spoke animatedly on his phone. An older man, with a face as brown and wrinkled as a walnut, 'Dovethorpe Town Council' emblazoned in red on his hi-vis jacket, was attacking blackened chewing gum spots on the paving with a steam cleaner strapped to his back. Even from a distance, it looked a Sisyphean labour. Ten o'clock came and went. Had he and Liv made an error with the map grid reading? Surely not – this was a likely spot. At ten past ten he thought he'd give it another few minutes before beating a retreat to the supermarket cafeteria or a café in the town to take stock. He tried to gauge his feelings. Tenseness was still there, but also a sense of anticlimax and even a tinge of relief. Maybe he could contact Andy Nolan himself and let the police take over. He wondered, as he always did, about his invoice, but who would he send it to?

'Mr Sterling? Frank Sterling?'

Sterling started. He'd been too busy looking into the pedestrianised square, and too busy daydreaming rather than concentrating. He was losing his grip. The surveillance work he'd done in his police career in the next town along the coast, Fenningstone, was a long way in the past.

Sterling looked at the man who'd managed to sidle up to him. He was about five foot ten, roughly the same height as Sterling himself, and overdressed for the day, compared to most of the people in the square, in a long brown greatcoat and slip-on tan shoes. Stubble covered the lower part of his face, the kind of stubble that quickly grows into a beard without shaves morning and evening. Crumbs from some recent pastry or croissant speckled the areas close to his lips. His skin was dark and his jowly face looked Arabic, even obscured by dark-framed spectacles with thick lenses which indicated chronic short sight. The coat could not disguise his roly-poly figure. There's a borderline between scruffy and unkempt. The figure in front of Sterling was in no man's land.

'Who wants to know?'

'There's no time for this, Mr Sterling.' Sterling's reply had confirmed his identity. 'I've been waiting for you for some while. Mike Strange will have told you about me. Clearly he couldn't come himself. We're exposed here. There's a Discovery Centre on the other side of the square – a kind of adult learning facility, they call it.' He peeped around a pillar as if expecting a sniper shot and indicated with a tilt of his head. 'It's just up past the museum. We'd better go separately. Meet me there. Don't go straight across the square. Ease around by the edges.'

Sterling watched the man set off in a kind of determined, rolling, ambling gait. He crossed the road and kept close to the estate agents, shops and bars on that side of the square. Then Sterling set off himself, his awareness sharpened by having just been caught unawares. There was no choice if he wanted to make further progress.

As he walked up the steps to the Centre, it wasn't noise that alerted him. Apart from the low rumble of traffic from the nearby ring road beyond the concrete monolith of the museum, and the gusty wind, it was relatively quiet. It was movement that he sensed behind him. With his contact framed just inside the automatic doors of the Centre, Sterling glanced back into the square. From each side, two groups of men were converging rapidly on him, as if they had been disgorged from nearby vehicles. He'd been led into a trap. He needed to get out of the open. There might be more of the gang in the Centre, but going back the way he'd come was out of the question. He'd be taken, silenced, bundled into a car and driven off. In the building, there would be people he could shout to. If it were only the scruffy man in there, Sterling would have a good chance of getting the better of him and getting out.

As the automatic doors hissed open, there was another surprise. The two girls at the fountain and the skateboarders motioned him in whilst Liv Eliot emerged from the left, barely recognisable at first from the tousled, dressing-gowned girl of yesterday evening and earlier in the morning because of the Doc Martens laced four inches up her ankles, the flared green-and-white hooped Glasgow Celtic mini-skirt and the short, diagonally-zipped suede jacket a shade or two lighter than her hair. 'I've fixed the door,' she said. 'That gives us a bit of time.'

'Right. Handy,' said Sterling. 'Hang on a sec.' He went up to the scruffy man near the adult education area, grabbed his coat by its greasy lapels and pinned him against the wall. 'You bastard. You led them straight to me.'

The so-far nameless man looked back without fear at Sterling through his pebble lenses. 'Not me, Mr Sterling. They want me as well. They're killing two birds with one stone.'

Liv tugged at Sterling's coat. 'We haven't got much time, Mr Sterling. Is he with you or not? We can get you away but only if we go now.'

Sterling released his grip. He turned back to the doors. Flanked by two others, a tall man in an expensive suit and a white collarless shirt locked Sterling with his fierce, angry eyes. Sterling held his gaze for a long moment. The man spoke to his underlings and they peeled away. Liv tugged again. 'With me,' said Sterling, and he, Liv and his new associate hurried away to the back of the building.

At the emergency doors, Liv turned to Sterling. 'Those blokes can't get around the back of this building for a good few yards – it's part of a block that follows the shape of the ring road – and they probably don't know the town anyway. Where do you want to go? The railway station at the priory across the ring road is too obvious, I reckon.'

'West,' said Sterling. 'We can't go any further south.'

'Agreed,' said the man with no name.

'OK, I'll put you on a bus,' said Liv. 'We'll go around Market Square in a wide loop. There'll be one dodgy bit where we'll have to cross a road. They probably won't expect us to double back.'

The motley group set off. The skateboarders went

ahead, in the role of scouts. The plump girls, one at the front and one at the back, acted as outriders. To Sterling's right, the inner ring road continued to hum with the vibration and noise of traffic. To his left was the block of brutalist concrete, including the town museum, the library and the adult education centre, that partitioned the road from the town centre, as Liv had indicated. They hurried on in a sharp leftward curve along a path that diverged from the ring road and went back to the town. Moments later, the group pulled up at the street leading from the town centre and filtering as a slip road into the ring road. The skateboarders emerged from behind some commercial-sized waste bins. 'It's clear for now,' said the taller one. An orange beanie on his head didn't prevent some unruly hair sticking out at every angle from underneath it.

'Let's go,' said Liv. The group hurried across the road and into the narrow one-way street opposite. Sterling was sweating. He could hear the nameless man's rasping breath and realised he was more out of condition than he was himself. The group plunged down Fishmongers Lane, bricked and featureless on either side. Three security shutters, completely down, protected Sandimede Dental Studio. At the end were blue-painted railings and a small footbridge. A sign told cyclists to dismount and another indicated that the group was crossing the River Dove – in fact little more than a stream. The group plunged on by the side of a pub, made a sharp left, a right and then another left.

In his confusion, Sterling consoled himself that the men in pursuit, if they were anywhere near, would be even more flummoxed. Only a few metres away from the town centre, Dovethorpe's bleakness was overpowering.

Under the shadow of the castle, an abandoned, decaying multi-storey car park had given way to a patch of forlorn wasteland. Down Dolphin Passage, more derelict buildings on each side funnelled the fugitives' progress. Then, after the skateboarders had motioned them across another junction, Sterling was astonished to find himself in front of the supermarket where he had had his breakfast. His companion leaned against the wide glass frontage.

'We need to stop. I'm completely done in,' he wheezed.

'Not yet,' said Liv roughly. 'It's too open. We go up Stembrook here, and into the park. You can conk out there. There are benches,' she threw out as a sop.

The big man peeled off the glass and lurched on. Liv looked at Sterling and rolled her eyes slightly. He wasn't feeling tip-top himself, but he had appearances to keep up.

The supermarket frontage and the car park opposite abruptly gave way to a park, without even a gate or railings to separate them, and as Liv had promised there were benches up ahead. Sterling realised that they had reached the River Dove again, only further up and away from the sea. The big man, stumbling and arms stretched out in front of him, struggled to a seat serendipitously hidden between trees and water, and sat heavily. He leaned back and puffed desperately, as if each breath might be his last.

Behind them, beyond the car park, the greensward buzzed with activity, clanging and general noise as a fairground was being set up. From the middle of the half-constructed rides and stalls a woman with bleached blonde hair in T-shirt and shorts, her face, arms and legs weathered from a life spent outdoors, emerged with two tiny Chihuahuas on fluorescent leads, one orange and one green. Sterling turned back to the sad little river. Gradually, the nameless man's breathing returned to normal.

'We can wait here while Jack checks the buses,' said Liv. 'I've told him you want to go west.' She smiled. 'I had to tell the silly sod which way that was.'

Sterling nodded. The girls had taken up positions on the path at opposite ends of the bench. The taller one hitched up her jeans and adjusted her bra. We're all a bit discombobulated, thought Sterling. He had many questions – for Liv and the man – but everyone was busy recovering and it wasn't the time.

Five minutes later, the boy in the orange beanie glided to a halt next to Liv. 'There's a bus to Fenningstone in five minutes.' The rescuers seemed to report direct to Liv without reference to Sterling and the other man. Liv tilted her chin at Sterling.

'That'll do,' said Sterling. His companion's elbows now rested on his knees as his face stared at the ground. He didn't seem to care much where he went next – the current adventure had taken too much out of him, but he got to his feet when it was time to move off.

'It's just across the park,' said Liv.

Sterling looked over again to the bustle to the left of the perimeter path the group was following. Articulated lorries circled the park like settler wagons in the Wild West. Young men clambered over the steel struts of half-completed rides with wrenches and hammers. Blocks of sturdy wood lay scattered on the ground, their purpose currently obscure. Nearest to the path, a teacup ride was almost finished, and next to it Sterling could see dodgem cars neatly stacked and wrapped up in a large container lorry, like bullets in the chamber of a six-shooter. Seeing his distraction, Liv picked up the pace, and at the far end of the park were the bus stops. 'That one,' pointed Orange Beanie at a new-looking double-decker.

The scouts and outriders faded into the background. Sterling and his companion joined the queue to board.

'Thanks, Liv. We'll see what's what when this is over. Is your mum OK?'

'I think so. Last I saw, the whole family was turning out.' She paused. 'Mr Sterling? This mess – here in Dovethorpe – I said this morning – it was my fault. I didn't keep shtum like you asked. Stupid. Someone must have been looking at my Facebook. That's why I came down with my mates. We're quits now, aren't we?'

'Quits?' said Sterling. Quits suggested he had done something wrong. 'I don't get it. What have I…?'

'You think I don't know about last night? Between you and mum?' Liv's eyes twinkled and she produced a small smile.

Sterling coloured. 'You cheeky minx. That's none of your business…'.

'Are you getting on or not?' said the bus driver.

'Thanks again,' said Sterling to Liv as he followed the nameless man on board. 'And thanks to your crew.'

'See you,' said the girl.

Chapter 18

From the top of the double-decker, halfway down the aisle, Sterling looked up and down Dovethorpe's main street. He could see male figures, mostly in twos, some white, some dark-skinned, scurrying up and down, ears to mobiles. Long experience, on the job as a policeman, and more recently riding on buses, told him they wouldn't look up, and even if they did, his image would be obscured by the light and the glass. Many people could remember the exact layout and order of a row of shops or houses at eye level in a street, but if you asked them about details of the second and third storeys, they'd more often than not be unable to tell you anything. The man beside him didn't share his confidence. He sank as low as he could in his seat, and as he did his bulk spread out and put the squeeze on Sterling in the window seat.

As he shifted to get comfortable in the small space available, Sterling totted up the narrow escapes he'd had. It depended on how you classified them, he reckoned, but at least five. Ranking them was just as tricky. He'd been more terrified in the boat off the coast than, say, under it when the thugs came searching for him on the shingle at Sandley Bay. It had been hairy at Stacey's, and then at the Discovery Centre at Dovethorpe. But curiously, the face-to-face confrontation with his main adversary there, only the glass doors separating them, had eased his fear. If your opponent was not faceless and remote, but there in the flesh, you knew what you were up against. Gradually, his heartbeat, racing from a combination of being hunted and lack of fitness, returned to normal, and the sweat on his skin dried.

The bus moved away from the town centre and began its long ascent up one of the many hills that radiated in fat fingers from the town. As it passed the station concourse and the mainly Victorian terraces that lined the road, Sterling's companion relaxed, straightened his back and marginally relieved the pressure. Soon they were on the seven-mile-long ridge that separated Dovethorpe from Fenningstone, the sea out of sight to the south and downland to the north.

'You first,' said Sterling.

The big man seemed to understand the lack of preamble. 'OK. Except... Obviously you're here, and not Mike Strange, so, as far as you are aware, is he all right?'

'I don't know. He gave me what you gave him and then disappeared. The blokes who are after us were just about to catch up with him. I only just got away myself. It didn't look good.'

The big man nodded, as if it was expected. 'Where do you want me to start?'

'Your name, I reckon, and then take it from there.'

'Well, Mr Sterling, I am Mohamed Husain. How do you do?' said the man with grave courtesy.

Sterling nodded. 'You obviously know who I am.'

Husain nodded back. 'The most important thing for you to know is that I'm a member of the British security services – dealing with threats from internal and foreign sources.'

'Now we're getting to it,' said Sterling. 'So there's a terrorist dimension to all this.'

'Not so loud, Mr Sterling,' said Husain, hunching instinctively back down in his seat.

Sterling eased his shoulder behind the bulky one hemming him in, and craned his neck around to survey the rest of the top deck. There wasn't anything to surprise him. Two young Eastern Europeans sat on the back seat in deep and animated conversation, the boy in a bright red puffa jacket and pitcher's cap with 'San Diego' emblazoned on it, the girl all long dark hair, mascara, foundation, blue-painted nails and skinny jeans. Somehow a white-haired woman had managed to get her granny trolley and its shopping up the stairs, which sat erect next to her seat, uncannily like a dog begging. An old man, also white-haired and with a backpack on the seat beside him, the sort Sterling's familiarity with buses told him was an all-day traveller with a free pass, stared out of the window. Sterling could spot the tell-tale transparent tubes winding up from the moulds in his ears around to the hearing aids tucked behind. A younger man, perhaps unemployed, flicked boredly through a redtop with dull eyes.

Sterling squeezed back to his original position. 'Well, Mr Husain, (a) I doubt whether anyone up here would be much interested in our conversation if (b) any of them could understand it or (c) even hear it properly. This is not exactly a hub of vibrant activity.'

'Even so – walls have ears, and maybe buses too.'

Sterling shrugged. 'Anyway...' he said more softly.

'Anyway, after a long operation during which I went undercover – since October last year – I managed to penetrate and gain the trust of a cell of an organisation planning some kind of attack somewhere here in the UK. I was in charge of internal communications.'

'Al-Qaeda? ISIS?'

'Neither of those, Mr Sterling. Something new. Something we previously haven't known about, and something without any discernible religious or political affiliations at all. If anything, it seems to be an organisation for hire. The terrorist equivalent of Western defence contractor organisations, if you like. So many of these groups mushroom out of nowhere. As usual, this one is organised in cells, and the cell I penetrated is multinational. The cell leader, Kurjak, is a Bosnian Serb, and the core is British, but the second in command, Zahra, is an American-educated Iraqi. He's the one coordinating the search for you. He's the one we saw at the doors of that centre in Dovethorpe where your young friends rescued you. He's the dangerous one. Virtually a psychopath.'

'Well, thanks a lot, Mr Husain, for landing me in this.'

'I had no choice, Mr Sterling. My department is compromised, maybe even my handler. That's why I had to leave the cell and go on the run. I was sure I was about to be betrayed. Mike Strange is a former colleague. I worked with him in Dubai, before he was captured and... Anyway, there was no one else to turn to. You probably know some of this. We met at Waterloo. I handed him a memory stick, which you say you have in your possession – otherwise you wouldn't have been at the rendezvous. The arrangement was that, when we parted at the station, if he was taken, he said he'd pass the baton to you. Apart from Becky, and he didn't want to involve her, there was no one else. He thought you'd be competent in this morass.' Husain paused for a beat. 'After your own fashion.'

'Thanks a lot to you too, Mike,' muttered Sterling.

'You've done well, Mr Sterling – better than I would have expected. It was the technological aspect that Mike had most doubts about, though he didn't always see it as a disadvantage, since not being very interested in that keeps you under the radar, relatively speaking.'

Sterling stared long and hard over the downland to the north. It looked as though the weather was breaking. Heavy cloud in a sharply delineated line was coming in from the northwest. 'Let me get this right. You are a member of the British security services. Seven months ago, you managed to infiltrate a cell – not Al-Qaeda, not ISIS – here in England – London?' He cocked an eyebrow and Husain nodded. 'Having gained the trust of the group, you stole – or you copied, or you intercepted – the cell's instructions about a terrorist event or attack or whatever – we don't exactly know yet – and put it on a memory stick, with a password, and with the rendezvous in Dovethorpe we've just made. Now the cell is after us and its instructions. I've seen the instructions, I think, but they're in code. The codebook is *One Thousand and One Nights*.'

'Impressive, Mr Sterling. 'You are' – Husain searched for an expression – 'right on the button. Just one point of clarification. There are two memory sticks with the crucial information. You have one, and I have the other – two chances for success, not one.'

'And you've got the codebook?'

Husain patted his pocket.

'I hope Mike is OK,' said Sterling.

'I hope so too. I shouldn't have involved him, or you.'

'But so long as we've got the memory sticks, no terrorist event, or whatever it is, is going to take place, right? Because your cell doesn't know what it's meant to be doing.'

'Unfortunately not the case, Mr Sterling. My cell, as I have found out over the last seven months, constitutes some sort of support group – to make sure that what is planned happens. Another cell is the actual delivery group. The event will likely take place in some way or another, whatever my cell is doing.'

Sterling sighed. 'It's getting worse and worse. When did Zahra turn up?'

'About four months ago, nominally as second in command, but he's really in charge, whatever Kurjak thinks. Up to that point, everyone was a bit sloppy and amateurish. Zahra isn't though. It became much more difficult for me after he arrived, and the group became much sharper and more effective.'

The two men were silent for a few moments. Before, the bus had been travelling through countryside interspersed with a few settlements. Husain had shown great interest in the Battle of Britain memorial, glimpsed through a leafy vista on the cliff top, vowing to visit properly 'when all this is over, as I am a true patriot'. Now suburban sprawl was overtaking fields. In fifteen minutes they would be dropping down sharp slopes onto the road next to the coastal railway and into the centre of Fenningstone.

'Thin,' said Sterling. 'It's all pretty thin and far-fetched, Mr Husain.'

'But true, Mr Sterling. In every detail.'

'Hmm. OK. What now?'

Husain said nothing for a few seconds. He stared ahead out of the window. His brow furrowed. Then he spoke. 'The best outcome would have been for me and

Mike, two experienced intelligence operatives, to rendez-vous in Dovethorpe and take things on from there. I expected it to be me who was taken and Mike to escape. If neither of us had managed it, of course, in the national emergency we are facing, it would have been reasonable for you to carry on. But I have managed to keep one step ahead of the cell, so I think it only right that we remove you from the danger. The situation is unfair on you as an ordinary citizen. It's for me to try and manage alone. We can split up at Fenningstone and you can make your way home, with my sincere thanks for your efforts.'

Sterling laughed. Perhaps there had been a time when he wouldn't have minded handing over the 'baton' and getting out of it. But now he'd come too far for that, and he knew too much. 'No way, Husain. Just off the top of my head, I can think of three reasons why that's a very bad idea. Firstly, forgive me for saying, but didn't I just save your skin back there, with that little band of irregulars? You may be a spook, but you're hardly the James Bond type. You need a minder. Secondly, I know Fenningstone like the back of my hand, every road, every alley, every arcade, because I was stationed here when I was a plod. I can find us somewhere safe to hole up. Thirdly, I've got to be in this for the long haul now. Is that bloke Zahra – with your ex-comrades – going to say, when I turn up again, "Oh right, Mr Sterling, so you've handed over the information stolen from us. Never mind. No hard feelings in this quarter. Sorry about chasing you, shooting at you and all that stuff. Off you go home and don't trouble yourself anymore"? I don't think so. You're stuck with me, and I'm stuck with you. Oh yes, and I've thought of reason number four. Who's going to pay my expenses and my bill when it's all over? We've got the information and the codebook. We can cooperate.'

Husain put his podgy hands on the headrest in front of him and leaned his forehead on them. He closed his eyes and then opened them again. 'All right, Mr Sterling. I can't deny it's been a successful and productive partnership so far, even if short.'

'Good. Sensible,' said Sterling. 'It's the right decision. What now?'

'We find somewhere to hide out, as you suggested. We decode the instructions. Then we take it from there. We can't use a hotel or bed and breakfast establishment because it would be too obvious. We could find a flat, or some sort of self-catering place. Zahra and the cell have a very clever technical man – well, boy more like. He hasn't got access to all the surveillance tools of the state, but he's good – which is one of the reasons they found you in Dovethorpe, I imagine – so we can't go anywhere public. At least Asif can't get hold of CCTV – not to my knowledge anyway.'

Sterling stared up at the grey CCTV bubble at the front of the bus. CCTV was everywhere, but ordinarily only useful after an incident like an assault or a disappearance – not for monitoring and pursuit purposes. He remembered early instructions to junior members of any investigating team when he was in the job – 'Go and get the CCTV.' He hoped Husain was right about the cell's techie and the disadvantages he had to grapple with.

The bus was finishing its steep descent into Fenningstone, the coastal railway diverging to the left towards the harbour and the bus itself going past the large concrete-and-glass monolith that was Fenningstone's

Grand Hotel. Sterling leaned past Husain and rang the bell. 'We'll get off here and cut through into the old town. I've got an idea.'

In the chilly, gusty breeze, the two men reached the Old High Street and started up the hill. The street was little more than a wide alleyway in parts as the overhangs above the shopfronts shut out the light and created a claustrophobic effect. This was a district of small restaurants and teashops, art galleries and emporia full of bric-a-brac and ephemera. Costume-hire shops shared blocks with tanning and nail salons, newsagents and charity shops. Sterling stopped outside a clothing alteration premises, its door and window frame painted bright yellow, with the name 'MayHem' in purple italics above. Through the window, passers-by could, if they wanted, watch the elderly tailor, with a grey fringe of what remained of his hair around the back and sides of his head, at work behind a counter on his sewing machine, all the other tools of his trade scattered around the surface on which he laboured. The results of his efforts hung on a rack to his right, whilst work pending was on his left. A separate yellow door next to the shop, lightening the gloom of the day, was the one whose bell Sterling rang.

He looked at his watch. It was approaching midday. 'It's late enough,' he muttered to Husain.

After a few moments, the door swept open. A face appeared, attached to a stocky body. Recognition flared in the rheumy young blue eyes. 'Bloody hell,' said a high-pitched voice. The door slammed shut. 'Plan B, then,' said Husain, making to carry on up the street.

'Hang on a second,' said Sterling.

The door swung open again, and this time the face

was cracked into a warm, delighted smile. 'Frank bloody Sterling. It's about time you paid a visit, you old bastard.'

'Hello, Joey. I said I would, but I've been a bit diverted lately.'

Joey's shrewd eyes took in Husain. 'And this is...?'

'Mohamed Husain,' said Husain gravely. 'An... associate of Mr Sterling's.'

Sterling looked up and down the multicoloured street. 'It's a bit public out here, Joey. Can we come in?'

'Sure. Follow me.' The young man turned and started up the stairs in a kind of determined waddle.

Husain turned to Sterling with a look that combined surprise, unease and something else that took a moment for Sterling to recognise – distaste.

'What?' said Sterling sharply.

'Well, is this wise?'

'Is what wise?' Sterling wasn't inclined to let his new associate off the hook.

Mohamed persisted. 'Are we really looking for help from...'.

'If you're coming up, hurry up, and shut the door behind you,' said the high-pitched voice from somewhere at the top of the stairs.

'You do what you like,' hissed Sterling, 'if you've got a better idea.' He began to clamber up the narrow staircase, and, after a moment of obvious uncertainty, heard Husain follow.

Sterling had been to Joey Miller's flat once or twice before. The first time was about eight years ago, when he was still a copper in Fenningstone. Joey had been beaten up near The Cliffs area of the town, and Sterling had taken his statement, and later managed to secure a conviction for the assault. They'd been friends ever since, and something more. Joey's membership of the town's dubious subculture – on the boundaries of criminal, but more akin to dodging and weaving – had made him useful as an informant. Sterling's arrest and conviction rate had made him a star in the local nick. Joey had developed a lucrative and relatively safe little sideline. The friendship had blossomed, based on a shared sense of humour and a fondness for beer.

'Still snitching, Joey?' said Sterling as he slipped from the hallway and into the lounge.

'I'm not a snitch, Frank, and never was.' Joey raised his eyebrows and put on an official voice. 'I facilitate the work of the police in the execution of their inquiries.'

'Yeah, yeah,' said Sterling. 'Well, you certainly helped me. Any chance of a cup of tea?'

'You can have tea, or I've got something a bit stronger. Newkie broon?'

'Good man.'

Meanwhile, Husain perched himself on the edge of one of the sharply angled grey sofas in the neatly furnished flat, whose wide bay window looked down on the Old High Street. The room was decorated in neutral off-whites and greys, with the emphasis on squares and rectangles rather than circles and ovals. It was neat and spotless, much like Stacey's house, though more masculine in style and decor, with a widescreen TV expertly affixed to the wall with a digital box and matching modern equipment. As Sterling and Joey Miller renewed their acquaintance, Husain took in the smaller man's flattened head, mobile, protruding tongue, nose flattened like a boxer's, short neck and slanted eyes. He noted too the beautifully, precisely cut short blond hair, layered and styled in a modern fashion, the well-fitting blue jeans, the pristine white T-shirt, black leather jacket and the jewellery – a gold neck-chain, and matching index-finger ring and bracelet. Husain had come from a world of privilege to a world of espionage – both in their ways limited. Something wasn't adding up.

Joey Miller had left the sitting room for a room at the back. There were sounds of a fridge door opening and closing, the clink of bottle-openers and other evidence of hospitality. Husain leaned forward on his sofa as Sterling sprawled comfortably back on the one at right angles. 'I still think…' started Husain. 'This isn't a game. We can't put ourselves in the hands of a…'. He stopped. He had the vocabulary – or he had a vocabulary – but he wasn't sure of it.

'Cretin? Moron? Handicapped person? Bloke with learning difficulties? Get over it, Husain. One, Joey is a pal of mine, and two, he's just the person to help us in our current fix. In fact, I can't think of anyone better.'

Joey came back into the lounge with a tray of beer glasses. It wasn't clear whether or not he'd heard the exchange, but he did not mistake the atmosphere. He offered the beer and turned to Sterling. 'It's my extra chromosome, isn't it, Frank? He wishes he'd got an extra chromosome like me, eh?' Sterling laughed. Husain squirmed. 'Don't worry, mate. Us disableds are used to it. Sometimes it's handy.' Joey put a plump finger to his flattened nose and tapped. 'You see more. You hear more. No one pays you much ear back. Sometimes they think they're being all trendy, having a drink and a laugh with you. Frank knows. Cheers.' He held up his glass. 'So, Frank, what brings you to Fenningstone and my little flat – after all this time,' he added slyly.

'Yeah,' said Sterling. 'I should have been down earlier

– or got you to bus over to Sandley for a pint. Still, here I am.' He leaned forward, rotating his beer glass in his hands. 'The thing is, Joey, Husain and I are on the run.' He felt he was getting more articulate. He'd practised the spiel enough. 'There's a gang of blokes who have been after me from Sandley since yesterday lunchtime, and after him,' – he jerked his head towards the spy – 'since, well, before that. It's a long story, but he stole information about some kind of terrorist attack, and it found its way to me. We need somewhere safe to rest up and see what we've got,' – Sterling looked around the flat – 'and probably some equipment to help.'

Husain sat back, not relaxed but acquiescent, as if recognising that he had no choice.

Joey took a pull of his brown ale. His rheumy eyes glittered. There were possibilities and opportunities here. 'The blokes... they don't know you're here.'

'Correct,' said Sterling. 'At least, we're pretty sure. We lost them in Dovethorpe. They're sharp, or at least some of them are, but their resources are sort of limited.'

'And you've got information they want.'

'Yup.'

'How long would you need to stay?'

Husain sat silently and listened. Negotiations seemed to have started, and Sterling seemed competent to conduct their side.

'Dunno. It depends on what we find out. A couple of days at the outside.' Sterling looked to Husain, who nodded.

'I've got quite a lot on, Frank, and it sounds a bit hairy. The gaff's small. If it was just you...'.

'We'd see you right, Joey,' said Sterling.

Husain twisted sideways and withdrew a fat roll of

notes from his trousers pocket. 'Of course we would, Mr Miller. Say, a deposit of £100, and then £100 for each day we stay.'

'£150 deposit, non-returnable, £100 *each* per day, plus expenses and extras – food and that,' said Joey.

Sterling covered his mouth and smirked discreetly. How could Husain know that Joey drove the hardest bargain on the south coast? Husain's rash intervention with his wad of cash had made everything much more expensive – not that Sterling minded, since he wouldn't be paying.

'All right,' said Husain. A look passed over his face – not quite surprise and not quite shock. 'And access to your computer.'

'Haven't got a computer, Mr Husain. The only things I've got are a mobie and the telly. A computer – a laptop – which I will have to source,' Joey said in an officious voice, 'comes under extras.'

Husain unrolled £150 and slapped it down on the glass top of the coffee table, an act of desperate bravado in the face of outmanoeuvre. 'The whole deal. Done.'

Chapter 19

Asif knew all about intelligence-gathering and search techniques. He could glean much from open source intelligence – the stuff anyone with a bit of nous could find from the Internet. There were more specialised techniques like data-mining – discovering patterns in large sets of data – that he knew about but had never practised. ANPR – Automatic Number Plate Recognition – might have been useful to him and his cell if he had access to the technology, but that was the province of the police, and anyway, neither Frank Sterling nor Husain had cars and were almost certainly moving around in another way. Buses had CCTV, and CCTV batoning was useful – tracking people from one bus to the next, or one CCTV location to the next. That was another established police technique for missing or wanted people, though the quality of the CCTV was often very poor.

Traffic analysis – in the sense of analysing computer or other communications – was useful, whether or not data was encrypted. Asif vaguely remembered how an over-conscientious German army coast commander's regular-as-clockwork message at a particular time every day – 'Weather fine; one overflight' – had helped the Bletchley Park code-breakers with their advances during World War II – they had arranged the daily 'overflight' with the RAF to get the repeated message. Not that Asif cared about a history to which he was so tenuously connected. Accessing Liv Eliot's Facebook page was probably in the category of traffic analysis. He knew about radio base stations and phone cell masts, the aprons that represented their coverage, and how mobile users could be located within the aprons. But Sterling and Husain were not even carrying phones.

Asif was good at what he did. He'd had some luck with the Facebook thing, but he'd made the most of it. The trouble was that Zahra didn't understand. If Asif didn't have the resources and the connections, or time to hack into systems, and if Sterling and Husain were abandoning technology, no amount of skill and ingenuity could get a result. Asif rubbed his eyes and returned from the window to his machine. How had he got into this? He was just a young bloke from a washed-up northern town on the outskirts of Manchester, destined for work somewhere as an IT technician. All this was meant to be worthy and exciting, but he'd been idiot enough to join the wrong group, and he might as well have been working in an office block in Salford Quays – no less boring and much safer. It wasn't just the stolen memory sticks, the information they contained and the fall-out from all that. He was working for a maniac.

The maniac in question sat in the Green Café in Dovethorpe's pedestrianised High Street. Although the café was crowded, he sat alone at a table for two, the aura around him discouraging proximity in the crowd of shoppers, idlers, lovers and children having their morning coffee and snacks. No one was listening to his phone conversation in the hubbub, but if they were they'd be unlikely to understand. He spoke softly but urgently, and a close observer would have seen the vein bulging out in his sallow forehead. 'Look again, Hamid. Get the others working harder. They must be somewhere. Come to the café in twenty minutes. Make sure the news is good.'

Just as he ended the call, a toddler, making a break for freedom, cannoned into his leg, wiping a sticky, ice cream mouth against the tall man's trousers. Zahra looked down fiercely, furious at another diversion, but seeing the little boy, his face broke into a smile that for once extended to his eyes. 'Where are you off to, my son?' He picked the grubby little boy up and looked into his naughty blue eyes. Soon the eyes became mesmerised, and the face fretful. His mother bustled up. 'Come here, Kyle, you little mischief.' She smiled nervously at Zahra, and whisked the boy away.

Zahra stared down at the table. He was Ma'dan – a proud marsh Arab from the Huwaiza marsh in southern Iraq. The little boy made him think of his family in the countryside of southern Iraq – his young nephews and nieces growing up in a refugee camp on the causeway to Iran, their way of life destroyed by dams, drainage, poison gas and bombs. He, Hamid and Rashad were the last to grow up in their marsh village. Zahra's father had been a sheikh and a landowner who raised cattle and grew rice. Now he was dead and his family had nothing. Five thousand years of culture and prosperity had been destroyed in three years. Only money would help Zahra's family. Nothing else mattered, and that's why he did what he did.

Reminiscences were pointless. His thoughts veered back to Husain and the man Sterling. Words from his time in America came to him – 'two-bit', 'dumb-assed' – and yet the men to whom the words should apply were still eluding him. If they weren't in Dovethorpe, where were they?

He reached again for his phone and heard Asif's alert response. 'They were where you said they'd be,' said Zahra. It was a statement, not praise. 'But we didn't take them.' Another statement followed, without explanation or anything approaching apology for not following up on good work. 'So you need to keep vigilant for any signs about where they are or might have gone.' He ended the call without waiting for a reply.

Hamid strode into the café and sat opposite Zahra. 'Nothing, Irfan.' He believed in getting bad news out of the way as soon as possible. What was the point of prevaricating? Zahra's knuckles were white as he gripped his coffee cup. Hamid sat quiet and still. He wasn't scared of Zahra, whom he'd grown up with, or anyone for that matter, but to say anything then would have been provocative.

'Keep everyone here on alert. At some stage we'll get something. What do the English say about cats? They have nine lives. If these two were cats, they'd have used up almost all of them. There's going to be a reckoning, Hamid. A reckoning.'

Chapter 20

Husain had been hungry, and Sterling was learning that this was an almost permanent condition. Under the category of 'extras', Joey had ordered in pizzas and 'trimmings' – coleslaw and cola. Now there were pizza cartons and cans untidily scattered over the coffee table and the arms of both the sofas, and Husain was half-sitting, half-sprawled on the sofa opposite the television. The flat was at the stage of still being immaculate but under a kind of scruffy assault.

Joey appeared from the kitchen with a large plastic bag. Whilst Husain remained oblivious, Joey put all the detritus in the bag, a moue of distaste on his small mouth. He rolled his eyes at Sterling and gestured him into the kitchen. His tongue worked rapidly against the roof of his mouth. 'He can't even aim properly, Frank,' he hissed, lisp accentuated in his agitation. 'I've twice wiped drops of his piss from the toilet rim. He's only been here two hours and he's doing my head in.'

Sterling shrugged and offered his palms in sympathy. He'd done some wiping of his own, after another of Husain's trips. It was clear that he had a bladder problem as well as, or because of, an appetite problem. Joey was Sterling's friend because of their 'professional' relationship, but they'd shared other qualities, including neatness,

OCD tendencies and wry humour. 'There's not going to be time to train him up, Joey, but I'll have a word.'

For the moment, there was nothing to do, so Husain did nothing. Having struck the deal, he believed he had carte blanche to act like a slob, at which he was a natural. Early on he'd taken possession of the TV control box, and was now watching a reality show featuring tanned, expensively turned out women basking and sniping at each other in the American sunshine. His eyelids drooped and soon he was snoring.

'I'm off out,' said Joey. 'I suppose that when His Nibs wakes up he'll be looking for a laptop. I tell you, Frank, I'm not far from pulling out of this deal.'

'It won't be for long, Joey. Put a big mark-up on whatever computer you manage to get hold of, and be imaginative with the extras. I reckon the bloke's loaded.'

Joey scowled. He shook on his leather jacket. 'Keep it tidy, Frank. I'm relying on you.'

Sterling watched from between slats of the bay window's venetian blinds overhanging the street as Joey made his way out of sight up the hill to the centre of town. He wouldn't be going to Curry's. He'd be going in and out of the pubs and amusement arcades, having soft conversations in the corners of bars and in the narrow spaces next to slot machines. He'd be going into bric-a-brac shops, whose owners weren't averse to receiving stock of dubious provenance, payday loan offices and pawn shops. Everyone knew him, and knew the kind of deal he cut.

Rays of afternoon spring sunshine, broken up by electricity wires, skittered across the window's highly polished white surface. He thought again of Stacey and their night together. He hoped she and Liv and all the

Sunningtons were safe. Surely Zahra would have no use for them after the tussle in Dovethorpe. A young woman came up the street pushing a large modern hybrid pram and pushchair, all pockets, trays, string mesh and transparent plastic. Her eyes were glazed and the vehicle moved as if on autopilot. Near her, two school-age children darted about like gnats, chasing and tormenting each other. The little girl started to cry and complain. Her mother stared on.

In the other direction, moving down towards the harbour, a slim teenaged girl in figure-hugging blue jeans and leather jacket that looked too old and big for her was clinging, two handed, to the arm of a taller, older boy in a duffel coat and skinny black jeans, pressing his arm between her breasts. She looked up into his face, her eyes full of anxious love. The boy looked ahead, his expression a mixture of surly and confident. Sterling was reminded of a poster at Sandley Guildhall bus stop – a picture of a young girl drinking from a bottle of beer and the caption 'She thinks he loves her, but he controls her,' and a helpline number. The boy and girl were overtaken by an elderly man with a pink face, rheumy eyes and wispy white hair in a comb-over undone by the brisk wind, manoeuvring a mobility scooter with deft experience.

He wondered again what had happened to Mike Strange yesterday. The whole situation was a dangerous mess. He should have been getting ready to finish his chores and go over to the pub with Angela for a pint and the prize crossword. Now he was in a desperate race against time. Kind of. Once his companion was back from dreamland, and Joey back from his quest for hardware, and they could discover the next challenge.

At four o'clock, Husain, now sprawled across the sofa,

his shoes kicked off and lying untidily beside it, woke up. The cushion he'd requisitioned for his head fell softly to the floor, where it stayed. He tipped himself heavily upright, swinging his feet around and knocking the coffee table out of its parallel alignment. A long belch, generated by pizza, cola and sleep, escaped from his mouth, his hand over his lips seconds too late. 'Sorry,' he muttered. There was a long moment's orientation. 'What time is it, Mr Sterling?' Politeness was in inverse proportion to slovenliness.

'Four o'clock. You've been asleep about two hours. Joey's gone out to get us a laptop.'

'Good, good. I needed that nap. As you can imagine, I've been on the go since Waterloo yesterday. I wonder if there's any chance of a cup of tea.'

It was tempting to point Husain to the kitchen and tell him to get his own bloody tea. Sterling thought of the cupboard doors left open in the search for teabags and mug; the milk spilled carelessly on the spotless work surface and the carton or bottle not returned to the fridge; the drips from the teabag in a trail across the kitchen floor to the waste bin, and even perhaps its falling off the teaspoon carrying it and being abandoned where it fell; grains of sugar scattered everywhere; the heat-ring of the mug on the only surface a heat-ring would be left. He could see Joey's shudders and feel his own discomfort.

He picked up the cushion, restored it to its allotted corner of the sofa, and straightened the shoes. 'How do you take it?'

'Use the coaster, Husain,' said Sterling a few minutes later. 'You'll leave a ring on the coffee table. Try not to spill it. Surely you can work out that Joey's pretty house-proud.'

'Not really,' smiled Husain. Charm would absolve him. 'I've never paid much attention to such things.'

'Clearly,' said Sterling. Here was an opportunity to find out more about his new companion, and he reckoned some background would be useful. He sipped his own brew. 'So, how come a bloke like you is a spook?'

'A bloke like me, Mr Sterling?' Husain's eyes twinkled – or perhaps they were glittering. It was hard to tell.

'Well, are you actually British for a start?'

'What difference does it make to you? Mike Strange trusts you. You trust him. We wouldn't have met without him.'

Sterling leaned forward on his own sofa. 'I like to know who I'm working with. You know something about me. Why shouldn't I know something about you? For all I know this might be some big trick and you might be working for the Saudis or someone.'

Husain sighed. 'All right. Some context. Whilst Joey, hopefully, gets us a machine we can work on. That should confer some reassurance.' He paused and continued. 'Although I have the colouring and look of a Middle Easterner, I am in fact British – I was born in London thirty-one years ago – but my family was originally from Jordan. My grandfather was in the Arab Legion, broadly speaking under the British in the Second World War. The family settled in England after the war. My grandfather and father, who is a civil engineer, were always Anglophiles, and the family found the resources to send me to Dulwich College. Is that enough background for you? Are my credentials satisfactory?'

Husain glanced sideways and caught Sterling's deadpan look.

'Perhaps a little more then. I have degrees in Theology

and the History of Religion from the School of Oriental and African Studies at London University. I am a Muslim but also a patriot. I try and live a proper life. I love this country, and always will, for the freedom and opportunities it has given me and my family, although I know it's not perfect. I don't go in for politics. I just think it's a bad, dangerous world, generally speaking, and the best government is the one that most diligently looks after British interests.' A hint of amused irony came into Husain's voice. 'My football team, for my sins, is Crystal Palace.' He patted his stomach. 'As you may deduce, I love my food and, sadly for me, I am always hungry. I try to have a completely vegetarian diet, but sometimes lapse. When I do, meat has to be halal, though I am not too diligent in checking. I am meant to be teetotal, but I have been known to slip, especially when things are stressful. I am far from perfect.'

He held Sterling's gaze. 'Most important of all for our purposes, I am an undercover agent, as you already know, working for a branch of the security services, which is where I met Mike and Becky Strange, and very keen, hell-bent you might say, on averting a catastrophe.'

'Tell me about Zahra and his group.'

'Ah, Zahra. Well, I have never come across someone like him. You'd think he, and the other two from southern Iraq, were motivated by a warped theory of religion, but that isn't the case. Their motivation is cash. My theory is that what they are doing currently, and what they have done globally, is to fund relief for their persecuted families back in the marshlands they come from. Zahra has some of the characteristics of a psychopath, and with his men he's the hardest of taskmasters. He can be cruel and ruthless. I know that first hand. But sometimes you see something more – a kind of tenderness triggered by things that remind him of home, and why he's chosen to do what he does.'

Sterling sipped his tea and listened on as the patriotic theologian-spook expanded on all his themes and experience, deploying erudition, shrewdness and insight. Watching Husain in action, it was easy to see him as a shambling, wheezing joke. Hearing him talk revealed someone quite different – someone focused and formidable, and far from a buffoon. Sterling came upon an insight of his own. The big man wasn't casually or wilfully untidy and disordered. He was simply too busy on more important things to notice. The aura of messy havoc and chaos surrounding Husain and on him – the disordered sofa, the new patch of tea on an otherwise pristine carpet, the stains on his shirt and the fingerprints on the coffee table – still grated. Sterling went off to the kitchen for a damp cloth and some Vanish.

Chapter 21

There was a scratch and rattle of a key in a lock, and then Joey Miller appeared in the sitting room, his eyes darting suspiciously over the furniture and around the whole room, as if a localised Armageddon might have occurred in the flat while he was absent and he feared the worst. He homed in almost immediately on the damp patch near the coffee table where Husain had spilt his tea. Sterling held up the spray-bottle of Vanish and Joey's face softened.

Husain was alert. 'Well? Any luck?'

'I need a drink,' said Joey, but there was a slim, plain leather satchel on his shoulder and a smile playing across his pale, dry face. He returned from the kitchen with a large tumbler of Baileys and sat on the opposite sofa from Husain. '£350,' he said.

'Three hundred...' spluttered Husain. 'I could have gone to Curry's and spent half that.'

Joey shrugged. 'If you knew where Curry's was. If you didn't mind being out and about in the middle of Fenningstone for anyone to clap eyes on you. If we didn't have a deal.' He hugged the satchel to him whilst Husain unrolled his wad of notes.

'We might as well settle up most of it now,' said Joey. 'Give me £600 and that sorts today and tomorrow out, taking the deposit into account. Knowing Mr Sterling, you might need to leave in a hurry, and I don't want to be left short.'

Husain shook his head, more in acceptance and admiration than denial. He peeled off the twenties and handed them over. 'Tomorrow being...'.

'Yep, a minute after midnight. It's five o'clock now, pretty much too late to go anywhere tonight, even if you get what you want from this,' said Joey as he handed over the machine. He pocketed the cash. 'Well, this calls for a little celebration. I think I can do something without charging. Anyone else for Baileys?'

'Certainly,' said Sterling. 'Very welcome. Thanks, Joey.'

Husain nodded and muttered his own thanks. He opened the laptop on the coffee table and shifted uncomfortably on the sofa as Sterling pretended not to notice a Muslim with a generous slug of liqueur.

'I hope this isn't going to be problematic,' muttered Husain. 'It would have been better, and much cheaper, if you'd printed the documents,' he grumbled again.

By now, having heard the complaint a few times, Sterling was impervious to the tone of recrimination.

Husain found a plug for the cable, almost tipping over his drink as he did so, but frowned as the machine booted up. 'Damn. It's password-protected.'

'I don't know much about these things,' said Joey, 'but I got the password with the machine. The bloke said you could add your own account once you're in, whatever all that means.' He passed over a sticky note. 'It worked in the shop.'

Husain typed in the password and his face brightened. 'We're in. I think it would be safer if I just used this account.'

DAVID R EWENS

Husain plugged in his memory stick and after a few clicks Sterling once again saw the groups of numbers that he and Liv had looked at the evening before from the document on his own stick. From his jacket, Husain pulled a tattered book in Arabic with an exotic cover in the style of the East. 'Joey, do you have some kind of notepad and pen?'

'So that's the codebook, Husain,' said Sterling. 'I'd have struggled even if I'd got hold of a copy. I didn't know it was in Arabic.'

'Yes. Muhsin Mahdi's 1984 edition of *One Thousand and One Nights* – which you probably know in some version, as *Tales of the Arabian Nights*, featuring, among others, *Aladdin and His Magic Lamp*, *Sinbad the Sailor*, and *Ali Baba and the Forty Thieves*. One of the reasons I managed to get recruited into the cell is because I am fluent in Arabic.'

Sterling and Joey watched the spook at work turning cypher numbers into plain text, his eyes flicking restlessly from the computer screen to the book, the fingers in his left hand riffling through the worn pages, and forefinger and thumb of his right hand scrawling on the paper with the cheap biro, the tumbler of Baileys entirely neglected.

The light was rapidly draining from the day when Husain leaned back an hour later, took a long swig of his almost-forgotten drink and stared at the results of his labours.

Sterling took his own look at the pad on the coffee table. 'Well?'

'It doesn't look good,' said Husain. He leaned forward, tore his Arabic translation off the pad, put it on the coffee table and started writing on a new sheet.

When he'd finished, Sterling picked up the translation.

'Do not delay.

Ensure your group is completely ready for immediate deployment.

Collect your final instructions on Sunday 17th April between 9am and 9.30am.

Location: Waste bin outside the Grand Hotel, Harbour Street, Fenningstone.'

'We're in luck – that's just up at the end of the street. Or maybe not so lucky. Mike told me south and west back in Sandley.'

'Dead drop,' said Husain. 'With a difference. Only a half an hour window. This is pushing caution to extremes.' He held up his empty tumbler towards Joey. 'I wonder if I could have a top-up, Mr Miller...'. To the room in general, or perhaps musing out loud to himself, he said, 'It's time to take stock.'

A few drinks later, the discussion was still continuing.

'Surely,' said Sterling, 'there's someone you can contact if it isn't your handler or your department. The boss of another section. A pal in the same organisation? There'll be a phone box down at the harbour, or up near the bus station. A quick call. Information conveyed. Job done.' The Baileys had imparted a warm glow. Sterling felt articulate and sharp-witted.

'The phone box would probably be all right, Mr Sterling. But apart from that it's problematic. I told you my department is compromised, so we've got to assume the whole organisation is. What we've found out could well get into the wrong hands. That's why I got Mike Strange involved. Also, the telephone box number is probably safe enough as I'd be gone before any hostiles could arrive, but the number I'd be dialling wouldn't be.'

'What about another organisation altogether? What about MI6?'

Husain laughed. 'Yes, I've got the numbers and the contact details. We often get each other in to help. They'd know exactly what I'm talking about. They'd go direct to "Critical" state of alert and take immediate action – no bureaucracy involved, no jealousy, no inter-agency rivalry, no checking, straight to it. Easy. You were a policeman, Mr Sterling. How likely is that?'

'The local force then. I've still got a contact or two.'

'I reckon if they got information about a dead drop they'd either treat it as a hoax or go completely overboard, suspect it's a bomb alert, cordon off the area...'.

Sterling thought of a particularly officious, cautious, uniformed inspector in charge of Fenningstone town centre policing when he himself pounded the beat here – Gambleton was his name – and his moniker, acquired soon after he arrived, Namby-Pamby, quickly shortened to Namby. Namby Gambleton: Sterling wondered where he was now. Weary experience told him Husain was probably right. 'So it's still down to us, then.'

'I think so. You know, Mr Sterling, sometimes it's not a matter of brute force and going in with all guns blazing. Sometimes more can be achieved by nuance and discretion.'

'Yeah, well, maybe. But they're not much answer to Kalashnikovs and grenades, are they?' Was it the drink, moving him into a sombre phase? Probably, but the truth was that he was glad to still be in the thick of it, and glad that there would odds-on be excitement tomorrow and in the days beyond. As it turned out, it would be a more unexpected excitement, and of a darker hue, than he imagined.

Chapter 22

Drizzle had descended as a cold, grey blanket across the whole swathe of south and east Kent from Fenningstone to Ramston on the evening of Saturday 16th April. In the safe house in Ramston, publicans Mike and Becky Strange, and Sandley librarian Angela Wilson, were keeping a low profile. The Stranges' pub, the Cinque Port Arms in Sandley, was being managed by one of the bar staff, with the chef doing the lunches. Conveniently, the pub closed on Sunday evening and did not open again till Tuesday. On their advice, Angela was giving work a miss on the Monday, leaving her assistant Kerry to open up in her absence 'until the present storm blows over,' said Becky. Mike had recounted his experience of Friday and was recovering from his waterboarding ordeal. 'Physical restoration is easy,' he'd said. 'You just don't know when the mental side will hit you – if it does at all.'

The house was comfortable and well stocked. If Angela wasn't in her own home beyond the Guildhall in Sandley, then this was doing almost as well. She'd asked Mike and Becky more about what they were all involved with, including Frank Sterling, but the answers were vague. 'It's because we don't know much more than you,' said Becky. But Angela was too attuned to social interaction not to realise that there were disagreements between her friends, no matter how considerately they were expressed. Normally, in the pub, the two of them functioned in perfect unison – one at the bar, one stoking the fire in the snug, one serving tables, one pulling pints. Now, everything was out of kilter and the teamwork had all but broken down. A sense of waiting pervaded the house – not for the storm in general to blow over, but for something specific.

*

Further south, late on the same night, Stacey Eliot was making tea just as Detective Sergeant Bill Murphy liked it – strong, a small amount of milk, one sugar. The biscuits were not supermarket best-buys, but, as he was a visitor, top-of-the-range Belgian numbers from the delicatessen in Deeping. Murphy was overweight, and knew he should resist, but he couldn't help himself. The tea was served in an elegant flowery tea set on a tray covered with a pristine white doily. The cushion propping him up on the sofa had been plumped up, and the scents of furniture polish and air freshener pervaded the immaculate sitting room.

Stacey had telephoned Cantcester Police Station at work, after she'd heard from her daughter in Dovethorpe. But a combination of circumstances, bad luck and process failure, including the fact that the person Sterling had told her to phone, his friend DCI Andy Nolan, was off duty, meant that her message had not been passed on for some hours. Murphy had known Sterling for years, and had worked with him and DCI Nolan on a case at Earlsey Tech. When he'd seen the message slip on Nolan's desk, he'd realised its importance. He liked Sterling – few people he knew didn't – but Sterling could be a cussed, maverick sod with a low opinion of the force he'd left. If he'd told the message-sender to contact the police, the matter was important. If he'd particularly specified contact with his long-time pal Andy Nolan, it was doubly important. Murphy had phoned Stacey himself, and hotfooted it straight away from Cantcester over to the north of Deeping.

When Stacey had finished her part of the tale, from Frank Sterling's arrival early on Friday evening to his departure early on Saturday morning prior to her other, more sinister visitors (without details of their night together, regarded as irrelevant), her daughter took up the story.

'I messed up, I admit it. I did the dumbest possible thing and went on Facebook to tell my friends about my amazing evening. So after we got Mr Sterling away out back, through the alley, on my uncle's moped, I went down to Dovethorpe on the train and got some of my mates out to help. We managed to get Mr Sterling and another bloke he'd just met out of Dovethorpe. We put them on a bus to Fenningstone.'

Murphy sipped his tea and crunched into another biscuit. He could not escape the sense gleaned from the corner of his eye that the older woman was checking that crumbs were going on his plate and not the carpet.

He reviewed what he knew about Sterling. Murphy had already joined the CID in Marchurch when Sterling was on the beat, almost two decades ago, first in Marchurch and then over in Fenningstone. A good way to look at it was to compare Sterling and DCI Nolan. They had always been close – not in the sense of being two peas in a pod but more like chalk and cheese. Nolan was always going places, it had been obvious from the start. He was cool, analytical and well organised. Sterling on the other hand – well, any investigation he got involved with meant fireworks, action and excitement, and recent evidence of his work as a private investigator led to the same conclusion. So Sterling had been going places too, but places that brought trouble, and certainly not upwards. It wasn't worth saying in the present company, but this sounded like a typical Frank Sterling expedition.

He wished he'd got Stacey Eliot's message earlier.

'So, to recap,' he said. 'Frank comes to you – on the lam, he says – early on Friday night having sailed (sailed!) to Sandley Bay from Sandley in a small boat, and he walks along the causeway next to the golf course down here to you. You knew each other when you were kids, and you put him up for the night.' Murphy looked at the beauty in the chair opposite, her neck and cheeks beginning to glow, considered Sterling and his reputation, and did the easiest detective work of his life. 'Liv here helps him with a message, with bits in Arabic, on a memory stick. The part about a rendezvous in Dovethorpe is OK, but you don't get very far with the rest because it seems that it's encrypted and requires a codebook. Early this morning, two men come calling for Frank, but you get him away on a moped. Your father and your brothers, Stacey, help you face them down. These men – what did they look like?'

'Middle Eastern,' said Liv. 'That colouring. The taller one was in a good suit, but it didn't somehow fit very well on him. He had a long face and a curved nose. Dark eyes. Dead eyes. He had a slight accent – a mixture of American and maybe somewhere else. His English was good, but I don't think he was British. He was polite, but you wouldn't want to mess him about.'

'But you did mess him about,' said Murphy. 'That took some guts.'

'Liv is feisty, Mr Nolan, but I was scared. They searched the house but they went when my dad and brothers arrived. The other one wasn't so threatening – he was just his number two or whatever. When I heard Liv had gone down to Dovethorpe I was even more scared. You shouldn't have done that, Liv.'

'What about Mr Sterling, Mum? I had to do something.'

'More importantly right now, what about the man in Dovethorpe, Liv?'

'Middle Eastern as well – maybe not now but his family. Very polite and well-spoken with an English accent. But fa... plump. Unfit. It almost finished him off when we marched around from the Discovery Centre to the bus stop through the park. He had to rest on a bench. He was scruffy and disorganised. He and Mr Sterling didn't know each other. It was obvious they'd only just met, and it was touch and go whether they'd stay together.'

'And you put them on a bus to Fenningstone.'

'Yep.'

'What are you going to do, Mr Murphy?' said Stacey Sunnington.

Murphy worked his fingers in small circles around his temples. It was all so vague, and he was thinking about what crimes had been committed. There was some intimidation, and probably worse, but the only tangible infraction was Frank Sterling's – stealing a boat. On the other hand, whenever Frank was involved in something, it was more often than not serious. Murphy's gut told him that this was the most serious thing yet. Never mind about crime. This was about crime prevention – or something worse.

'I'll arrange patrols up here just in case. I'll get a couple of detectives up to Sandley to see if they can find out what went on up there. That's what I can do with the authority I've got. I'll get DCI Nolan in, and recommend that he contact the security services. They'll have a broader idea of what might be going on. But Mr Nolan and I will concentrate on Fenningstone. Frank was stationed there for some years, so I reckon that's where he'll feel safe. He and the man with him will be working out and pooling what information they've got before the next step.'

He looked directly at Liv – 'No Facebook activity,' – and then at both Liv and her mother. 'Keep this quiet. Tell your dad and brothers too. We don't want some kind of panic, and we certainly don't want any publicity.' Privately, he thought of his boss, Nolan – promoted relatively recently to Detective Chief Inspector, fast-tracked ahead of older incompetents, time-servers and even one or two decent rivals. He wondered if Nolan had the clout to get senior support for a full-blown preventative operation. There were always politics. Nolan was good in that sphere, even if he maintained he didn't like it.

As the girl opened the front door, Murphy saw her mother get out a carpet sweeper and busy herself with his crumbs. In his car, he found his phone and started the round of calls, starting with the DCI.

The fact that the new hotel in Dovethorpe was part of a worldwide chain, and the suite of rooms Kurjak had hired was consequently impersonal to the point of desensitisation, meant nothing to Zahra. Rage was building, and blocked everything but the mission out.

'We know the event is planned for tomorrow,' Kurjak was saying. 'We hope it's somewhere local. Other than that we know nothing, and we'll continue to know nothing until we catch Husain and the man Sterling. We have already lost the man Strange. Worse. We have lost our credibility within the organisation.'

Zahra said nothing, but his knuckles were a familiar white on the arms of his chair.

'Well?'

'What did you wish me to say, Excellency?'

'Don't chop logic, Zahra. What is the current situation?'

'We believe that Husain and Sterling have gone to ground somewhere local. Asif was successful with his monitoring before. I think he'll be successful again. We will capture them and find out the message in time.'

The other man sipped his tea. He checked the Rolex on his wrist – 11.30. 'This is our last chance,' he said. '*Your* last chance.'

Zahra stood up abruptly. 'I'll check Asif and the others,' he muttered.

*

Outside the small flat above the tailor's in Fenningstone, Saturday night was in full swing and there was constant hubbub. A group of young men in T-shirts and jeans was engaged in banter with a group of young women in micro-mini dresses and bare shoulders tottering up the hill in dizzyingly high heels. One of the men was bent over in a shop doorway, retching. Chip papers and similar trash skittered in the wind down towards the harbour. A pair of refuse workers in beanies and hi-vis green jackets, 'Fenningstone DC' inscribed in red on the back, were busy with their litter pick-up sticks, precursors of the heavy duty refuse trucks that would appear early on Sunday morning.

Inside, tensions had been rising, tensions ostensibly unconnected with the business to come in the morning. It had been essential, according to Husain, to assuage his voracious appetite, and that had entailed the ordering and delivery of an Indian takeaway. Joey Miller prowled the flat, constantly on the qui vive for curry-sauce-coated grains of rice and other detritus from the greasy cartons and bags strewn over the coffee table, and the plates on the knees of his guests. It wasn't just the mess; no air freshener had ever worked as hard as Joey's in combat with the cooking smells and eruptions from Husain. Sterling wondered what the odds were of his going directly from the home of a domestic goddess to that of a domestic god. He ran a neat, clean and tidy household himself, but Stacey and Joey were at another level, a wearing level, a level that suggested obsession.

It seemed sensible to cede the spare bedroom and its wide single bed to Husain while Sterling himself had the narrower, shorter sofa bed. The advantage to Sterling was the chance to look through Husain's carelessly hung up coat behind the flat's front door when he heard the big man snoring. Husain was outwardly open and easy-going, but, when Sterling thought about it, what did he really know about his companion?

The pockets reflected Husain's untidy habits, not his lucid mind. Used paper handkerchiefs, fluff, a pen, elastic bands, small change caught in the corners and other rubbish combined in grubby, tangled masses. A sheet of paper had been screwed up into a ball and forgotten. Under the coffee table lamp, Sterling smoothed it out and scanned it – a definition and analysis of extraordinary rendition by the civil liberties organisation, Liberty. He'd heard the term – Angela had probably explained it at some point – and from the sheet reminded himself of the definition – essentially, illegally transferring people for torture abroad when it was banned at home. After the side pockets, the breast pocket, where there was another shock. Astonishingly, unexpectedly, Husain was packing a gun.

Later on, after Sterling had screwed up the sheet of paper and returned it, and everything else he'd disturbed, to the pockets, sleep was restless, and he regularly got twisted up in the thin sleeping bag Joey had produced. Stacey appeared, and appeared to be dusting, after they had been lying naked together. At 4am a shadowy figure flitted into his dream – or was it into the dining area? Sterling felt unease; a sense of things not adding up, and not having added up for a good while. In the morning, a sentence at the end of the Liberty analysis recurred in Sterling's addled brain: 'The extraordinary rendition chapter is not over'. And on the breakfast counter, the cradle in which Joey charged his phone was askew.

Chapter 23

Zahra's dreams were of the marshes and wetlands, the reeds and the narrow boats in the countryside of his birth and childhood, before the draining, the shriek of the jets, and the bombs, and later the exodus to the city.

'Brother, brother.'

Zahra realised that it wasn't his fisherman-grandfather all those safe, prosperous years ago shaking his shoulder but Asif – urgently yet gingerly. Zahra roused himself. 'What time is it?'

'Eight o'clock, brother.'

'Well?'

'There was a call, about three hours ago, to the secret service number we have been monitoring.'

'Three hours ago? Why is it only now that you are telling me?'

Asif proffered sheets and sheets of printouts. 'There are so many numbers to cross-check. There is only me. I have been working through the night.' He blinked his sore, bloodshot eyes, as if to demonstrate his devotion to duty. He knew better than to curry sympathy. He kept thinking of the film he'd enjoyed when he was a teenager – *Groundhog Day*.

'What was said?'

'I don't know, brother. With our surveillance level, I

can only get call number lists. It's impossible to get more.'

'So why have you woken me up?'

'I have almost exactly pinpointed the location of the transmitting phone – an address in Fenningstone.'

'Where is Fenningstone?'

'About eight miles west along the coast. It's possible – likely, brother – that Husain borrowed the phone from its owner.'

'It's thin, Asif. This could lead nowhere.'

Asif looked down at his hands. He didn't want to say what he knew to be the case: there were no other leads.

Zahra stared at the abundant, straight, dark hair on the crown of Asif's head and tapped the speed dial of his phone. 'Hamid? Gather everyone together. We're going to Fenningstone right now.' He motioned to Asif for the address and read it out. '15A, Old High Street, Fenningstone FR7 8QT.'

At the address in question at the same time – 8am – there was quiet havoc. Husain had created a slum in the second bedroom and was in the process of flooding the bathroom as water from the shower splashed everywhere. Already, the sink was full of short dark hairs from his beard, and smears of toothpaste were drying on the taps and the previously pristine tiling above the sink. On the mirror, a crude handprint remained from when it had been steamed up and hurriedly wiped.

Joey roamed the flat, his tongue silently tapping against the roof of his mouth, his hands and fingers jerking and flicking convulsively and his eyes darting.

Sterling had managed to get himself ready before the Muslim maelstrom emerged from the bathroom, a wet towel discarded carelessly onto the carpet. 'Think of the cash, Joey,' he said softly. 'It's not going to be for much longer. Then you can do some spring-cleaning.' Joey could not engage with him. 'I'll make it right, Joey. Honest. When it's all over. I'll come back and make it right.'

Finally, the small man looked at him. Sterling gave him a light punch on the shoulder. 'I promise,' he said.

There was time for further disorder at breakfast, involving dollops of marmalade and tea spillages, and then Sterling and Husain were ready to go.

'Thank you very much for your hospitality, Mr Miller,' said Husain. To the end, his habits continued to be as messy as his manners were impeccable. 'I'm sorry for the… inconvenience. The stress makes me… careless.'

Joey nodded. His expression struggled in a stalled transition between understanding and acceptance, his eyes flicking to the mess on the breakfast table.

Sterling went to the bay window and looked up and down the street. 'Let's go, Husain. See you, Joey.' He clattered down the stairs, opened the door at the bottom and slipped into the street, sensing the large man behind him.

Again he looked up and down the narrow, old-established street, and then at his watch. At a quarter past nine on a windy April Sunday in the centre of town there were few people about. Husain did his own tradecraft sweep.

'Down here,' said Sterling. 'The hotel is just a bit further along from where we got off the bus yesterday. We'll reach the bin in a couple of minutes – plenty of time.'

Husain continued his scanning. 'OK,' he muttered.

Was he checking that there were no threats, or was he expecting something?

The Old High Street came out like a narrow tributary into a great river. 'Damn,' said Sterling. 'I'd forgotten how open this was.' He picked up his pace towards the large glass-and-white-concrete mass, jutting at right angles towards the sea, more like a 1960s office block than a hotel catering for the south coast Kent and Sussex well-to-do. As he approached the only bin just short of the entrance, he realised in an instant why the dead drop time frame had been so tightly prescribed. Behind him he could hear the harsh grind of bin-lorry machinery.

Already, Husain was struggling for breath beside him. 'How come there's rubbish collection on a Sunday?'

'You heard central Fenningstone on a Saturday night, didn't you? It's like all the coastal towns, and the inland ones for that matter – Cantcester and the like. The result is strewn all through the streets in the morning – paper, plastic beer cups, burger wrappers, fag ends, blood, vomit, rubbers, needles, footwear, tights. Some towns send their cleaning teams out in the early hours, but that's probably even more expensive than double time on Sunday morning. Whichever way they organise it, they don't want to scare the tourists and more respectable clientele off, do they? Here we are.' He approached the bin. 'Keep your eyes peeled.'

Sterling peered into the bin. Many of the things he had just recounted appeared to be in it, but so was a small brown envelope to the side. He reached in and retrieved it, wrinkling his lips and nose at the slime over one corner and that familiar melange of seaside and Saturday night smells. He and Husain looked over the Arabic script on the sheet of paper within. 'That's got to be it,' said Sterling.

A wiry young man in hi-vis orange overalls and a baseball cap that was turned backwards on his small head came up to the bin. 'Find anything decent?' he grinned as he whipped the top off the bin, released it from its housing and strode off to the back of the bin lorry. 'Just in time,' said Sterling. 'Or, if it's not this, just too late.'

Something in the corner of his eye begged his attention, and at the same moment Husain tensed. A young man, alert and sharp-eyed, had come around the corner into view from the direction of the Old High Street and Joey Miller's flat. Sterling trawled his memory for the layout of the town. The Old High Street and the one almost parallel, Tontine Street, connected the commercial, culinary and shopping centre at the top of the town to the harbour at the bottom. Both snaked down a steep hill. Further along to the west, the top was separated from the shore by a cliff, once exclusively chalky but now covered with vegetation. Along the shore behind the hotel was a series of graciously built Regency crescents and more prosaic blocks, now, if he remembered rightly, turned mostly into flats and the occasional bed and breakfast establishment. Interspersed between the blocks were a coach park and a car park, and a long esplanade beneath the cliffside. Where they currently were felt horribly exposed, but they were cut off to the east by the young man from both the harbour and the old town on the cliff top.

'Come on,' said Sterling. He turned his back on the young man a hundred and fifty metres away and plunged up the steps and into the foyer of the hotel. 'All right, Marcus?' he'd said to the doorman in his top hat and brown-and-gold livery, a local he'd known well in his Fenningstone days and who, fortunately, remembered him. 'Marcus and I sorted out fights and spats together outside here back in the day,' he muttered to Mohamed. 'Through here and out the back.'

At the corner of Harbour Street and the Old High Street, the young man was struggling with his phone and its speed dial. 'Hamid? It's Nevin. I think I've spotted them going into a hotel opposite the harbour.' He searched for the hotel's name. 'The Grand – so I'm off after them.'

'Keep your phone on. I'll send some others. Don't let them get away.'

Hamid turned to his boss, who was looking, almost dreamily, into the window of MayHem. All that was lacking among the needles and swatches and racks of clothes and fragments of cloth and the large sewing machine on the counter in front of a functional olive-green work chair was the tailor himself, but because it was Sunday the shop was as empty as the street it belonged to. 'Nevin thinks he might have seen them. I'm going to send some of the others to the harbour to help him.'

Zahra nodded. 'While they do that, let's see what the owner of the phone can tell us. He motioned to the doorbell with a slight incline of his head, and Hamid pushed the button. A trill echoed tinnily up the stairs as it had the day before for Sterling and Husain. Joey appeared at the door. 'I thought you'd gone...' he started, and then his high-pitched voice tailed off.

Hamid put his hand on the door and pushed, forcing the small man backwards, and he and Zahra stepped over the threshold and closed the door behind them.

Upstairs, Hamid drew the curtains of the bay window.

The blinds were also drawn, but Hamid knew to take no chances. In a street like this, there would be a window opposite at the same height.

Joey sat on the sofa, his small, slanted blue eyes blinking rapidly. On prompting from Zahra, Hamid retrieved a stool from the kitchen, and swapped it for the coffee table. Zahra perched himself on the stool, his hands clasped and his legs crossed at the ankles, a large dark brooding vulture. He looked down at Joey Miller with a face of competing and complex expressions, including, in large measure, distaste.

'You've had two men here. One of them used your phone.'

'I-I-I-... d-d-d-don't know what you're talking about. I live by myself.' Joey swallowed with a struggle. His large Adam's apple bobbled in his pale-pink throat. 'My girlfriend's coming round in a little while. She'll tell you.'

Hamid returned from his sortie around the flat. 'There's no one here, Irfan.' He leant in and whispered in Zahra's ear. 'No sign that anyone's *been* here either. The place is very clean and tidy. There was this cash in the main bedroom.'

Zahra sat still. 'Check the rubbish.' He turned back to Joey Miller. 'Tell me about them. Tell me about them – Sterling and Husain. When were they here? What did they do here? Where have they gone? Tell me about the money.'

Joey's foot thumped the floor like the hind leg of a rabbit. Sterling and Husain had taken the laptop with them, but Joey had spotted something else that might interest these men, in the tray under the coffee table, and knew he had to keep quiet. Hamid returned from downstairs with pizza cartons and foil containers. Zahra examined them with fastidious hands.

'You can't just come in here like this,' said Joey. Perspiration dewed on his flaky brow.

'Enough,' Zahra shouted, muffling the sound through gritted teeth. He hurled the cartons and containers at Joey's head, and the diminished figure put up his forearms to his face and flinched.

When he'd taken his arms down, something in Joey had changed. He no longer cowered. His back straightened. Obstinacy descended on his handsome flat features. He folded his arms and his lower lip jutted out. 'F-f-f-fuck you.'

Zahra recognised the moment. He'd seen and experienced it often enough in the gaols and interrogation centres of his shadowy world, in men very different from Joey Miller. It did not mean that you would not break the person defying you; it simply meant that it would take much longer, and be much messier. The rage he'd struggled to contain, from the moment Husain had broken his cover and disappeared with his wad of cash at Waterloo Station, to the escape of the man Strange, to the defiance and luck of the man Sterling and to all the other recent little mishaps and conspiracies against him, boiled over. His leader and his men were incompetent; the world was against him; he'd never get what he aspired to and deserved. And now this cretin defied him.

Zahra launched himself from the stool into Joey, knocking him back, straddling his chest and pinning him down on the sofa, the cartons and containers strewn on and around him. He pummelled Joey's flat head, and then his strong, slender hands closed around the thick throat. His ears roared and his rage hummed as he grunted with effort and determination. Under him, Joey writhed and clawed and choked. His tongue protruded grotesquely from his gasping mouth and his eyes bulged out from their narrow slits. Gradually, life was ebbing from him, almost to the point of no return.

Zahra felt strong arms envelop him. 'Irfan, Irfan,' said Hamid, 'you know this will achieve nothing. Come. Let go.' Firmly, the second in command prised his leader's hands from Joey's neck and swiftly Zahra responded. Panting heavily, he dragged himself from the body on the sofa, like a horseman dismounting after a hot day's ride. He paced the sitting room, flexing his fingers and rubbing his hands. The dam had burst. There was no need, in this, the end game, to kill the young man, or go back to the Sunningtons in Deeping, or even Captain Cavendish in Sandley, for punishment or revenge for their deception and misinformation. The future was what mattered, not the past.

Hamid looked on without expression as Joey lay unconscious and motionless on the sofa. All the tribulations they faced were an inevitable part of the mission. An inevitable part of something, anyway.

As Zahra shifted restlessly back and forth, Hamid stirred himself to check the flat meticulously to remove evidence. He wiped Joey's pink neck, and, after a final survey, indicated it was time to go. Zahra's almost-murderous rush to the head had upset the rhythm. Without it, there would have been a more thorough search, and a more thorough search would have turned up the vital evidence that remained loosely concealed.

In the street, Zahra stood as the other man gently clicked the front door closed. Surreptitiously, Hamid used his cuff to wipe the door and the doorbell button.

He followed as Zahra strode off down the hill towards the harbour. If Hamid had had the ability, the imagination and the inclination to ascribe feelings to actions, he'd have described Zahra's demeanour as carefree, almost jaunty, almost relieved, as if a great burden of anger and resentment had been lifted from his shoulders, and it was clear that his boss's migraine had gone.

Chapter 24

It all came back to Sterling: the reception desk to the left, the receptionist in the same livery as all those years ago; the silver-doored lifts beyond the desk to the left; the bar, all bright and beguiling with the beer and lager taps and the fancy lighting; the restaurant area with its isolated clusters of late breakfasters; the chairs and tables and décor, modern fifteen years ago and now somehow out of kilter with the world outside; and at the left towards the back, the conference rooms, open doors showing the projectors suspended from the ceilings, the screens and the flip-chart stands. He'd taken his wife here more years ago than he cared to remember, when they were courting, when they had to hurry back to their room for sex in the afternoons. Before the bitterness, the walkouts and the recrimination, and later, the tears – and not just hers.

He strode through with the feigned confidence of a registered guest, Husain wheezing behind him. There was a door in the huge glass panelling into a patio courtyard at the very back, abutting the kitchens on the right. The parasol-umbrellas were tinged green at the crown with moss and algae stains, and the patio heaters and flame towers were dark, cold and silent. Cigarette butts circled the nearby bins. Sterling pushed the release bars of the emergency exit and stumbled through into the dustbin area hotels never want their clientele to see – or smell. A complex bouquet of cooking fat, rotting vegetables, yeast and beer assailed Sterling's nostrils as hazy steam and waste gas wisped lazily into the clear spring air from extractor fans and ducts on the kitchen walls.

Another door, whose panels were rotting at the bottom like jagged teeth, led the two men into the hotel car park. Sterling hurried them to the exit, which got them onto the road directly beneath the cliff.

'We can't go back, so we'd better push on west and find a spot away from prying eyes where you can do your translating.'

'OK,' said Husain. 'But don't go too quickly.'

Away from the back of the hotel they passed a one-storey block containing a fish bar and a separate kebab and burger bar catering for the day tripper trade. Parallel to the hotel was a plain brick 1960s block of flats divided by a road from a Regency block on the opposite side – utility and grace in side-by-side contrast.

They came out to the coach and car parks, and the other Regency blocks loomed like Arctic-white battleships in a grey tarmac sea. Then they were in the open, and for a few minutes making good progress away from the harbour. And then they were spotted.

Husain saw them first, ants running and gesticulating four hundred metres away. 'Lord,' he said. His eyes flicked ahead. 'There's nothing up here. We haven't got a prayer.'

Sterling looked back. 'They'll have to come after us on foot, unless they really know the area. There was a barrier back there, and it's not straightforward to get a car up here along the esplanade.'

Up ahead, about a hundred metres away, he spotted a familiar building nestling under the cliff like an old rural primary school or railway station, all red Kent brick, pantiles, long vertical windows and sharply angled gables. His eyes moved up the cliffside to the rails like ladders set against chalk. They'd reached the water lift and the funicular railway. His mind raced. What day was it? Sunday. When he was stationed here on the job, the Baptist church at the top of the cliff had an arrangement with the council to open the lift in the morning to get an important part of its congregation, the folk in the flats below, to come to its Sunday service. If he and Husain were lucky, really lucky, it would be working.

There were Jacob's ladder staircases up to the top, steps zigzagging this way and that up the side of the cliff, with starting and end points disguised among the vegetation, but Husain was not fit enough for those and they'd be caught before they reached the top. The lift was a better bet. Once they were on it and going up, there'd be no following for at least ten minutes – plenty of time to disappear back at the top of the town.

'Come on,' said Sterling. 'We're going for a ride. Hopefully.'

The small ticket hall looked exactly the same as in about 2010, when Sterling had last been in it. The ticket office manager and lift operator might not have been the same man as before, but he was from the same mould. His pebble-lensed, black-framed spectacles were slipping down his nose and no amount of automatic finger poking lodged them back above the bridge. Strands of his wispy comb-over fluttered in the draft from the dilapidated door. He exuded cantankerousness, developed through years of deflating the high spirits of kids coming off the beach, teenagers made rowdy and over-relaxed by cheap lager, and of course the compulsion of Sunday morning opening.

'Two tickets, please,' said Sterling. Husain peered anxiously towards the esplanade.

'Not opening for ten minutes,' said the liftman.

'We're in a hurry. It's probably life and death.'

'Can't help that. Opening time is opening time.'

'A hundred quid.'

'What?' The liftman, his small pot belly protruding over his shapeless trousers, was startled.

'A hundred quid to open now and get us up the top.'

'A hundred just for that?' The liftman's eyes were shining. He'd be able to have a couple of pints on his way home at lunchtime and still have plenty left. The beer would inoculate him from his wife's incessant complaining over the roast.

'Husain, where's your wad?'

The liftman slid the door back and Sterling and Husain climbed into the boxcar. They watched as the outer gate was shut and the man moved over to the control room. Sterling sat on a hard, square brown seat, torn and tatty with age and the weight of a thousand backsides. He couldn't see the entranceway. There was a jerk and he and Husain were on their creaky, arthritic way. On the glass panes on the outside canopy housing, salt had evaporated from the sea and crystallised into thousands of snowflake patterns. Sterling was a slow-getaway specialist and had case-files to prove it, but this surely broke all records. Halfway up, the other boxcar crossed on the way down.

Within spitting distance of the exit platform at the top, the boxcar jolted to a halt, so sharply that it juddered on the rail. Someone at the bottom had pressed an emergency stop button. Sterling looked down through the grimy window at the back, straight into the sharp eyes of the young man, he was certain, who had chased him in Sandley. Sterling opened the boxcar door. There was no newfangled locking system on this Victorian contraption that prevented exit until the car docked at the bottom or top. The only obstacle was the uneven slide of the door, which kept sticking on the grooves as the door's bottom caught and the top overshot. There was an iron support bar like a girder under the platform overhang. It wasn't even a leap away from the door. Sterling stretched up and put his arms over it, then levered and scrabbled the ankle of his right leg further along the beam. Awkwardly, he twisted and worked his body from the girder and onto the platform above, with the help of a wrought iron pillar, breathing heavily and sweating from the exertion. Outside the glass door of the top terminus he saw a pair of small sandals and looked up to see a little girl with auburn ringlets pointing right at him, her mouth an astonished little 'o'. He turned back down to the boxcar. Husain looked disconcertingly large and heavy as he raised his worried dark eyes upwards.

'Right,' said Sterling. He made his voice confident just as his heart was sinking. 'Wrap your arms around the girder like I did. Then I'll help you get your legs up.' He was sure that Husain didn't lack bottle. The man had infiltrated a terrorist cell, after all, and lived on his wits in a hostile environment for however long. But there was bottle and bottle. Sterling himself did not mind most physical pain, or even the prospect of it, but for example he certainly wasn't thrilled about being in enclosed spaces. One of Husain's blind spots was clearly hanging out of boxcars on water lifts, and he might have stayed where he was, looking down and then looking up, wavering and havering, had it not been for the lurch of the boxcar at the beginning of its descent. He did as Sterling commanded and a moment later was left stranded as the car moved away.

'Swing your leg, Husain,' urged Sterling. 'Go on, swing it.'

The other man's sweat-stained face, growing darker and darker, registered panic and growing despair. Prone on the platform, Sterling reached for the seat of Husain's voluminous loose trousers, struggling to grab a purchase. When he did, he could feel himself sliding forward and in danger of getting tipped onto the rails. He started to feel despair of his own. Either he let Husain go, and who knows how long Husain would be able to hang onto the girder with his arms, all fifteen stone of him, or he was finished himself.

'Bloody hell,' said a voice from behind.

Sterling felt his own ankles roughly wrapped around with large hands, and a kind of tag-wrestle followed, with limbs flailing, grunting and oaths. A few seconds later, Husain had been rolled and manhandled onto the platform where he wheezed next to Sterling like an old elephant seal as a tall, neat man in shorts and T-shirt, with short dark hair, five o'clock shadow and a gleaming, multi-jointed grey-and-silver prosthetic right leg, stood over them.

'Thanks,' said Sterling. He stood up and brushed himself down and then helped Husain to his feet. He peered down over the edge of the platform. The car he and Husain had come up in was just above the other car as it ascended. 'Uh oh.' He scoured the small boarding and alighting area and found what he was looking for, banging the red emergency stop button with the flat of his hand.

It was Husain's turn to lean over the platform. There was a puff, and then the whine of a ricochet as something rattled around in the domed top of the lift. Husain flinched back but put his thumbs up. 'It's stopped.'

'Let's go,' said Sterling. Fear, and the surge and ebb of adrenaline, rendered him laconic. At the top of the cliff, on the western edge of the town centre, he looked around. It seemed dismayingly open. 'We've only got a minute or two. Those blokes will be up out of the lift, and I bet another lot will be coming over from the high street.'

'Follow me,' said the man with the prosthetic leg. He led them to an old Mr Whippee ice cream van parked on the kerb almost opposite the water lift and opened the passenger door. 'Go in the back and lie on the floor.'

'Eh?' said Sterling. He'd stopped with one foot in the well of the passenger's side and one foot on the pavement. 'We need you to drive us out of here without any pussyfooting around.'

'Ah,' said the man. 'Problem. Snafu in fact. The van won't start. I'm waiting for roadside rescue.'

'Jesus Christ and all the saints and angels.'

'No time, Mr Sterling,' said Husain. 'We'll have to chance it.'

Sterling scanned the view through the windscreen and side windows and sighed. After all this, were they going to be cornered in the back of an ice cream van?

He slipped into the space on the floor at the back and Husain joined him amongst the freezer compartments, the cone dispensers, the scoops and the soft ice cream machine. There was a cold, sweet aroma redolent of Sterling's expeditions as a boy with his father to the local sights and sometimes those further afield.

The ice cream man locked the van and joined them in the back, propping his forearms over the sill of the dispensing window. There was barely room for his feet. Staring at the prosthetic leg and the bottom of the freezer, Sterling could hear the soft hum of the generator and felt Husain's warm breath on his neck. Pinned together, they settled down to wait.

'What can I do you for, gents?' said the ice cream man two minutes later. Sterling could hear harsh breathing and sense agitation.

'Two men came out of the lift just now. Where did they go?' said Nevin.

'Two men... From the lift,' echoed the ice cream seller. 'Hmm... Big bloke, Middle Eastern, and a smaller one, more English-looking.'

'Yes,' said Nevin. 'Exactly.'

'I'm not sure. I had a bit of a queue. I think they went along there and around the corner.' From the bottom of the van Sterling could see the man stretching out from the window and sensed him pointing to the west.

'Thanks,' said Nevin. He stepped back and put his ear to his phone again. 'They're going west. We should get them shortly.'

The ice cream man called in vain to the backs of Nevin and the two others. 'Fancy a cone? A "99"? Fuck off, then,' he said under his breath. 'This poxy ice cream van business.' Then his tone changed again as he edged away from the bodies on the floor and into the driver's seat. 'Whoa, guys. Just when it's bad, things get better. The breakdown van's arrived.'

'Good news,' said Sterling. 'But we'd better stay here till the problem's fixed, don't you think?' More softly, he addressed the prone figure squashing him. 'Husain, why don't you get out your codebook and decode the message from the dead drop while we wait. Given what business is like for this bloke, I reckon that if you get your cash out again we've got ourselves transport for wherever we next have to go.'

Sterling felt the big man shifting next to him. 'That would be the best and most obvious thing to do, Mr Sterling, were it not for a snag.'

'A snag,' repeated Sterling.

'In our rush this morning, I'm afraid I left *One Thousand and One Nights* in Mr Miller's flat.'

Sterling started banging his forehead on the freezer compartment.

Chapter 25

'They're geniuses, those blokes,' said the ice cream man, as he watched the breakdown and recovery man drive off to his next rescue. 'They go unerringly to the problem, and seem to know exactly what to do to fix it. They've got everything they need in those little vans.'

'I'm getting cramp down here, mate,' said Sterling. 'Can you park up somewhere quiet so we can sit in the front and sort out what we do next?'

'I should be selling ice creams,' said the man. But he started up and pulled away, finding a parking space a mile further along amongst the grand Victorian piles on Fenningstone's west cliff.

The three men settled in the front, Husain squeezing Sterling against the passenger door. Sterling leaned forward and twisted around so he could see their rescuer. Husain introduced Sterling and himself. The ice cream man was called Al Chambers, a man full of urgent, suppressed energy and clearly someone who relished action and involvement. His speech was rapid and full of slang, which Sterling, deciphering the torrent, worked out as a mixture of British army and American cop shows, with a smattering of Cockney rhyming slang.

Sterling didn't believe in beating about the bush. 'Where did you leave your leg?'

'Afghanistan,' said the war veteran. 'Helmand. IED. I

was a non-com. Makes a change. Normally, people want to know, but it takes two days and fifty conversations before they come out with it.'

'You came over to the lift just in time. How did you know there was something going on?'

'The kid. She was hopping from one leg to the other and pointing, but her mum just told her to come away. I thought I'd check for myself.' The ice cream man shrugged, as if something like this was just in the normal course of things. 'My turn. One of those blokes who came up to the van fired a gun in the funicular. They meant business. What's going on?'

Sterling nudged Husain. 'Go on. Give him a summary.'

At the end, Husain shuffled in his seat. 'So that's it, in broad sweeps, but unfortunately I left the codebook in the flat.' He glanced at Sterling. 'I was much more hurried than usual, or it wouldn't have happened.'

Sterling ignored the barb. 'We need to get back in the flat. It would be too risky for me or Husain...'.

Chambers stared out of the windscreen and drummed his fingers on the steering wheel. An old man with a stick emerged from a door in one of the big nineteenth-century blocks, tottering unsteadily down the steps, tapping gingerly with his stick, as if the hard stone would turn to jelly in a treacherous trice. 'Don't get me wrong. I don't mind a bit of excitement in a good cause,' said the ice cream man, 'but I'm barely keeping the wolf from the door here. We've just left a good pitch back there, so I'll have to find another one, maybe not so well placed. It's dog eat dog in this game, you know. When you're starting out, they don't tell you about the bans and licensing, the unsocial hours, the competition from supermarkets and all that stuff, never mind the customers you get. And of course, no one wants an ice cream when it's pissing down.'

Sterling, whose eyes had long glazed over as Chambers warmed to his theme on the merits and demerits of mobile catering, which had started to encompass complex comparisons between ice cream vending and burgers and hot dogs, nudged Husain again. Husain unfurled his wad of cash. 'Will £100 cover the half an hour required to walk down the high street, knock on Mr Miller's door and recover what we require, with a hint of caution for possible surveillance?'

Chambers looked at the money. 'Certainly, squire.'

Ten minutes later, Sterling and Husain were looking down on the centre of Fenningstone from the multistorey car park fused into a shopping mall. Chambers's last words as he left for the lift were an entreaty to sell cones, '99s' and ice lollies to anyone chancing upon the van and fancying a treat. 'You wouldn't believe where I've done my best business. It might start a craze – ice creams on top of a multistorey. If it went viral…'.

They watched the man with the prosthetic leg emerge briefly from the car park-cum-shopping mall and stride off into the shopping centre opposite and out of sight.

'Can we trust him, Mr Sterling?'

'What choice have we got?' Sterling chose not to harp on about the agent's carelessness. What was the point? What was done was done.

Because it was Sunday, the car park and the town were relatively quiet. He put his forearms on the railing and looked out around. There was a miscellany of buildings just next to the centre, as if architects had just plonked them down without a thought for coherence of any sort, some mainly glass, some mainly brick, some square and some round. Among them, the bus station had been shoehorned in. Next to the brutalist new order was the older, more intimate centre and then residential areas radiating away in waves reflecting different eras, mainly from Victorian to the present day, like a rolling, predominantly red-brick carpet over the area where the Kentish North Downs tapered down to the sea. Out to the left, a long, dramatic railway viaduct bisected the whole urban area, and closer below, straight ahead, an enterprising house owner had painted the huge head of a seagull on the side of his dwelling. Churches and spires dotted the townscape, including a Grace Chapel of late Victorian design. A mile away east to Dovethorpe, a mysterious, stubby, white, circular tower squatted redundantly in an expanse of greensward, framed against the cliffs behind.

It was quiet out in the open, and a cool breeze blew up from the sea.

Husain joined Sterling at the railing. 'He should be OK. Ex-army and everything. I got the impression that he finds selling ice creams a mixture of boring and stressful, so this is a diversion.'

'Maybe,' said Sterling. 'Your wad of cash is probably pretty effective. What do you reckon's in this latest message?'

'I don't know, Mr Sterling. I'm racking my brains to think of a target, or an event, or a location, down here. It would be easier if there were a summit, or a royal visit or something. Easier...' he laughed wryly, 'only easier in that I'd know the scope and scale of the problem.' Despite all the action already during the morning, Husain seemed preoccupied.

'Look,' said Sterling. 'He's coming back. And he's not hanging about, either.' The two men watched as Chambers scuttled across the gap between shopping centres and into the car park complex. Sterling was slouched on the hood of the van, with Husain close by, when the ice cream vendor strode up the ramp.

Husain's hands were clasped as he went to meet the messenger. 'Well? Success?'

Chambers tossed *One Thousand and One Nights* at the agent. 'It was exactly where you said – the tray under the coffee table.' He moved over to Sterling. His face, even with the effect of five o'clock shadow creeping through, was ashen. 'I shouldn't have got into this,' he muttered. 'I should have stuck to selling ice creams.'

'Tell us,' said Sterling. He knew the news wouldn't be good. He just didn't know how bad it would be.

'There was no answer when I rang, but the latch was up and the deadbolt hadn't been turned. Someone was careless. So I just opened the door and went up. What was your mate's name?'

'Joey,' said Sterling. 'Joey Miller.' He felt a hollowing in his stomach, a sudden lurch as when you drive fast over the brow of a hill and the car leaves the ground for a moment.

'Joey,' repeated Chambers. 'Well – he's alive, but he's in a bad way. He's had a beating, and someone tried to strangle him. You didn't tell me he was…'.

'Did you call an ambulance?'

'Of course I did. What do you take me for? That's the first thing I did after I checked him and made him comfortable. His pulse was strong, so he'll be OK.' Chambers caught Sterling's look. 'I was in Helmand, mate. I know when a bloke is going to make it and when he's not.'

Sterling went back to the railing. This was his fault. Not the whole sorry business. Mike Strange, or Mohamed Husain, or both of them, had started it, at least Sterling's involvement in it. But he had chosen to get Joey mixed up in it, and Stacey and Liv for that matter. *Christ, supposing…* It was difficult to think clearly. He'd seen Joey in action in some of the toughest bars in Fenningstone. He was plucky. He'd have been nervous with Zahra and the others, but he wouldn't have backed down. Zahra had done it, Sterling was sure, and Zahra would pay.

'I'm sorry, Mr Sterling,' said Husain. 'Perhaps we shouldn't have…'.

Sterling put his hand up. 'Just get in the van and work out the message, Husain.' He turned to the ice cream man. 'You must trust us, Al, or you wouldn't have come back.'

'Don't worry, mate. I had a good think down there in the town after I got out of the flat, the big question being why you two blokes would send me back to the crime scene if you were the perps. If you were the perps and you'd forgotten the book, you'd have been more likely to go back yourselves, before someone discovered the poor bloke. And don't forget, I saw there were some men after you, and I spoke to them.'

'Have you called the police as well as the ambulance?'

'No. I don't want to get involved with them. You know how it would go. Your pal was all right with me or without me. I left the door of the flat open. The paramedics will get the police. It will be fine. I know it.'

'OK, well when Husain's sorted the code out, we'll find a phone box and tell them as well. We'd better do it anonymously. Let's get back in the van.'

Husain was still busy, his fingers and hands working hard with the paper and the codebook. Eventually he sat back and rubbed his eyes. He looked at Sterling and then quickly away, out over the town, again preoccupied and disengaged.

Sterling reached for the paper and read it.

'Final instructions to the Eagle Company, Team 2
Location: The Old Lighthouse, Drangeness
Date and time: Sunday 17th April, 12pm
Action required:

1. Secure access to the lighthouse, coastguard cottages, café, station, approach road and surrounding area beforehand to facilitate the suicide attack.
2. Withdraw after the attack and await instructions.'

'South and west, just as Mike reckoned at the beginning,' said Sterling. 'Today. In a few hours. Just along the coast. Some kind of attack. Bloody hell. We've been through a lot for this, Joey's nearly paid the ultimate price, and the actual details are sketchy.'

'It's classic spy craft,' said Husain. 'If you work on the principle of keeping information to a minimum, and sealing it so that no active agents have the full picture, and no cell in a cell structure knows what other cells know or are doing, this is exactly what to expect. I stole the information on Friday. It's Sunday now. It's all just-in-time, need-to-know stuff. What's puzzling me is what's being attacked at Drangeness.'

Husain caught the glances that Sterling and Chambers exchanged. 'You know, gentlemen,' he said, 'don't you?'

'Drangeness, and the small area around it,' said Chambers, 'is said to be Britain's only desert. Actually, it's just somewhere with a few features akin to a desert, sand and scrubby bushes and the like. There are a few good pitches around there in the summer,' – the temptation to weave in ice cream-oriented comments was irresistible – 'but that's not it. That's not it at all. No, what's relevant to you is that plonked right in the middle is Drangeness B nuclear power station.'

Chapter 26

Brer Rabbit was hopelessly stuck, fore and back paws, to the tar baby made by Brer Fox, when Andy Nolan's wife came with the telephone into the living room in their semi-detached house in the north of Cantcester. The two young children had heard the story a hundred times but its charm never seemed to pall, not even with Andy Nolan himself.

'Wait a moment,' said Nolan. He took the phone to the French windows and looked out over the back garden. The grass needed a cut, and the whole garden had a bedraggled but bright mid-spring look. A squirrel was foraging by the hedge at the end, possibly looking for nuts buried a while before. 'Nolan,' he said.

'Duty sergeant from Fenningstone here, sir. We were notified to contact you if anything significant happened here. It has. We were alerted by paramedics and then had an anonymous 999 call from a public phone box in the Sandstone Road sending us to an address in the Old High Street. A man with serious injuries. His name is Joey Miller. Suspicious circumstances – in fact he'd been beaten and half-strangled. No particular sign of forced entry. Forensics are in there now, and a couple of our detectives are also at the scene. That's about all I have at the moment, except... well, the victim has... learning difficulties – to be specific, Down's syndrome, and although he hasn't got a record, he's known to us.'

'How so, Sergeant?'

'Well, he's a ducker and weaver really, in the dodgier circles in Fenningstone, and he hears things that are useful to us.'

'Is that why someone went after him?'

'It should certainly be a line of enquiry, sir.'

Nolan saw a blackbird dive-bomb the squirrel, probably because he had a nest to defend. Nature was a war. Behind him, his wife was finishing off the story. Brer Rabbit's excellent and intuitive use of reverse psychology had culminated in his joyous escape, and the children squealed with delight as they and their mother shouted out the final line that goaded poor, stupid Brer Fox.

'I've got to go out,' said Nolan, when the commotion had died down and he'd finished his call. 'Fenningstone.'

His wife nodded. It had always been like this, and it would always continue like this, but Andy Nolan was going places, and she was lucky enough to share his ambition. 'Is it to do with Bill Murphy's call last night? About Frank Sterling?'

'Almost certainly. Bill's looking after Sandley, Deeping and Dovethorpe, so it's Fenningstone for me.'

On the way down, Nolan realised that he knew of Joey Miller already – he just hadn't made the connection. He'd never been stationed down in Fenningstone himself. His squad car years with Frank Sterling had been in Marchurch. But he'd heard Sterling talk about Miller and all the help Miller had supplied. The duty sergeant's 'line of enquiry' amongst the Fenningstone underworld might well be the one that led to an assailant, but it surely couldn't be a coincidence that Frank Sterling had almost certainly been in the vicinity around about the time of the assault. He wouldn't have done it, of course he wouldn't, but Frank found trouble without even looking, so he was bound to be mixed up in it somehow.

Nolan made a connection with the hands-free. 'Sergeant, the phone box in Sandstone Road where the emergency call came from. It's a long shot of course, but can you get someone to fingerprint it?'

'In hand already, sir.'

That nick was competent. 'Thanks. I'll be at the scene in about twenty minutes.'

Nolan's musings drifted back to Sterling. The view in the force was clear. Sterling was a hothead and a loner, but he was talented, intuitive and got results, and the ride was always exciting. Jim Selby, the Police Fed rep, always complained that Frank bloody Sterling took up more of his time in casework than all the others combined.

Nolan didn't disagree with any of that, but he knew Frank better than anyone, and his view was more nuanced. He'd seen him defend a homeless man from a mob of drunken bullies, unafraid about getting stuck in. He knew about his sense of right and wrong, and how he separated it from law and justice. People responded to the honesty that he exuded. He could be awkward and stubborn, but people stepped up to help him.

Down in Fenningstone town centre, the blue light casting its sombre glow in the narrow street told Nolan that he was close, and a young female constable, when he'd shown his credentials, pointed to the entrance of Joey Miller's flat. The plastic bootees on his shoes were all right – easy to put on, a little slippery underfoot – but he never got used to the tight surgical-style gloves, which squeaked and stretched as he struggled to squeeze his fingers into them. Upstairs the flat was still immaculate, and in no way affected by the forensic team in white plastic onesies as they went about their business. Miller had already been taken off to hospital. Frank would be upset if he knew what had happened. When he'd mentioned his friend to Nolan, affection mingled with admiration.

The detective in charge was called Jepson, a tall, painfully thin man with a lugubrious expression seemingly permanently fixed to his long face, as if in all his life he'd seen nothing but woe. There were few detectives in the Kent force that Nolan didn't know. This one was methodical and competent, and he gave a succinct and clear summary. 'It was a savage, determined attack,' he ended. 'It's surprisingly difficult to try and strangle someone, even someone as small as Mr Miller, and as you can imagine, he had a thicker neck than what you might normally expect.'

He and Nolan were interrupted by a voice from the bottom of the stairs. 'Sir, I don't want to get kitted up again. Can you come down? I've got a witness.'

Nolan went down and found that he knew the detective sergeant as well – Maria Tenwick – also competent, and very ambitious. She was as short as her boss was tall, and was perhaps carrying a few pounds more than she was comfortable with. Nolan couldn't help thinking of the wisecracks that might be circulating around the main Fenningstone nick about the investigating team.

'I'm here,' said Nolan, 'because this might be connected to something big – bigger than a possible feud or score-settling or whatever here in central Fenningstone. So I'm not interfering but hopefully complementing and adding to your inquiry.'

'Right, sir,' said Tenwick. 'Well, we've been doing a canvass of the street. It's been slow-going to an extent because, being Sunday, a good few of the shops are closed. Even so, I reckon we've struck gold. Follow me.'

She led the two men to a doorway across the street, almost opposite Joey Miller's, but the narrow staircase was dingier, darker and dirtier. Nolan could smell damp, biscuits, stale cigarettes and what might have been vanilla on the way up. The flat at the top, when they had knocked and entered, could not have been more different from Miller's. His was all light, angles, modernity, minimalism and spotlessness. This one, in an atmosphere of spicy blue smoke, was full of yellowing lace, dusty bric-a-brac and figurines, bamboo screens and colours of rich dark red, purple and blue, like a fortune-teller's fairground booth – a Victorian booth at that. Nolan half-expected to see a crystal ball and tarot cards on the heavy, scratched old table at the back opposite the grimy bay window. The picture of a young wedding-day couple stood on a small round table next to a large armchair that looked out over the street. The bride, dark-eyed and raven-haired, looked radiant, the groom tall and proud. The background appeared to be an exotic, old hotel in a Mitteleuropean style. Beside the photo was an ashtray full of pale yellow stubs, and one cigarette whose thin whorl of smoke disappeared in and added to the fug.

'This is Mrs Dostavich,' said the detective sergeant, with a small sweep of her hand towards the elderly woman in the armchair. Mrs Dostavich had thin, orange-dyed hair through which her pale scalp was visible, the kind of dye job where the grey overwhelms the peroxide and brightens the final result. Her dark face was criss-crossed with tiny lines and wrinkles no make-up could entirely conceal. She was more enveloped by the armchair than sitting in it. Her tiny, liver-spotted hands rested in her shrunken lap. An ornately patterned shawl in the dominant colours of the room draped her shoulders. But despite her diminished state, her eyes were bright and lively.

'Mrs Dostavich, Detective Chief Inspector Nolan and Detective Inspector Jepson.' Something in the setting and in the elderly woman in the armchair next to the window required courtesy and formality. The woman inclined her head. The men gave slight bows. To Nolan's ears, his rank sounded outlandish. He'd never heard anyone say it before. He and Jepson perched on cane chairs that didn't match on the other side of the window.

Maria Tenwick was short enough not to loom over them. For a moment, it looked as if she was a child made to stand in a teachers' staff room. 'Can you tell them what you told me earlier?'

'Could you not have told them yourself, dear?'

'You're an important witness, Mrs Dostavich, and we don't want a kind of Chinese whispers situation.'

Mrs Dostavich smiled. 'So it's straight from the horse's mouth, then, me being the horse. Well, from yesterday around midday poor Joey had lots of visitors. First there were two young men, one English, or at least he looked English, and one who looked more Middle Eastern. Joey let them in, and he seemed pleased to see one of them.'

'Any chance of a bit more description, Mrs Dostavich?' said Jepson.

'Well, I only really saw the backs of them. They were both the same height. What is average these days – five foot ten? The English one had dark brown wavy hair. He was quite slender and was wearing a short, grey-black coat. The other one was in a longer overcoat and had glasses I think. He was fat. Am I allowed to say that anymore? Anyway, you could see it even from the back. They went in and didn't come out till this morning, although I did see Joey go out and come back in the afternoon. He waved. He was OK.'

Nolan tried to remember if his friend had any distinguishing features from the back. The description of the English one could have been Frank Sterling, but it could have been a hundred other men in Fenningstone high street yesterday. On the other hand, he remembered Murphy's comprehensive briefing. Liv Eliot had put a large Middle Eastern man and a white man on a bus from Dovethorpe to Fenningstone. What were the odds that Sterling was not the white man?

'I saw the two men leave the flat at about quarter past nine this morning,' continued the old woman. 'I don't sleep much, so I was up at seven and had already had breakfast. I didn't see Joey. The blinds were down and the curtains were drawn, but that's not unusual. Fifteen minutes later, two more men knocked at Joey's door. They both looked Middle Eastern. One was very tall, with a hooked nose and dark eyes. His clothes looked expensive but he didn't wear them very well. I don't think he cared, to be honest. My phone went – my daughter phones every Sunday morning – so I didn't see any more then, but they weren't there when I got back. I don't know if Joey let them in, and I have my coffee then, so I didn't see them come out either. Maybe they were just delivering leaflets or something.' The old woman looked at the three police officers with a furrowed brow. It was common for witnesses to be anxious, and do everything they can to be fair and accurate, as if they've already been transported to the witness stand.

'You've been very helpful,' said Jepson. 'My colleague here has taken notes that she'll write up, and we'll get you to sign a statement.' He and Nolan stirred in their chairs, half in and half out, their arms helping to lever themselves up.

The old woman put up her hand. 'Actually, I haven't finished.'

The men sank back down. 'Sorry, Mrs Dostavich,' said Nolan. 'We move quickly in the early stages of an investigation as experience shows that this is the key time. But please carry on.'

'After all that, it was quiet for a while, or it was while I was sitting here. Then there was another visitor. This time it was another man with black hair dressed in shorts and T-shirt.' The street-observer's eyes gleamed. 'I couldn't see what was on the back of the T-shirt – it was all skulls and Gothic lettering – but I don't think that matters too much because' – she leaned forward conspiratorially – 'he had an artificial leg.'

Chapter 27

'His false leg looked really sophisticated,' said Mrs Dostavich. 'My grandfather lost a leg at Gallipoli, and his tin leg was awful, a heavy thing that chafed his poor stump. He had to put Vaseline on every day. Anyway, this one was a silver-and-grey contraption, all properly jointed and probably very light and flexible.'

Tenwick was writing furiously in her notebook.

'Don't think I'm nosy,' continued the old woman. 'I'm not one of those curtain-twitchers you always see on telly. I've had a wonderful life of my own with my dear Anatoly and our children.' She reached for the photograph on the small table and looked at it almost reverently. 'At one time we had three businesses on the go here. But I get lonely, and the window connects me to the world. Lots of people know me and wave as they go past. I hope you catch whoever assaulted poor Joey. He's a kind man – does my shopping sometimes, and gets my Balkan Sobranies.' She gave the detectives a sly look from under her eyelashes. 'He always gets me a good price.'

In the street outside, the three detectives conducted an impromptu update, conference and review, with the smoky air of the flat still clinging to them.

'Obviously follow all the conventional lines of enquiry,' said Nolan, 'but this bigger thing I mentioned should be the priority. It's all hypothesis at the moment, but here's what I think happened. On Friday lunchtime a friend of mine, Frank Sterling…'.

'Frank Sterling,' said Maria Tenwick. 'Blimey. And a friend of *yours*, sir.'

Nolan looked at her. 'Sorry,' she muttered.

'… suddenly seems to have become a fugitive. Somehow he got information that a gang had lost and needed back. The gang might be a terrorist cell. From what I gathered, there are some Middle Easterners in it. Sterling got out of Sandley, apparently by boat, and ended up at a friend's house at the top of Deeping. He got some information on a memory stick, with the help of his friend's daughter, about a rendezvous yesterday morning with someone else in Dovethorpe. According to the girl, there was other stuff on the stick, but it was encrypted so she doesn't know what. The cell caught up with Sterling in Dovethorpe but he and the man he met escaped here. I reckon it was Sterling and this other man who knocked on Joey Miller's door on Saturday afternoon, and they were the first people that Mrs Dostavich saw.

'They left Joey on Sunday morning, and then it was two members of the cell that Mrs Dostavich saw a few minutes later. I'm speculating of course, but I think they did the assault.'

'What about the man with the prosthetic leg?' said Jepson.

'Someone phoned 999. He was the last person Mrs Dostavich saw going into and leaving the flat. The timings fit. I think it was him. Sterling and the other man went to Joey Miller's flat to hide. Sterling knew Miller from when he was stationed in Fenningstone, so that makes sense. The two other men turning up also makes sense.

They have sophisticated tracking equipment because they infiltrated the Deeping girl's Facebook account. It's not clear where the man with the prosthetic leg fits in.'

'Why didn't Sterling just get official help at any stage of this business?' said Jepson.

'I don't know. He's not always a team player. It might be something to do with that. Perhaps he and his associate are afraid of being compromised in some way. We might know the bare bones of this, but there are a lot of gaps.'

Tenwick started to say something and then stopped.

'Go on, Maria,' said Nolan. 'Spit it out.'

'Well, Sterling's a friend of yours, but... don't you think there's a possibility that he might have done it? An argument with the victim, and some involvement from the man with him?'

'You're right to ask. I'm trying not to let personal feelings get in the way. But Frank's not the kind of man to do something like this, not even spontaneously. And it doesn't fit with what we know. Remember, as well, that he told Liv Eliot to contact me.'

'Yes, but that was yesterday morning.'

'True,' said Nolan. 'Still...'.

'The hypothesising is useful,' said Jepson, 'though of course we mustn't let it get out of hand, and we must be ready to adapt. What we need to do, with your agreement, sir,' said Jepson, 'is alert all our people to what's going on. We can't ignore the wider connotations, even if we don't know any details. I'll put out an alert for officers to keep an eye out for and if possible detain Sterling and his associate, and the man in shorts and T-shirt, as well as all these other men. We should have details and maybe a picture of Sterling. There can't be many men with prosthetic legs in and around Fenningstone. The man might be ex-army. I'll get a team onto that. It's sensitive, but I'll need to emphasise that the others are Middle Eastern. I'll organise a press conference with the focus on the assault. At that point, we can go public about wanting Sterling and the others to help with our enquiries. Everything else is in hand.'

'Good. I'm happy to leave all that with you. Where's your incident centre, Fenningstone nick? I'll go and establish myself there and check if the detectives Jim Murphy sent to Sandley yesterday have come up with anything.' Nolan went to the harbour car park where he'd left his car. Could he have done more after Jim Murphy had briefed him on Saturday night? Could he have prevented the attack on Joey Miller? Was something bad going to happen that earlier action could have stopped?

Back in the Old High Street, Tenwick turned to Jepson. 'Do you remember Frank Sterling, Guv'nor?'

'Before my time, Maria,' said Jepson. 'I was still at Eastbourne.'

'And mine,' said the detective sergeant. 'But I heard plenty about him. The stuff of legend, as they say, and not always for the right reasons. I reckon DCI Nolan is right. Half-strangling and beating people up isn't Frank Sterling's thing.' She smiled. 'But everything else in this adds up to a classic Sterling caper.'

Chapter 28

From the top of the car park, Sterling, Husain and Chambers looked down into the town. There was a shadow of blue light flickering around the buildings down towards the harbour, and an unseen sense of bustle and activity.

'You found a phone then – assuming those blue lights are outside Joey's.'

'Yep,' said Chambers. 'By the bus station.'

'OK,' said Sterling. 'Sitrep. You called a bus; the police are there. The hunt for the perps will have started.'

'10-4.'

Classic, thought Sterling. *Chambers is not getting the piss-take. He's spent so long in the army, and watched so many US cop shows, the language is in his bloodstream. He knew that 'bus' is New York slang for 'ambulance' and all the rest of it.* One corner of Husain's mouth went up involuntarily and he stared fixedly ahead. The irony hadn't passed him by.

'Well, there's nothing to keep us here, and plenty to divert us somewhere else. Are you in?'

'Roger,' said Chambers, 'but I'm losing money.'

Husain took out his wad and peeled off more notes. Even so, it didn't seem to be getting any thinner.

'That helps,' said Chambers. 'A lot. Next stop

Drangeness. I haven't had this much excitement since Sangin 2008. Hop in.'

He eased the van down the ramps and to the exit, and after the one-way system had whisked them compulsorily eastwards, managed to turn back and move out of Fenningstone in the opposite direction. Quickly, the Westcliff's Victorian piles were behind them, and the large town atmosphere was being replaced by a locale that was not quite suburb and not quite satellite town. Then they were in Sanditon, an old established fishing village under the influence of a gentrification process epitomised by antique shops and restaurants. Sterling remembered Sanditon Castle, really little more than a small stone fortress, surrounded by much newer houses and cottages that he had visited with his father when he was about eight or nine. Elizabeth I had visited in the 1570s, if he remembered correctly.

Beyond Sanditon, Chambers took the coast road. Now, in the crisp spring lunchtime air, the terrain between the sea to the south and the downland in the north was laid out in stripes. The pale gold shingle beach was lined into the distance by a pink-hued esplanade, and beside the esplanade was the road and its double yellow lines on which the ice cream van laboured, buffeted by the fresh wind. A pavement, the same grey as the road, separated it from the scrubby, marshy, no man's land of yellow-green sward. In turn, the sward abutted a low bosky embankment hiding the beginning of the Napoleonic canal that continued through Hykewood and Rye and fell just short of Hastings. Near and far, the landscape was speckled with white houses and villas.

Ahead, Hykewood's taller buildings loomed, and Sterling knew that soon the canal would sheer away from its parallel course next to the road and in the long, wide gap, Hykewood golf course would appear, as if squeezed in. In the distance, Sterling could see their destination on the far tip of the wide bight that started at one end at Fenningstone and ended at Drangeness itself. From this vantage point, the nuclear power station was a miscellany of low-slung grey blocks blistered on the surface of the horizon.

Apart from the hum of the engine along this flat stretch between Sanditon and Hykewood, and the rattle and vibration of various components in the back, it was quiet in the van, the three men disinclined to speak and all looking out at the vista in front of them. Sterling wasn't a vindictive man, and he wasn't one for revenge. His long experience of the criminal justice system demonstrated that there was, to his mind, only a tenuous connection between wrongdoing and the appropriate punishment. But he knew that he owed it to Joey to make sure that the people who beat him up got their comeuppance. Sterling stared through the windscreen. A young golden retriever was sniffing energetically at a lump of tar or seaweed on the shingle, clearly ignoring his impatient owner, a white-haired man in a parka. Animal and owner faded to specks in the wing mirror. Sterling had put a lot of people in danger this time. He'd behaved like a user, and it didn't feel good.

The straightness of the road was unsettling. All they could do was drive straight on to an inexorable fate, or that's how it seemed. Sterling looked at Husain's profile, and noted a man subdued and busy with his own thoughts. Chambers was whistling and tapping his fingers on the steering wheel, almost carefree and, like the squaddie he had once been, content that decisions were mostly the responsibility of other people.

Hykewood announced itself in a sign just before the entrance to the golf club, twinned with a coastal town in Brittany. A handsome whitewashed Victorian hotel, taken over by an international chain, was set off from the coast road, and then the van was wending its way through the town itself, crossing the canal which divided it into upmarket blocks of flats, houses and villas on the northern side and the more louche settlements of small cottages, terraces and ancient pubs between the canal and the sea.

Just beyond the centre of the town, the main road to Drangeness and the canal came together again, the road in a one-way system on each side of the canal. It was on the westward side that the van's hum turned into a judder. Chambers pumped the accelerator, but the power surges quickly died down and then faded away altogether, causing the van to hiccup and buck in the busy line of traffic. Chambers banged his hands on the steering wheel.

'Bloody hell, what a time for a Charlie Foxtrot.'

Husain turned to Sterling. 'You don't want to know,' said Sterling. 'Cock-up just about gets it.'

Chambers managed to get the van half into a gap in a line of cars parked in front of an Edwardian terrace. 'Those breakdown rescue blokes... They just turn up, fiddle about a bit, tell you nothing, say it's fixed when it isn't and pretend it's job done, and onto the next one. Load of Jackson Pollocks.'

'Wait a moment,' said Husain. An apparently natural sense of fairness wouldn't allow him to let it go. 'Didn't I hear you say how marvellous that chap was just earlier near the lift?'

'Hmmph,' said Chambers. 'You need to get out and push this heap of shit further out of the road. Traffic is backing up.'

Finally, the van was wedged between a small, battered old Peugeot saloon and a sleek Mini Cooper with the union flag sprayed on the roof.

'What now?' said Husain. On matters of transport he deferred to the locals. 'Can we catch a bus to Drangeness? Or get a taxi?'

'There's a Sainsbury's over the other side,' said Chambers. 'There'll be taxis there, or we can phone.'

'I've got a better idea,' said Sterling. 'Come on.' He set off at a brisk pace westward, confidence and determination drawing the others along with him. At the same time, the spark of an idea fixed itself in his mind. If he thought it through properly, he was sure he could pull it off. At the end of the one-way system two hundred metres further on, he turned right.

'Gleaming,' said Chambers.

Husain shook his head. The language was English, but not as he knew it. Then he saw the sign, 'South Kent Marsh Light Railway', and things began to make sense again. 'So this goes to Drangeness,' he said.

'Correcto,' said Sterling. 'In fact, straight to the Old Lighthouse. Discreetly, quietly, and disguised amongst a bunch of tourists. Come on. We're in the open here, and, let's face it, we don't exactly fade into the background. I reckon my ex-mates in the police will be joining up the dots by now, and taxi companies are among their first points of call, investigation-wise.'

Hykewood Station looked like the pre-Dr Beeching station it might once have been, set apart from the road and pavement by a short, smartly painted picket fence that matched, in colour and pattern, the awning above the entrance.

'I could do with a brew,' said Chambers, eyeing a kiosk in the small entrance hall next to the gift shop area. 'This is thirsty work. Anyone else?'

'Get them in, mate. I'll go and get the tickets. We couldn't be luckier. The train goes in five minutes.'

Husain got out his roll of notes. 'No,' said Sterling. 'You've forked out since Dovethorpe one way or the other. This is my shout. Why don't you help Al carry the drinks?' He hurried off to the ticket counter with his head down. It sounded false and hollow even as he said it, his voice hoarse and unusually shrill, his sudden generosity jarring with his previous acquiescence in Husain, a proxy for the powers-that-be, paying for everything. Timing was going to be crucial.

Two minutes before the train started. Sterling could see beyond the ticket collector and the barrier down to the long platform stretching out of the canopy. Steam was hissing and rising from the small locomotive at the far end. Sterling remembered the miniature carriages and their sliding doors on wooden tracks from outings with his father when he was a very young boy. He looked at the ticket collector in his blue serge uniform, 'SKMLR' silvery and glittering on the badge of his cap. They were almost all volunteers on this narrow gauge track, but this man clearly knew his stuff, and Sterling was encouraged by his tallness and bulk, his no-nonsense expression and a peppery toilet brush Fuehrer moustache. A jobsworth was just what was needed.

Chambers and Husain arrived at the barrier just before Sterling, Chambers with a tenuous grasp of two paper cups of tea. Sterling plunged forward with his ticket. The light railway dictator got to work with his clipper and ushered him through. 'That was the last but one whistle before it goes,' he said.

'We're with him,' said Chambers, pointing with his chin as Sterling strode off down the ramp.

'Tickets,' said the ticket clipper. He put up his hand and moved his body into the space between the barrier and the wall.

'He's got them,' said Chambers.

'No, he ain't. Or if he has, he ain't shown them to me.'

'This is important, sir,' said Husain the emollient.

'No tickets, no ride. Rules are rules. We'd quickly be bankrupt if not.'

Sterling slipped into the last carriage with a slim young woman in a ponytail with her two young boys in identical chunky black-framed spectacles, looking like owlets. The train whistle sounded for the last time, and the train moved off in a series of wheezes and lurches. He jerked open the sliding window in the carriage and looked back up the ramp. Chambers was hopping from one foot to the false other, the paper cups still in his hands, a picture of annoyance, anger and confusion, like Rumpelstiltskin with a prosthetic leg. Husain's gaze held Sterling's eye. Sterling struggled for a moment to recognise the look. The big man should have been disappointed and crestfallen. Instead, he raised his paper cup in a small toast, with an expression that looked unmistakeably like relief.

Chapter 29

'Fubar,' muttered Chambers. 'Completely and utterly fubar.'

'Fubar?' said Husain. Sterling was no longer there to translate.

'Fucked up beyond all repair,' said Chambers. 'The sneaky bastard. Why did he do that?'

Husain shrugged.

'OK,' said Chambers. 'What now?'

Husain turned to the ticket man. 'When's the next train?'

'An hour and a half. It's a single-track line mostly, and there are only one or two double-track passing places. If you're going to Drangeness it's worth the wait. You could get a bit to eat in the caff.'

Husain sensed that the man was feeling twinges of conscience about his inflexibility. 'Let's go over to the café, Mr Chambers, and drink our tea. We can discuss it then.'

'We haven't got time for this,' said the ex-army man in the café.

Husain gave him an appraising look for a long moment and then made his decision. 'You saved us back in Fenningstone, Mr Chambers, not just at the lift but from a criminal investigation when we needed to keep going. You have done so much. I don't think you can directly do any more.' He pushed the 'Queen and Country' button. 'This really is about the national interest, and how you can best serve it. At the moment, it's by going back to your van, getting it fixed, selling ice creams and letting me get on with my job. I'll be honest. If the police catch up with you, and I expect they will eventually, after they have asked for witnesses in the High Street,' – Husain looked down at the prosthetic leg – 'it would be excellent if you could... deflect things for as long as possible.'

'What about Sterling?'

'Well, he is doing his own deflecting. Of course it was irritating, but I have time to sort that out – in the national interest,' Husain stressed again. Then he pushed the other button. The bundle of money came out of his pocket and he peeled off note after large note, a month of mixed weather ice cream sales. 'I won't sugar-coat anything.' He looked down again at the silver-and-grey leg. 'As I said, the police will almost certainly identify you as someone they want to talk to in connection with Joey Miller and this whole thing. But it would be most helpful if you delay telling the truth for as long as reasonably possible. By the time you have told your story and been exonerated, everything will have been resolved.'

'You're paying me off,' said Chambers. He was indignant, but Husain's flag-waving was a masterstroke. Besides, Sterling's desertion had been deflating, and the cash... what a difference that would make.

'For all you've done, in the national interest,' repeated Husain, 'and to protect you from further danger. This could end so badly, Mr Chambers. Please, go back to your ice creams. When the story is told, you will be a hero. A patriotic hero.'

He watched the ice cream seller pad off back towards his broken-down van, and then went to the payphone next to the gift shop. As expected, taxi company cards were stuck on the wall beside the phone apparatus and the booth, by the looks of it installed circa 1980, in which it was housed. Husain debated with himself. Best to stay independent, he concluded, rather than involve the department. He dialled and waited. 'Speedy Cars? I'd like a taxi at South Kent Light Railway Station, Hykewood, straight away.'

'Certainly, sir,' said the despatcher. 'It will be there in five minutes. Where are you going?'

'Lydcote Airport.'

As Husain transacted his business, from the small green next to the canal and opposite the station and its facilities, a young Police Community Support Officer spoke into her phone. 'Control?' She waited and then spoke again. 'I think I've spotted one of the men the assault investigation team wants to speak to. He's in shorts and T-shirt and has a silvery-grey prosthetic leg. He's just come out of Hykewood station and is heading back towards the town.'

'Keep him in sight and await further instructions.'

In the major incident room in Fenningstone police station, Chief Inspector Andy Nolan was trying hard to analyse and make sense of the information relayed to him. Sometimes, when he couldn't work things out, couldn't make the intuitive mental leaps, couldn't join the dots so important to his rapid progress in the job, he thought he'd lost the ability forever. The Middle Easterners were off the radar for the moment, probably in vehicles. He was waiting for CCTV footage on that aspect. But Sterling, the big man, and the man with the prosthetic leg were nowhere to be found. It was likely, surely, that the big man was the same one that Liv Eliot had rescued with Frank in Dovethorpe. They had gone to Fenningstone together and ended up staying at Joey Miller's. Somehow, the man with the prosthetic leg had joined the party. Nolan cracked his knuckles. How did everything link up? The assault was a priority, of course it was. But now that he'd received news that Joey Miller was sedated but was going to recover, more important was the possibility of a terrorist attack.

A constable came into the room. 'Sir, we think we've picked up one of the people we've been looking for in connection with the assault – the man with the false leg.'

'Where?'

'Hykewood, sir. He's got an ice cream van which has broken down. We got him on the pavement next to it.'

'Get my car. Tell the officers down there to keep hold of him. I'll be ten minutes.'

With Jepson, siren and flashing blue light scuttling out of Fenningstone, Nolan thought through how he'd approach the interview. He felt a sense of urgency that meant an unconventional approach. By the time they'd arrived behind the broken-down van and the squad car, he had explained to Jepson how he was going to proceed.

'Get him out of the car,' he said to one of the vehicle officers. He motioned to a shop doorway, a hairdresser's that was closed up, whose sign – 'Beyond the Fringe' – was peeling from the fascia.

Nolan leaned on the door jamb. The wind rustled sweet wrappers and cigarette packets in eddies around his feet. The man joined him, moving without any hint of a limp on his prosthesis. He took up station on the other side of the doorway, showing no fear.

'I'm DCI Nolan,' said Nolan. 'And you are...?'

'Al Chambers.' He jerked his head towards the van. 'I sell ice creams.'

Nolan noted posture, demeanour and prosthesis. 'Ex-army?'

'Yep.'

'Right. Well, I won't beat about the bush, Mr Chambers. I'm going to tell you, informally, what I think, just between the two of us, and then we'll take it from there. I don't think you were responsible for the very serious assault of the young man we found in a flat back in Fenningstone a short while ago, but I think it's likely that for some reason you were the one who found him and called the emergency services. Somehow I think you're connected with a large man of dark complexion, whose name we don't yet know, and someone whose name we do – Frank Sterling.' Nolan was looking for tells, and so far he had not been disappointed, especially when he mentioned Sterling. Chambers was stony-faced, but he was wringing his hands and rubbing the join between prosthesis and what was left of his upper leg.

'We're certainly going to take you in, and you'll probably need legal representation, even if we think of you as a witness rather than a suspect. But the reason we're talking in this windy doorway and not in an interview room under caution, Mr Chambers, is not because of Joey Miller in Fenningstone, serious as his case is. It's because I have information that some kind of attack is in the offing, connected somehow with Mr Miller, Frank Sterling and the big man, and other men we think are involved, and at the moment I'm more intent on doing something about that – preventing it in fact – than something that has, regrettably, already happened. My instinct says you can make a vital contribution. It will stand you in good stead, and probably do a huge amount of good in a short amount of time, if you exercise that choice quickly. If you don't, well…'.

Chambers looked out towards the canal and the greenery on the other side. He was used to taking orders, used to black and white. Current nuances and complexities were turning him into a ditherer. 'You sound as if you know Sterling – Frank.'

'I do. He's a friend of mine. We go back a long way.' Nolan dredged his instincts and experience to come up with the right phrase – the trigger that would get him the information he needed. 'I expect you found yourself helping him, maybe against your better instincts. He has that knack of drawing people into his schemes. He's an honest bloke and people sense that as well. He's got that sneaky sense of humour. But the thing about Frank that you've obviously also already found out is that he's not a team player, and that gets him into trouble. He ploughs on by himself even after it's time to call in the cavalry.'

For the first time Chambers smiled. 'Tell me about it.' Husain was all right, but the patriotic card had been trumped. Not only that, Chambers still had Husain's cash. Why was it important to stonewall anyway, given the circumstances? His allegiance switched to Nolan, Sterling's proxy. 'Frank's gone to Drangeness on the train – to the Old Lighthouse. It's all kicking off down there – or more likely the power station next door. Husain, the other man, is probably following him.'

'Thank you, Mr Chambers,' said Nolan. 'We will need to ask you more questions, and Detective Inspector Jepson is going to do that now in the car. Then these officers will take you to the police station.' He stayed in the doorway as Chambers was led away, allowing himself a small smile of relief as he turned to the glass and put his phone to his ear.

'Control room,' he said. There was usually a competent young sergeant in such places, and he wasn't disappointed. 'Listen carefully,' he said to the young woman. 'Contact Drangeness B nuclear power station and have them put their emergency plan into action – danger of attack. Activate our major incident plan, including liaison and communication with our partners. Get armed response vehicles out to Drangeness, both to the Old Lighthouse and the nuclear power station. Do it now.'

'Yes, sir,' said the young woman. She paused for a heartbeat. 'And you are taking full responsibility?'

'Yes,' said Nolan. He'd not been a chief inspector for long. Would this be the shortest tenure in the history of the Kent police? *Frank, you bastard, what have you got me into now?*

Chapter 30

Suburban back gardens on each side of the track were what Sterling had unexpectedly forgotten on the South Kent Light Railway as he trundled along in the doll's house carriage towards England's only desert. He'd thought it was desert most of the way, but back gardens certainly came first.

There were gardens whose fences contained small glass viewing windows, and gardens with messages for passengers – 'Hello, have a good journey', 'See you on the way back' and other permutations on the theme. Some gardens had decking, and on some decks barbecue paraphernalia was set up. Some gardens were derelict, with wood panels like rows of rotten, broken teeth, weeds and shattered beer bottles. Some had washing lines, with and without clothes, and some were reduced by back-wardly encroaching conservatories. Sterling saw car wrecks and hulks of white goods like lopsided mini icebergs in seas of weed. There was every variety of boundary line – railings, palings, pickets and wickets, fencing and elaborate arrangements of rush-work. Some gardens were immaculate and some merely tidy. Many were scruffy or not tended at all. There were flowerbeds, lawns cut in circles or stripes, and gardens only with vegetables.

And behind the gardens was every permutation of housing – terraces, bungalows, semis, detached houses and almost as many that were neither one nor the other, but instead weird hybrid constructions with extensions, protrusions, loft conversions and additions of every conceivable nature. All middle England and below was represented on that long ribbon from the town to the desert – a narrow strip of chaotic civilisation between the coast and fields.

When there weren't back gardens, small recreation grounds appeared where children and dog-walkers waved, and gaps between the settlements where the view stretched down almost to the sea. Through one brief vista, Sterling spotted and remembered the tall, nineteenth-century brick water tower, like a thin, pale-red stick in hazy sunshine, built by a Victorian property developer with delusions of grandeur.

His chin sank into his chest as he hunched into the small seat. The whole business stank, right from the moment Mike Strange had burst into his office on Friday. Mike had said 'south and west', and here Sterling was, south and west, almost as if it had been prearranged. Mike, a highly trained and effective ex-security service agent, had then been abducted by a cell or gang that hadn't been nearly as daunting as he had indicated. Sterling's own continuing liberty was surely evidence of that. Liv Eliot had done well with the memory stick and the code, but how difficult had that really been?

There had been something hinky about meeting Husain in Dovethorpe, and even about the presence of his pursuers. Then in Joey's flat, Husain hadn't made much of a fuss about translating and sharing the coded message. All that guff Husain spouted about 'no communication' on Saturday night, and then he uses Joey's phone – with almost fatal consequences.

How did the ice cream man fit in? Had Husain phoned him? Was he another agent? It was very convenient how he'd turned up at the top of the cliff in a broken-down van, and he hadn't really batted an eyelid about all that had happened, including Joey's assault and getting involved himself. Even a squaddie would have second thoughts. *Especially* a squaddie. The riffing about ice cream and ice cream-selling from the side of a van was too glib, as if he'd got it from a website. Other things did not add up. The overall sense of following a path set out by someone else came back strongly.

On the other hand (there was always 'on the other hand'), maybe paranoia was taking over, or at least something that Angie had told him about over the crossword in the pub one evening when she'd explained the very rudiments of transactional analysis and the OK Corral quadrant. 'So Frank,' she'd said, 'I reckon you're a kind of "I'm OK, you're OK" kind of a person most of the time, but when the chips are down it changes to "I'm OK, you're not OK"'. Maybe she was right, or maybe she wasn't. Maybe a complex idea had been oversimplified.

He trawled through the evidence again. Mike was pretty straight. Husain seemed genuine. If Sterling had been manipulated, it was a risky strategy and very dependent on his ingenuity. When Chambers had mentioned the kid at the entrance at the top of the lift, Sterling had seen her himself. The other stuff could be explained in a similar way.

He squeezed his eyes shut. Whether it was a dose of paranoia, or whether he'd swung into that TA quadrant or not, he reckoned he'd made the right decision. He had a bit of a head start, and what happened next was up to him and nobody else.

Images from his adventures over the last three days flickered in his mind: the crazy chase around Sandley's alleys; the escapade with the boat down to Sandley Bay; Liv's rescue in Dovethorpe and the bus to Fenningstone; Joey fussing and tutting around his flat; and then the water lift on the Westcliff and getaway by ice cream van. He thought of Stacey, her warm, slender body, pretty, unlined neck and shapely breasts, generously given and gratefully received. When all this was over…

'Wanted man,' said the young woman with the ponytail a few moments later. A smile played across her attractive, flat, strong face. The ponytail, pulling back her thick brown hair, accentuated a high forehead. Her skin was pale and clear, but her eyes looked tired and careworn.

'Eh?' said Sterling. The two young boys, about eight and nine, neatly dressed in jeans and bright-blue quilted jackets like their mother, peered at him through the large glasses identically perched a little way down their button noses. When one poked the frame up with his forefinger, the other one followed almost straight away.

'Wanted Man,' repeated the woman. 'Sung by Johnny Cash, some say written by Bob Dylan, some say co-written by them both. You were whistling it.'

'Was I? I wasn't really concentrating. Impressive. Not really your time.' The two boys were looking up at him, their mouths slightly open.

'My grandparents brought me up. Johnny Cash was my grandad's hero. Dylan too. Richard Thompson. All those folkies, American and British. How could I avoid it rubbing off on me?'

Sterling tipped his head from side to side as if making an appraisal. 'You've got a point.'

She started to speak, stopped, and then plunged on. 'Forgive me for saying, but you seem a bit agitated.'

'Yeah? Well, maybe I am.' He looked out of the window at a mare calmly grazing in a small enclosure, a foal nuzzling her flank. It probably wasn't a good idea to get into an involved conversation, not as things currently stood. Look where involvement with him had got Stacey, and Joey worst of all. Angela regularly told him off – 'When you've got your teeth into something, you forget about people, or worse, they are just pawns in whatever it is you're fixed on'.

'And travelling alone on a miniature railway,' the young woman persisted, her sons a fascinated audience, 'principally for children and families.'

'Yeah.'

'We've been to Hykewood for the day. Drove to Drangeness from Lydcote and took the train. We had a row in a boat in the canal, didn't we, boys? We caught loads of crabs.'

'We didn't, Mum.'

The woman smiled at her secret joke. 'Where are you going?' she said to Sterling.

'Drangeness.' He looked away, back out of the window again. *Yeah, Drangeness B Nuclear Power Station to be exact, or as close as possible – i.e. the Old Lighthouse. To stop a terrorist 'event'. By myself. Frank Sterling's one-man anti-terrorist army.*

He'd been so busy getting paranoid and working out ways to dump Husain and Chambers so he could go it alone, he hadn't thought things through. The training sergeant at Ashtonleigh, when Sterling was a cadet, had summed it up in his final report: 'enterprising, resourceful, determined, fearless, hotheaded, impulsive, not always a team player'.

And this was the current consequence – rattling along in a miniature carriage into Kent's bleakest landscape without the slightest idea about what to do or what to expect when he arrived. He checked his watch. It, whatever 'it' was, would be kicking off somewhere in Drangeness in about forty minutes.

He dredged his memory for security arrangements at the power plant. Based at Fenningstone police station, he'd attended regular liaison meetings with the plant's security team. The approach road to the plant, the imaginatively named 'Power Station Access Road' was long, straight and monitored all the way by CCTV cameras. Not even Google Street View could get close. Google was banned, he also reminded himself, from the roads and settlements in the vicinity of the power station and the access road to the neighbouring nature reserve. Fences were tall, topped with barbed wire and electrified. Emergency and disaster plans dovetailed with those of the police and other services.

The more Sterling thought about it, the more far-fetched his mission, if it could be called that, seemed to be. As he remembered the layout of Drangeness SKLR station and the sparse little colony around it, he wasn't even going to get that close to the plant – perhaps a quarter of a mile from the perimeter.

The owlets stared. Sterling didn't mind kids, so long as, after a kick-about, a game or a conversation, someone else came and took them away or at least exercised some responsibility for them. He was even godfather to one of Andy Nolan's.

They steamed on, past the back gardens, the recreation grounds, the tiny stations where adults were Gullivers and everything seemed just out of kilter, and the brief vistas across fields and level crossings. Then, with a shrill whistle, the locomotive and its carriages burst joyously from the shackles of civilisation into a terrain that could not have been more different from the one before – England's only desert. Through either window, as far as the eye could see, sand and scrub intermingled in a grey, ochre, dirty-green, pancake-flat endlessness. Marooned and dotted randomly here and there, like abandoned moon craft, were sheds and primitive corrugated dwellings, sometimes in the shape of containers.

Apocryphal stories had it that some of these structures were abandoned railway carriages from a Victorian railway company that had been appropriated by local fishermen, hauled off into the wilderness and converted into homes, but it seemed a stretch. The decayed skeleton of a fishing boat lay on its side. Telegraph poles carried cat's cradle power lines across the wilderness, final destinations at each end, from the carriage, entirely a matter of speculation. A small bird of prey, perhaps a hobby straying from nearby marshland, hovered, its wings beating urgently before it swooped. At least one shack was occupied, the tatty clothing on its primitive washing line fluttering and twitching in the light breeze. Something, a bottle or a tin close by, glinted and flashed like a semaphore.

Sterling made a decision. Disengagement, against his natural sociability, was all very well, but if he could keep this little family from danger, that was his duty. He leaned forward, clasped his hands together and rested his elbows on his knees. 'My name is Frank Sterling.' He turned to the older boy. Let him have some responsibility. 'Who are you?'

'Danny Monkton. My brother is Freddy.'

'And your mum?'

The boy looked sideways and up to his mother's face. He was so used to calling her 'Mum', it looked as though he might have forgotten.

'Jess,' she smiled. The boy looked relieved.

Sterling held out his hand solemnly and shook the boys' hands and then their mother's. 'Nice to meet you. Sorry I've been a bit… off. Are you going anywhere when you get back to Drangeness, or is your mum taking you straight home?'

'She said we can have an ice cream in the café and then go up the lighthouse,' said the older boy, words gushing from his mouth as if previously stoppered by politeness and now released.

'Right, OK. Good,' said Sterling. 'Well, the thing is, I'm not sure it's a good idea for you to go up the lighthouse.'

The young woman cocked her head.

'It's a bit difficult to explain.' Sterling's eyes moved across to the two boys. 'But what I'd do, if I were you, when we get off the train, is go over to the car park, hop in your car, and drive off home to Lydcote.'

'And not go up the lighthouse?' said the younger boy.

'And not go up the lighthouse,' said Sterling.

'While you…?' said the young woman.

'Well, sort things out, like.' Even knowing what he knew, it sounded thin to Sterling.

'Why?' said Freddy.

'Why what?'

'Why can't we go up the lighthouse?'

'We'll go another time, sweetheart. I'm sure Mr Sterling has good reasons.'

As Jess Monkton spoke, there was a whistle from the locomotive, which Sterling saw for the first time as it curled with its load in a long wide arc towards Drangeness, the final stop. To the north and east, the land stretched away into the distance, empty, sandy, barren and parched under the wide blue sky. Through the other window, Sterling could just make out a roundhouse with whitewashed stone walls and slate-tiled roof, weathered from black to dark grey, accompanying single-storey blocks in the same style and one or two other meagre dwellings that made up the hamlet of Drangeness itself. Louring over all of them was the tall black presence of the lighthouse, its latticed beacon housing at the top like the eye of a Cyclops.

On the station platform, the quartet shuffled in an uncomfortable gaggle. Sterling could see an elderly couple with wavy white hair in matching red fleeces and logos, perhaps married, perhaps twins, eating fish and chips in the café attached to the station. There was a smell of cooking fat mixed with the sweet odour of confectionery.

'Remember. Straight to the car,' said Sterling. 'Get an ice cream in Appledore and eat it next to the canal. Nice to have met you, Jess, lads.'

The young woman put her hand on his arm. 'What about all the other people?'

'I can't do anything about them. Even if I could, it would start a panic. And it might be for nothing.'

Sterling strode off down a winding slatted wooden path across the sand that separated the station and café complex from the Drangeness hamlet. The path was weathered grey and pitted, but firm and solid underfoot. He felt the gaze of the trio of mother and sons on his back, Jess's hands probably still on Freddy's shoulders. They needed to get out along the lonely approach road and across the desert, into the marsh and then to the safety and normalcy of Appledore and Rye.

The black lighthouse was about three hundred metres from the station, with the whitewashed roundhouse immediately behind. Sterling looked at his watch. 11.45. He had fifteen minutes. As he approached, he knew something was wrong. A small group of people milled about, some clutching mobiles. A young father enveloped his two small children, his large hands on their backs, their tiny arms wrapped around his thighs, their cheeks buried in his trousers. Sterling plunged through the door and into the lighthouse – far more light and airy than he ever remembered.

A white-faced woman was securing the ticket office area. Grey edged from the parting of her brown hair. Behind her, and all around, the walls were adorned with marine and lighthouse paraphernalia – barometers, compasses, shipping maps, spoked wheels and photos of men in sou'westers and long beards. On the counter was a chart showing all the wrecks claimed by the Goodwin Sands around the coast beyond Dovethorpe. She looked terrified.

'Tell me what's going on,' said Sterling.

'A maniac pointed a gun at me and went upstairs.'

'Describe him.'

'A maniac. A maniac. What don't you understand?' Sterling's low-key manner did something. The woman put a brake on her hysteria and focused more closely on Sterling. 'Who are you? Police?'

'Detective,' said Sterling. He wanted information, not argy-bargy about his status or credentials. It wasn't a lie. 'So...?'

'Young. Thin. A small white face. Had big, thick boots. Camouflage trousers. I couldn't see anything else. He was wearing this huge, long, blue greatcoat.'

'Like you get from military surplus?'

'Yeah, and a kind of grey-coloured peaked cap. His head was tiny compared to that big coat.'

'And he went upstairs?'

'The woman nodded. 'About five minutes ago. With a really big heavy bag. He was struggling as he started lugging it up the stairs. He told me to get out. Which is what I'm going to do. Right now.'

'Good plan,' said Sterling. 'There'll be reinforcements shortly.' There might be, if Husain and Chambers were on the way, or if someone in the group outside had dialled 999, but perhaps not, and probably not for at least half an hour. 'Apart from this man, is there anyone else up there?'

The woman shook her head. 'I don't think so. Everyone came rushing down as he went up.'

'Right. You've done well. It would be best if you tried to gather everyone in the vicinity and get them over to the café. That will make it easier for backup.'

'What are you going to do?'

Yeah, what are you going to do, Frankie-boy? Go upstairs unarmed and unprotected, and, as the ice cream man would almost certainly say, 'kick ass'? Not much of a scheme – and maniacal enough in its own way. 'Sort it out,' he said.

Chapter 31

However quiet Sterling tried to be, his footfall made a slight echoing clang every step up the open cast-iron spiral staircase. As he ascended, marine and lighthouse paraphernalia, seemingly randomly hung and surplus to the exhibition at the lighthouse base, provided a continuing backdrop. At regular stages, windows gave him panoramic views, now the car park and single-gauge railway line to the north, now the long approach road bisecting the wilderness to the east, now the sea from Drangeness Point to the south, and the metallic grey mass of the power station westwards. Sand and scrub curved in streaks away to the skyline.

Halfway up, the staircase merged into a second floor, obviously cleared of machinery previously essential to the running of the lighthouse and similar in character and ambience to the floor below. This time there was a thorough attempt at curation, showing the development of warning systems for ships passing Drangeness Point from crudely maintained beacons to privately financed early lighthouses to the current arrangement, a new, slimmer, automated white lighthouse half a kilometre southeast having replaced the one Sterling was clambering up.

So far it had been straightforward, and, given that something was planned to happen at twelve o'clock, better that Sterling had come up rather than waiting at the bottom. Now he felt butterflies as he crossed the floor to the staircase leading to the very top. The staircase narrowed as he ascended, and he felt a fleeting wave of claustrophobia. The door at the top opened onto the circular platform around the obsolete beacon itself, whose latticed windows had been visible from the train. Sterling was within the eye of the Cyclops. He edged himself forward as quietly as possible, working to control his breathlessness from the long climb. He didn't think he'd find the man inside, and he was right. Fortunately also, the door gave onto the beacon room to the east, and the beacon blocked out the power station to the west, and west was where he expected the danger to be.

The final door, the door that linked the inside area at the top to what had become an outside viewing platform, was a couple of steps away. Through the salt-encrusted glass, murky like a car windscreen whose cleaning fluid has run out, Sterling could see a vague shadow low down, making blurred movements. He eased open the door and immediately recoiled from the sharp, fresh, robust and gusty wind that suddenly assailed him. It was noisy too, and he could smell the nearby sea. Accustoming himself to the changed conditions, he slipped onto the outside platform, a grilled metal arrangement enclosed by a generously high, white-painted barrier all around the beacon behind the glass.

The figure had discarded the greatcoat and was crouching next to a large, military-style duffel bag. Gun, or more accurately, armament parts lay strewn on the platform. The young man, ascetically thin, with narrow shoulders, a matching narrow, pale face and a wispy blond beard, caught Sterling's movement in the corner of his eye, and looked up. 'Stop there.' He reached for a small pistol amongst the gubbins.

Sterling pulled up, his hands going forward, half in the classic pose of a person surrendering and half in supplication.

'Stay back,' said the young man, motioning with the gun. Sterling did as he was told. It would be a dramatic ending at the blustery top of the lighthouse, and his name would surely live on, if only in Wikipedia, but he'd much prefer a long postponement. The young man muttered to himself, and Sterling heard fragments, gathering, as he knew already, that backup had been expected but not supplied.

'There's no need for this,' said Sterling.

'Fuck off,' said the young man. His accent, even in those two brief words, sounded distinctly northern.

'You're from around Manchester, aren't you? British. You've probably watched Corrie with your mum.'

The young man looked at Sterling, his expression a mixture of puzzlement and contempt. Sterling was racking his brains. He'd pretty much run out of ideas before he'd started about how you talked down someone hell-bent on blowing up a power station. He tried again. 'When it's over, it's prison. You'll be put away for a very long time. Life. With no chance of parole, I'd imagine. They'd probably be reluctant to put you in the general population. It'll be lonely – and dangerous.'

The young man smiled and shook his head. 'I'm not going to prison. When this is done, I'm out of here. My backup will be here shortly. With what I'm getting, I'll be set up for life, starting with some clubbing somewhere in the Med.'

Sterling passed his hand over his eyes. The wind was

roaring. He felt sick. 'Come on. There is no backup. If there was, it would have been here already. Why do you think I'm here? You've been abandoned.'

The young man's eyes shone. 'Crap. Utter bollocks.' Eyeing Sterling, and making sure that he was far enough back, he put the pistol aside and clicked the final parts of the armament into place. Sterling could see that it had taken the shape of a rocket launcher.

Perhaps it was an optical illusion. Perhaps it was his mind playing tricks, but to Sterling, the power station seemed startlingly closer than when he'd looked over at it from the station, and so did the pylons behind as they stretched off into the distance towards Lydcote.

There was a click as the missile slotted into the front end. It was a kind of diamond shape, tapered at the front and back, and bulging in the middle. There could have been more in the large duffel bag.

The young man juggled the launcher and pistol. 'Get back inside the lighthouse,' he said. For a short moment, a small fraction of a second, Sterling calculated distances. Lunging forward and getting into an arm-wrestle, or any wrestle at all, was the direct route to personal oblivion. And for what? He couldn't stop a disaster, and equally there was no point in sacrificing himself for nothing. It wasn't being chicken. It was logic. He slipped back into shelter, expecting the whoosh of a launch shortly.

Through the opaque glass, he could see the young man's shadow and the launcher like a misshapen black bar. He sensed agitation in the young man's quick movements and the oscillation and waving about of the weapon. He wondered whether the missile could possibly be nuclear-tipped – surely not – it would be too heavy for a shoulder-launched arrangement like an RPG or bazooka. The trouble was, he knew nothing about such things.

But something wasn't right, or rather, something wasn't going according to plan. Time had stopped, but the agitation of the shadow show wasn't decreasing. Sterling stuck his head out of the door. Nothing in this whole case – if it could be described as that – rang true. Everything was smoke and mirrors. Sterling almost laughed. The rocket launcher was long, and the curvature of the beacon-housing meant that it was impossible for the young man to align it to point straight at the power station. If he stayed to the north, the launcher pointed south west. If he went south around the other side, it pointed north west. If he went to the west, the launcher simply pointed straight up into the air. Wrestling with weight and aim and frustration, terrorist had turned into clown.

Sterling took his chance. He sprang from the door and cannoned into the young man, grabbing the launcher as he did. The two men grappled and pushed. Fear and doubt entered the young man's grey eyes. None of this was part of the plan. As for Sterling, Saturday night tussles with drunks, reprobates and troublemakers on the seafront at Marchurch and outside the nightclubs of Fenningstone had prepared him well, and he was stronger, taller and heavier. He pinned his opponent back, looped his leg behind the other man's knee and pushed. As they toppled, Sterling on top, both clung single-mindedly to the weapon.

'Give it up,' said Sterling. 'It's over.'

A different look replaced the fear and doubt in the man's eyes, and a small smile spread upwards from his mouth.

'Oh shit,' said Sterling. He'd seen that look before, or something like it. Andy Nolan, back in the days when he and Sterling shared a squad car, called it the 'I-no-longer-give-a-fuck' look, 'inlgafl' for short, pronounced 'inolgaful', most common when drunks look at the uniform and decide to take a swing. Alcohol had the effect of dissolving the ability to think of consequences behind actions.

When the young man pulled the launcher trigger, Sterling thought that was it. But then the young man pulled again, and again, and again – each time more frantically. There was nothing. No fireball flared from the lighthouse, no explosion boomed out over the ness and no flesh, bone, glass, masonry and twisted metal debris mushroomed over the hamlet – just gusts of wind around the lighthouse, the smell of the sea, a look of angry surprise in one pair of eyes, and utter relief in the other.

Sterling roughly prised the launcher from the young man's grasp and put it out of reach. He pocketed the pistol he'd already grabbed and got to his feet, pinning the young man to the platform with a foot to his chest. He conducted a quick body search of the supine figure and found no more weapons. Then he got out the gun, aimed at the door and pulled the trigger three times. It was as he expected. There was nothing but sharp cracks and muzzle flashes.

The magazine was filled with blanks. The launcher couldn't aim at the power station, and, even if it could, it was fake too.

'Mate,' he said to the woebegone figure beneath him, 'you've been had.'

Chapter 32

Anger and defiance seeped from the young man with the wispy beard at the top of the lighthouse. He slowly eased himself upright, his back to the beacon housing, his legs bent and his knees pressing into his stomach. Already small, the experience seemed to have shrunk him further. He wrapped his arms around his legs, stared downwards and said nothing.

Sterling had questions, a torrent of them that he thought would help him understand what was going on – questions about where the young man had been recruited and prepared, not, as it turned out, for actually attacking a power station, but as a decoy. Sterling knew the business wasn't finished. He shivered. The adrenaline rush was over and now anger had replaced fright. If he didn't get answers quickly, he decided that there'd be rough stuff.

Then he sensed something, like a faint echo on the wind steadily becoming more substantial. He looked over the thin metal parapet. In the far distance to the east, across the desert, he could see and hear the blues and twos of police cars, armed response vehicles and fire engines out of Fenningstone, racing towards the road to the hamlet and towards the parallel road to the power station.

Now there was a decision: to interrogate, or to try

and slip away. Getting information quickly from the would-be power station attacker would be impossible, no matter how disoriented and demoralised he was. Slipping away – living to fight another day – would be tricky, but was more attractive. The last thing Sterling wanted to do was get wrapped up in the ponderous clutches of a police operation, where even the most innocent and detached bystander would be condemned to hours of checks and hanging about. He needed time to think – to work things out.

Quickly, Sterling scooped up the weapons paraphernalia, dud or not, into the large duffel bag. Leaving the young man, he slipped back into the shelter of the beacon housing. There was no lock on the small door, but it opened inwards. Taking the disarmed rocket launcher from the bag, he wedged it hard against the door, the rear end fast against the base of the beacon housing. The man had his greatcoat, it wasn't cold for April, and the police would be up the lighthouse rapidly once they arrived. He clanged down the stairs to the bottom and found it deserted. If the young man wanted to kill himself by jumping off the lighthouse, Sterling had no strong opinions, but that wasn't a likely option. The more he thought about this business, the more it seemed to be about money, not terrorism. Slipping behind the counter of the gift shop and ticket booth, he eased the duffel bag under the counter and made for the exit.

A knot of people shuffled about outside the black tower. Sterling spotted the gift shop and ticket manager among them, her white face even more ghastly in the sunlight. He beckoned her across.

'You can hear the sirens, so the police will be here in a couple of minutes. This is what to say. There's a young bloke at the very top who had some weapons up there. He's unarmed now, and I've wedged him in, taken the weapons and put them in a bag behind your counter. None of them work,' – he put his finger up to stop an interruption – 'but keep them safe just in case till you speak to the police. Got all that?'

'I thought you were the police.'

'I am – kind of – but I've got to get onto the next thing. What's important is – have you got all that?'

'Yes, but…'.

'Good.'

Sterling turned and plunged off towards the station and the car park next to it. If there was a train back to Hykewood, he could get on that. It might be stopped at Middlestone or one of the other stations on the way, but police-monitoring would be looser away from the immediate danger. By car, there was only one way out – east along the approach road, picking up the road two miles down that linked Hykewood in the east to Lydcote and Rye in the west. There would be roadblocks though – he remembered at least that from the disaster plan. There was another possibility. He looked to the north. He could just walk off into scrub past the railway track and between the parallel roads. It wasn't dangerous – after three miles the desert came up to the link road. He'd just be an eccentric bloke doing a bit of scavenging, or looking for a lesser-spotted desert warbler.

'Frank,' said a small, apparently disembodied voice, as Sterling approached the end of the car park and contemplated the wasteland in front of him.

Sterling scanned the cars. Poking out of the back window of a newish blue Ford saloon was the top half of one of the boys from the train. It was Freddy, the youngest, or was Danny the youngest? Sterling had forgotten.

'Freddy,' he guessed as he approached the car. 'I thought you'd gone to Appledore for an ice cream.'

'Mum thought we'd better wait.'

Behind the windscreen, he made out Jess's face, and a little wave of the hand. She leaned over and flipped open the passenger door, moving her handbag from the seat to the footwell. Sterling eased in and slipped the door shut.

'It could have been dangerous,' he said. 'You should have got out.'

'Mum thought it was sneaky just to leave you,' said the older boy.

'Danny,' chided his mother.

'That's what you said.'

'All sorted out, then?' said Jess.

'In a way,' said Sterling. 'It's going to take you ages to get out of here now. You can hear the sirens. The cops will be here soon, and at the other end they'll already have set up roadblocks. You should have gone when I told you. A disaster plan is swinging into action.'

'Well, we'll go now and take our chances. Seatbelts, boys.' The young woman started the engine. 'Do you want a lift, or are you going yomping?' She'd seen him contemplating the desert.

'A lift, please.' In the end, a lone man walking over the rough ground was hardly going to be inconspicuous. 'I could do with getting through that roadblock without any delay. The police will cotton on to the fact that there was a man in the lighthouse they'll want to talk to, and I really need to have a think about things.' He leaned over, put his hand over his mouth and whispered so that the boys could not hear. 'Could we be a family for a bit? That would help.'

'Yes,' said Jess, 'a family.' She smiled. 'A family with an emergency of its own. That would help even more.'

A small queue of cars was starting when they'd got halfway down the road out of Drangeness.

'Danny, Freddy, listen up,' said Jess. Sterling sat up a little in his seat. When this woman said 'jump', her kids jumped. It almost certainly wasn't just her kids. She was one of those people who had a natural air of authority. It came from knowing what was right, and sticking to it. 'There's a police roadblock up ahead, and we've got to get through it. For a few minutes, Frank's going to be your dad and married to me. Danny, start holding your breath so your face goes red – like you did when you were little, being naughty. Then start doing that breathing, as if you're finding it hard.'

'Is this safe?' whispered Sterling.

'Don't worry about old Danny. This is nothing. I've lost count of the number of times we've ended up in A & E or at least Minor Injuries, sometimes when I've been on duty, since I'm an A & E nurse at Ashtonleigh. The boy's an accident magnet, but he recovers just as quickly.' She glanced in the mirror. Danny's face had gone puce. 'OK, Danny, that's enough.'

Sterling saw a frown ghost across Jess's forehead. 'Yeah, not too much, mate,' he said. 'You'll go dizzy. Why not go onto the breathing?'

'Rummage through my handbag, Frank,' said Jess. 'There's an inhaler somewhere in there. Right, all ready?' She slipped out of the queue and up to the police car blocking half the road. Behind her there was a short cacophony of indignant hooting.

'You'll have to get back in the queue, ma'am,' said the young policeman, 'otherwise we'll have a riot. No one leaves until we get say-so.'

'Sorry, officer, but our lad's having an asthma attack, a bad one.' She held up the inhaler. 'It's run out. We've got to get him to hospital, quickly.'

Danny's breath was rasping. He leaned back in his seat and tipped his head back, gasping for air. The officer looked over at his colleague turning away traffic to Drangeness on the other side of the road.

'Please,' said Jess. Danny writhed.

The policeman dithered. Then he decided. 'You're all together?' He got out his notebook. 'Names please. Quickly.' Sterling discovered that he was now Frank Monkton. The policeman went around to the front of the car and took the registration number. 'Which hospital? Do you need an escort or an ambulance?'

'Ashtonleigh. No, it's happened before. We know what to do and where to go. We just need to get going.'

'Go on,' said the policeman.

Jess eased the car past the police vehicle and left towards Lydcote and Ashtonleigh. She glanced in the rear-view mirror and put her thumb up to the shrinking policeman. Sterling looked at Danny. The puce colour was fading and his breathing had returned to normal. Both boys were smirking.

'I did well, Mum, didn't I?' said Danny.

Jess said nothing and concentrated on the road. A few moments later, the newly constituted family passed a second police roadblock at the top of the road down to Drangeness Power Station. Soon the desert was behind them and the car was crossing a low causeway between two large blue lakes. If Sterling's memory was right, the one on the left was a bird reserve. Jess seemed to be looking for something as they drove along the causeway into the flat, bleak distance. Something was unsettling her, and it transmitted itself to him. He sank down in the seat, but it didn't make him any less conspicuous. Jess looked in the mirror, indicated and pulled into a small layby. A heron flew directly in front of the windscreen towards the lake. A line of telegraph poles, marching off Indian file to nowhere, added to the empty desolation.

Jess turned off the engine, twisted around and thrust her face between the front seats, all in a series of brisk, quick movements. Sterling leaned into the corner between his seat and the window. The boys in the back flinched back into their own corners.

'You did do well, Danny. You too, Freddy. You kept quiet and played your part. But let's be absolutely crystal clear. That was an emergency. We were helping Frank because he had to sort something out. It wasn't a game. It was something we had to do. In ordinary circumstances, we never show the police any disrespect. We never show anyone any disrespect. We're polite, honest and law-abiding. Got it?'

'Yes, Mum,' chorused the boys.

'Yes, Mum,' said Sterling.

Jess turned back and put her hands on the steering wheel. 'It's not funny, Frank. They've got to know what's what. I can't be doing with any disobedience or misunderstandings. I've got too much on my plate.'

Sterling put his hands up. 'No, don't get me wrong. I agree, and if that policeman gets into trouble, which I don't think he will because he got our registration, I'll personally see to it that he's OK.' He turned to the boys. 'Your mum is plumb right and you always do what she says.' Now it was time for a change of tack. 'I tell you what – let's go over to Appledore and have those ice creams. My treat.'

Jess slipped the car into gear and pulled back onto the road. 'Good plan,' she said, 'and I'm glad we're all on the same page.'

Sterling looked out at the wading birds riffling the surface of the lake. What he'd thought earlier was spot on. Some people you didn't mess with and you knew it straight away. Jess Monkton was one.

Chapter 33

In the car to Drangeness, DCI Nolan was restless. He'd set off the disaster plan at 1.45 and knew that a senior officer would be alerted and take over soon. Other, specialised agencies would be involved. But there were still numerous loose ends, not least the exact whereabouts of Sterling and his former companion. Jepson was competent though, and would make good progress with the man with the prosthetic leg. The mystery duo at Joey Miller's flat, and the associated group, had still not been tracked down.

The Control Room sergeant phoned. 'Chief Superintendent Elsworthy will be here shortly, as per the plan.'

'Good. Thank you, Sergeant. Make sure your team keeps searching for the people we want to question. Everything we're dealing with here is connected, from the Old High Street to Drangeness.' (*And who is connecting it?* he mused, keeping his thoughts strictly to himself. *Frank bloody Sterling*). 'Obviously, tell the chief when you brief him that I'm on my way to Drangeness. You know about as much as me, at the moment, so you're perfectly able to brief him. I'll give him another update when I find out what's going on down there.'

'Noted, sir,' said the sergeant. Nolan knew the young woman was going places – she was competent, with a no-nonsense manner and a willingness to take responsibility. The force needed more like her. 'One other thing before you go. We're hearing reports from the local radio station that something is happening at Drangeness. People are phoning in and sending pictures. It's very vague at the moment, but I thought you'd need to know.'

'Thanks. I'll find out what's happening at first hand soon enough, I hope.' Nolan resisted the temptation to have the radio turned on. He needed thinking time.

The driver was attuned enough to keep silent. Nolan paid no attention to the journey – the caravan parks with holiday lets, the Martello towers at regular inter-vals, the garish, neon-lighted, flashing frontages of amusement arcades, the ubiquitous retirement bunga-lows, isolated churches dotting the marshes, and the high sea wall looming over the low-lying shore for long miles. But it was clear that all his cogitations were getting nowhere. He closed his eyes and waited. Surely, there would be some answers at least at the Old Lighthouse in Drangeness.

At the Drangeness roadblock, the driver showed his ID, and then the car was bisecting the desert on the way to the lighthouse. The driver pulled in under the shadow of the glowering Cyclops, and another sergeant quickly appeared, also young, also seemingly competent and with a strong air of authority.

'DCI Nolan? Sergeant Moore, ARV team leader.' The remnants of teenage acne pockmarked his alert face, which managed to seem hard-bitten and youthful at the same time. In his military-style police fatigues and helmet he looked fresh enough to be more like a role-playing, computer war-game character than the real thing. He looked hard at Nolan, weighing up whether he could get away with speaking truth to power. 'If I may say so, sir, I think you were spot on to initiate the disaster plan. We've just made everything safe and secure down here, but it's clear that something was planned.'

'Tell me.'

'We're holding a man on the ground floor of the lighthouse. He's dressed in military-style gear. He's saying nothing. Behind the cashier's desk we found a very large duffel bag, full of weaponry of various kinds – hand-guns, rocket-style grenade launcher, AK 47 – enough to start something – except' – he raised his eyebrows – 'nothing was live. The guns were filled with blanks, and the rockets or grenades or whatever they are, are duds or dummies.'

'You're sure?'

'Well, not exactly. That's why my lads are guarding it, but we're pretty sure. The cashier has been helpful. She said that at around twenty to two, the man came into the lighthouse waving a gun and carrying the bag, told her and everyone in the shop and exhibition to clear out, and then went upstairs, clearing each floor as he went. About twenty minutes later, another man came in, said he was the police – no – sorry – said he was a detective, told her to call us, and went up. He came down about another twenty minutes later. Like the woman had said, we found that he'd wedged the door at the top shut – with a rocket launcher! – with the other man trapped outside on the platform, brought the bag and its contents downstairs and left it behind the desk. He told the woman that the weapons were safe and walked off.'

'This man – about five foot ten, dark wavy hair,

decent-looking, smooth, even complexion, ordinary clothes?'

'Well, that could be anyone, couldn't it, sir? With respect. But I can go one better. We've got some photos and a bit of video footage.'

The knot of people around the lighthouse had not dispersed. On the contrary, since the drama at the top of the lighthouse and the arrival, heralded by blues and twos, of the local constabulary, with the prospect of reporters to come, numbers had swelled. Sergeant Moore singled out three white-haired people, two men and a woman in their late sixties, all wearing fleeces, multi-purpose olive-green trousers, the kind that have half a dozen pockets, including halfway down the thighs, and sturdy walking shoes with thick laces and many eyelets.

'We've sent these images back to HQ, and we'll look at whatever CCTV there is,' said the sergeant to Nolan. Then he turned back to the trio. 'Can you show the chief inspector what you've got?'

The three jostled forward, each proffering their phone footage. Blurred images jerked out from the three handheld screens – people leaving the lighthouse, looking back with faces of anger, dismay, fear and indignation, parents clasping children. A figure approached from the other direction, only his back captured on camera. More pictures emerged, vague and contradictory, of the top of the lighthouse. There was a hubbub of noise – people talking, the gusty wind and a miscellany of unidentifiable other sounds. Segments of video started and stopped. Then a man came out of the lighthouse and walked towards the car park. Again, the footage caught his back as he went past, but not before a clear sequence from the door, before the videographers, in reflexive unison, turned their attention away from the retreating figure and back to where the action was.

DCI Nolan was not surprised to see the focused, determined face and figure of his closest, most exasperating friend, the person who, at this moment, he wanted to speak to more than anyone.

Chapter 34

In the safe house in Ramston, cabin fever and a nagging anxiety were Angela Wilson's overriding feelings at lunchtime on Sunday. The library in Sandley was all right. She had spoken at the end of Saturday to her assistant Kerry and she and the volunteers had managed without her, and, as agreed before, would do it again on Monday if need be. Mike and Becky had put their own Plan B into operation for the pub. Employing and developing a competent staff was the least Angie would have expected. But being cooped up and inactive didn't suit her, and she was worried about Sterling.

'We can't do anything,' said Becky. 'Not until we get some sort of update. The whole point about being here is that we're safe, but ready to go instantly if we're needed.'

'What about Frank? He could be anywhere. And where is this "update" going to come from? Isn't it time for the police?'

'And tell them what?' said Mike. 'You're right. He could be anywhere. As Becky says, we have to be ready.' He paused for a second. 'We care about Frank too. You know we do. I wish I'd never got him involved, but I've told you the whole story. It's a matter of national security. My back was against the wall, and I had no alternative. I got him into it. I'll get him out.'

'If he's not lying in a ditch somewhere, or dead,' said Angela gloomily. But she was astonished as well. Mike rarely said anything, and he generally showed his feelings through actions, not words.

'Frank's canny,' said Becky, 'and people help him. He should be OK. I reckon we'll hear something from somewhere soon.'

In the end, the source was banal – not a call or text from a burner phone to another burner, or even a landline, or an e-mail via a secure server to a secret e-mail address.

They were having coffee after lunch when they found out.

'Reports are coming in of a major incident at Drangeness Old Lighthouse, thought to be linked to Drangeness B nuclear power station. Locals and visitors are phoning in messages and photos of an aborted attack staged from the lighthouse. We understand that police and other emergency services are attending. We will deliver regular updates to this story.'

Mike turned off the radio. 'South and west – exactly as I told Frank on Friday. It's fifty minutes away. Let's go.'

'If this is about Frank,' said Angela – as one, the Stranges stopped, alert and attentive – 'no more funny stuff – you know – cloak-and-dagger. Frank's too important for that. We should be liaising with the police now.'

'Got it,' said Becky. 'At this stage, that's the way to go.'

Chapter 35

In the silver Mercedes in Fenningstone, listening to the same radio newsflash, Asif allowed himself a small, secret smile. The days when you could listen in to police radio communications with a scanner were long gone. TETRA handsets and Airwave had put paid to that. Even if you had the right equipment, you needed an authorisation code to access the system. Zahra wouldn't understand that, but he might have a small grasp of the notion of breaking news in a free country.

Asif continued listening, hearing how the attack seemed to have been by a lone man with no support and faulty equipment. Amidst the speculation, the newsreader suggested a bodged job. Asif peeled off his headphones. 'Brother, I am sure I have found the target – Drangeness nuclear power station, about sixteen miles west of here. Everything fits with what we already know.'

Zahra rubbed his temples. A migraine always seemed to be just below the surface. 'How do you know this?'

'It's on the radio, sir. What they say was "an aborted attack by a lone gunman". All the emergency services are on the way.' He stopped and bit his lip. 'It will be very busy down there. Perhaps we'd be a bit conspicuous...'.

Zahra looked at him, and then across to Hamid. 'Set the Satnav. How long will it take us?'

'About twenty-five minutes.'

Zahra turned back to Asif and nodded in the direction of the laptop. 'Find me a map of the Drangeness area.'

Asif's eyes returned to his laptop and then through the window. Something bad had happened in Fenningstone. Hamid knew all about it, but none of the others did – not the details anyway. Asif had the sense that things were spinning out of control, and had been since Husain had escaped them at Waterloo Station and during all the time that they had chased and failed to capture the man Sterling. At the same time, they were also coming to a head. He continued doing as he was told, finding the map. He was damned if he did and damned if he didn't.

He refined the thoughts he'd been having for weeks. He could have been an IT technician at one of the universities or colleges around Manchester, commuting in from the town where he was born and grew up, marrying and raising a family in his own community. He'd taken a very bad, misguided wrong turn. He wondered if he'd ever be able to go back. He wondered if he'd even be able somehow to slip away when everything really kicked off, which would be sooner, much sooner in his opinion, than later.

Zahra was speaking to Hamid in their own language, something he had rarely done recently. It was a variant of Arabic that Asif, with his own smattering, could barely recognise and certainly not understand.

'I'm tired, Youssef,' Zahra said.

Hamid looked across. He could only see Zahra's profile – the swarthy skin, beginnings of dark stubble around the jaw line, the long, hooked nose. He concentrated. Zahra never spoke like this, barely even used his first language anymore, and never called him by his first name. 'This country… All these obstacles. A man who always seems one step ahead – through luck and clumsiness rather than by design. That idiot who directs us, demanding everything but taking responsibility for nothing. The men we have to manage, never doing things as they should. The – what do you call them? – the kid gloves we have to wear. We haven't been home for a long time. My family deserves better. So do yours and Rashad's. This is our endgame. The gloves are coming off. After this, we should have enough to look after everything.'

Hamid said nothing and squirmed in his seat. What did 'endgame' mean exactly? Surely the purpose was to emerge intact with mission accomplished. On the other hand, he'd come too far – they all had – to be pulling back now.

Chapter 36

The silver Mercedes glided around the corner where the road from Hykewood to Drangeness that DCI Nolan had travelled down almost half an hour before left the coast and swept inland, in effect marking the border of the desert/scrub.

Zahra turned back to Asif. 'Where is Kurjak's car?'

Asif frowned as he looked at the GPS tracker screen on his laptop. 'It's about two miles behind us on the same road we came down, brother.' He'd been told to say 'brother' to this unnerving man, but as Asif was a Lancashire lad, it felt ridiculous.

Zahra showed no flicker of surprise. He studied the map on one of Asif's other machines.

'There's a police roadblock just up ahead,' said Hamid. 'Not this road, but the road leading off it to the south.'

Zahra nodded. He could see that the blocked-off road led down to Drangeness. The Old Lighthouse and its replacement were clearly marked. There was only one way in and one way out. 'Keep going,' he said. 'Calmly. We're just out for a Sunday afternoon drive, like all the English.' As they passed, a young woman was remonstrating with one of the policemen, phone in one hand and notebook in the other.

'A journalist following up the phone calls, pictures, video footage and all that stuff from the lighthouse,' said

256

Asif. He'd once done work experience in the office of a local newspaper. 'They'll be telling her it's not safe to let her through, and they've got to wait for a heads-up from the person in charge.'

Just under a mile later, there was another police roadblock, again on the road leading off it. Zahra rubbed his temples again. He pored over the map with increased concentration, glancing up only to tell Hamid to slip past the second roadblock. The roads leading off the current road combined with it to make a kind of π-shape. Nothing made sense. He and his cell had been expected to support an attack which they now knew was from the Old Lighthouse at Drangeness against the nuclear power station. But after the attack, how would they have got out? The attack had failed, but the difference between what was planned and what had happened was that he and his cell were on the right side of the roadblocks. Unless...

Hamid steered the Mercedes smoothly on. Now he and the others were going past the bird reserve and the lakes on both sides of the road, half an hour after Sterling had come through with Jess Monkton and her children on the way to Appledore.

Zahra looked keenly from side to side. 'Stop here, Hamid.' He pointed to the entrance to the RSPB reserve, where there was a small empty parking area amongst the only trees in any direction, trees stunted and struggling in the harsh landscape, with nothing to inhibit mostly westerlies sweeping in across the flatness. 'Phone Kurjak, Asif. Get him to meet us here. Get everyone else too.'

There was a steady stream of cars leaving the bird reserve, occupants glancing curiously over to the parking area. Zahra could see a small pebble-dashed cottage with plain red tiles beyond and half-hidden by the trees. He got out of the car and motioned Hamid to follow him. In the late afternoon, the wind gusted and swirled, and little flurries of dust spurted up from the parking area. The mid-afternoon sun was beginning to send slanting rays that made the Mercedes glitter sporadically. The hum of traffic on the road to Lydcote rose and fell in a steady rhythm. By the house, a ragged St George's flag fluttered on a shabby flagpole.

'I need somewhere quiet and out of sight for a short while. That cottage might do. If anyone's there, put them somewhere out of the way.'

Hamid nodded and went to the boot of the car, unlocking a concealed compartment containing guns, rope, duct tape and a range of other all-purpose assault and abduction material. He made a selection. Just at that moment, another car arrived with Rashad and Nevin.

'Explain quickly to Nevin and take him,' said Zahra.

Asif watched them go through the trees, hardly qualifying even as a copse, and out of sight to the house. His hands were slippery with sweat. He knew bad things were in prospect and that there was no way out.

Hamid emerged a few minutes later. 'Just an old woman. We put her in the shed and shut her up.' He waggled the roll of duct tape. Zahra motioned Nevin away and put the palm of his hand between Hamid's shoulders. Usually undemonstrative, he wanted to reinforce Hamid's so-far unquestioning loyalty, and he knew he had to be clear about what he wanted. 'Something is very wrong, Hamid. I don't mean everything we have had to tolerate over the last two days – this business with the man Sterling and his infernal luck. The man Strange escaping. Husain nowhere to be found. There is something else. Something more important. And it's inside our organisation. That's why I want to see Kurjak. We'll take him to the house and ask him some questions. Brief Rashad and Nevin and make sure the others are with us. You're the one I trust, Hamid, and you never let me down.'

Hamid nodded. He followed orders. He did what he was told. It all made sense to him, if he even bothered to think about it.

When Kurjak's driver swept him into the parking area in his black Range Rover, the rest of Zahra's cell had also arrived. Kurjak waited for his driver to open the passenger door. 'I am not at your beck and call, Zahra,' he began, 'especially during this whole fiasco.'

Zahra tipped his head. Hamid and Nevin stepped forward and grasped Kurjak by his wrists and elbows.

'What the hell?'

Kurjak's driver stepped forward. Rashad put his hand on his chest. 'Stay with us, brother. You owe him nothing. Zahra is sorting everything out.'

Hamid and Nevin frogmarched Kurjak through the dusty copse to the cottage. There was no garden, just a small bare area of scrubby grass in front of the door. Just inside, Zahra looked up a steep, short, narrow staircase. Stair rods kept a threadbare carpet in place, and the gaps on either side of the carpet going up showed worn wood of a nondescript colour. The parlour on the left of the front door was full of heavy old furniture too big for the room. A large paisley rug covered most of the floor. Ash and charred wood lay in the grate from a recent fire and an ashtray on the arm of an armchair was filled with cigarette butts. The glass lampshade in the middle of the ceiling had a brown, flyspecked tinge. The walls were papered in a small rose pattern which had yellowed and in places peeled from the surface. Random, intermittent acquisition and decoration marked the room rather than any sense of planning. It smelled of woodsmoke, stale cigarettes and a kind of musty decay.

The small room on the right contained a creaky-looking dining table and battered, ancient chairs. Behind that, at the back of the house, was a kitchen with a dresser for crockery, an ancient white-enamelled cooker powered by a canister of Calor gas and an ancient sink. A drip persisted from one of the taps, about every fifteen seconds. The room was clean, but spartan.

After his swift reconnaissance, Zahra settled on the kitchen. He motioned for Kurjak to be secured in one of the kitchen chairs, and Hamid got busy with cord and duct tape. Kurjak had given up blustering, making threats and protesting. The senior man's once-immaculate suit was rumpled, his black, highly polished shoes scuffed and his white shirt and collar stained with sweat that dripped from his face and neck.

The kitchen table screeched as Nevin pushed it under the windowsill. Zahra perched against the table edge, crossed one leg over the other and clasped his hands. He could have been casually networking at a conference, or dealing with pupils' questions in a classroom.

'Kurjak,' he said, 'you haven't been honest with us. I am very disappointed, not just for myself but for my brothers out there in the car park. We haven't been together long. They are not very experienced and they have made mistakes, but they have done what we have asked of them.'

Kurjak's eyes flickered and darted from right to left.

His body seem to hunch and shrink under Zahra's stare. 'I don't know what y…'.

In a lightning movement, Zahra slapped the bound man across the face. The crack of hand on cheek resounded around the small kitchen. The blow caused the chair to rock sideways on two legs before it settled.

'No, Kurjak. There is no time for this.' Zahra paused and composed himself. He'd been in America for many years and was educated there, so his English was of a high standard, but the verb tenses and constructions were complex. 'My brothers and I have been very greatly… inconvenienced the last two days, and the three months before it, all, it seems, so that we ended up trapped at the bottom of a long cul-de-sac in a sad little corner of this awful little country allegedly supporting a stupid, hopeless attempt at an infrastructure attack. Even if the attack had been genuine and successful, we would never have got out. What conclusions can we draw from this?

'Firstly, that you wanted to get rid of us. Husain did us a favour by disappearing, forcing us to go after him; we failed to get to him, or the man Sterling, in time. We were driving past the roadblock when we should have been somewhere within the cordon.'

'Secondly… well, secondly, why should I speculate when you are here and can tell me?'

Kurjak pursed his lips and remained silent. He closed his eyes, as if that might make his desperate position go away, or simply turn it into a bad dream.

'Nevin,' said Zahra, 'put the kettle on.'

Nevin wrestled with the tightness of the dripping tap as he went to fill the kettle. He knew it wasn't for a pot of afternoon tea, English-style.

Chapter 37

'Why didn't you just wait for the police at Drangeness? Surely, job done,' said Jess Monkton. She and Sterling were lazing on a bench licking ice creams, overlooking the military canal at Appledore. He knew the village because his father had been a sucker for uprisings against 'the Establishment' and it had been linked to Wat Tyler's Peasants' Revolt and Jack Cade, so they had had to explore. He was beginning to feel calm again. The trembling and the sweats, a delayed reaction from the recent near-death experience at the lighthouse, and indeed from all the hazards of the last two days, were abating. He hoped they weren't too obvious.

A few metres away, a pillbox, grim and grey, with a mean black slit for gun barrels, guarded the landward side. They could see and hear her boys exploring further down, clearly following instructions – 'Be sensible. Don't go too near the bank. Respect nesting birds and wildlife, so don't be too noisy. The biggest reward might be just lying in the grass, still and quiet, and seeing what turns up.'

'If I'd done that, I wouldn't be sitting on this bench with this ice cream with you and your boys, would I?'

Jess smiled and looked down at the cone in her hand. Then she held it up, bit off the bottom and started sucking the ice cream from the hole. 'This way you get ice cream with every bite, not just boring, dry old cornet.'

'Neat,' said Sterling.

'So why really?'

'Well, it is nice here. I like you, and your boys. I like the way you're bringing them up. But you're right, it's not just that. If I'd stayed, there would have been endless hanging around answering questions and making a statement. Depending on who from Fenningstone nick turned up, I might have been detained for more than a few hours – "just answering a few questions, Mr Sterling". I've got a bit of a rep over there, to be honest. And you can imagine how it works, you being at A & E. Once you're in the system, it's hard to get out.'

'Tell me about it,' said Jess.

'I got someone to contact a detective pal of mine in the force, Andy Nolan, on Saturday morning. Even if he'd turned up, he'd still want chapter and verse. But the most important thing is, what I'm mixed up in isn't over. I just don't know what's next.'

'Go over what's happened. Two heads looking at it might be better than one.'

'All right. Are your boys OK down there?'

'Sure. Are you OK yourself? I can't help noticing...'.

'Yeah, much better now. I won't tell you all of it. That will come out another time. I'll concentrate on the main bits. I got involved in something in Sandley, where my office is. I'm a private detective. I was given a memory stick and a gang that wanted the information on it chased me down to Fenningstone. In Fenningstone I managed to find out what was on the stick – plans for an attack on the power station from the Old Lighthouse. That's why

I was on the train, and that's why I told you to get out of Drangeness. With me so far?'

'The information was for the gang members. They were meant to support the attack, but they couldn't because they didn't know any details. So the man who went up the lighthouse to do it didn't have any backup. The cell structure in operation means that the left hand doesn't know what the right hand is doing until the last minute – or in this case, not at all.'

'But this is the interesting bit. When I got up to the top of the lighthouse, the young bloke up there had a large duffel bag of weapons, but he'd been conned. None of it was live, and the rocket launcher contraption couldn't even point at the power station because it was too long and the beacon housing got in the way. You can imagine how pleased I was when I found that out, and how fed up he was. So I wedged him in up there and joined you in the car park while the police were mustering. And you were right, I was thinking of traipsing over to the main road across the scrub. But the thing is, why all that trouble for a fake, ridiculous attack?'

Jess looked down the canal. It was getting on for four o'clock. It had never been a warm day, but now there was a distinct chill in the bright, sunny air. The placid surface of the canal dimpled and a circle of ripples spread out from the centre. 'The boys are probably lying quietly down there to see what comes up. They have their moments, especially Danny, but they're pretty good. What would have happened if everything had gone exactly to plan, do you think?'

'The young bloke would have had backup – men with real guns and real ammunition – though small arms, not rocket launchers. There would have been the same alerts – maybe later than actually happened. The hamlet would have been taken over – not just the lighthouse but the café and the station and so on. The whole gang would eventually have discovered that the armaments were all dud. The police armed response vehicles would still have turned up, and the roadblocks, and, eventually, air support from helicopters. The terrorists, if that's what they are, would have been trapped. There's only one road out, and they could hardly commandeer the train. Although someone at the top of their organisation had obviously let them down, they probably wouldn't have been inclined to surrender. The result could have been a great big stand-off lasting for hours – days even – with people like you and the boys caught in the middle as hostages. You should have got out straight away, Jess.'

'All's well that ends well. It did seem sneaky just to leave you. So basically, this was a completely pointless, even stupid, activity, unless…'.

'… unless the objective was not an attack on the power station but a red herring…'.

'… and the red herring was to distract the local Fenningstone emergency services for a long period of time.'

'But where does it get me, Jess?'

'Why has *it* got to get *you* anywhere, Frank? Like I said, you've done your bit. I'm speaking professionally now, but shouldn't you concentrate on recovery? Why don't you just contact your mate – what's his name? Nolan – and tell him all you know?'

'I don't work like that. If I start something, I want to finish it.'

There was a faint noise high above. Sterling and Jess

looked up and a silvery machine glittered in the sunlight as it droned off southeastwards.

Jess frowned. 'All right. So why the Drangeness power station disaster plan? Why the Fenningstone emergency services?'

'What are you getting at?'

'Well, if this Drangeness thing is all a charade, it's a charade that has involved people in a particular area, and that surely means it's diverted them from something else in the same area, and even if something else crops up, you don't necessarily take it so seriously. Human nature really. Me and the boys live in Lydcote, which is in the Fenningstone catchment area. And I tell you what, there's an emergency plan for around here as well as Drangeness.'

Sterling trawled his memory. It was a long time since he'd been a copper stationed in Fenningstone. 'You're right. Lydcote Airport.'

'There have been rumours in the town. Secret goings-on. Unrecorded night flights.'

'I should try there then. Long odds, but there's nothing else on the horizon. It'll probably come to nothing and I can go home.'

What he chose not to mention, so that Jess would keep thinking the odds were long, was the memory of the crumpled-up paper in Husain's coat pocket back in Joey Miller's flat – the Liberty analysis of extraordinary rendition, and how it might still be going on. That, and everything else so far, made Lydcote Airport an even more plausible next destination.

There was a rustle in the grass behind the bench. Jess pretended she hadn't noticed, and Sterling cottoned on. They stared quietly ahead as they waited for ambush, and were suitably terrified when the boys attacked.

'We saw a heron, Mum,' said Danny.

'And moorhens and their chicks,' said his brother.

'Excellent,' said their mother. 'You don't always have to be still and quiet, but it sometimes pays dividends. And you managed to creep up on me and Frank. Come on. Let's go home. I've got to get into your great-grandfather's shed, and then we've got to drop Frank off at a footpath at the other end of the town.' She looked at Sterling, her face full of irony. 'A man's gotta do what a man's gotta do. Right, Frank? Even if it's a stupid wild goose chase.'

Sterling was savvy enough to know that her anger was somehow displaced and not directly to do with him. She hadn't mentioned the boys' father. Perhaps it was to do with him. It wasn't any of Sterling's business. 'Something like that,' he said.

'What's in Eddy's shed, Mum?'

'Wire cutters,' said Jess.

Chapter 38

'You know him, sir?' said the pockmarked sergeant as they looked at the camera footage.

'Yes,' said Nolan. 'That is one Frank Sterling.'

The sergeant's eyebrows went up.

'Name familiar, sergeant?'

'Yes, sir. A bit of a...' – he searched for a word – '... legend in Fenningstone, possibly not for all the right reasons. A reputation as a maverick, amongst other things.'

'Too right,' said Nolan. 'Well, he was heading towards the car park, but I highly doubt whether he had a car, and if he did, the roadblock would have stopped him. He probably came on the light railway, and we've stopped that. But... he's personable, sergeant. Somehow people always seem to trust him, and when they trust him, they help him. Have a word with the officers at the roadblock and see if anything odd has happened up there. We might even get lucky – he could be in one of the cars in the queue.'

The sergeant dipped his chin and spoke into the radio strapped to his chest. Then he turned back to Nolan.

'How did the man with the weaponry get here?' said the detective. He chose his words carefully – to say 'terrorist' or anything similar would be jumping to conclusions.

'There's an SUV in the car park which we think is his. We've managed to match people to vehicles in every other case. We checked for booby traps. It's clear.'

'And there was no one with him?'

'We've searched. We've spoken to everyone up here. The roadblock's in place. Really, all the indications are that the guy was by himself.' The sergeant's phone buzzed. 'Hang on a second, sir. The roadblock team is coming back to me. They let one car through. A kid was having an asthma attack. They took names and registration number. Four in the car – wife driving, husband and two kids, the oldest having the attack.'

'That's it,' said Nolan. 'I'll bet you a pound to a penny the "husband" was Frank Sterling. Have the registration number traced and we'll take it from there.'

'Right, sir. There's something else. A van's arrived and the three people in it say they have important information for the officer in charge.'

'Give me your phone.' Nolan spoke to one of the roadblock officers. 'DCI Nolan here. Give me the names of the van people.' He listened. 'Let them through. I'll meet them up here.' He listened again. 'No, no press – not at the moment – not until things have settled down.' He handed the phone back to Moore. 'Let's go and see the prisoner. While we're doing that, can you get a couple of your men to section off an area of the café as a kind of command centre? Have them take the people in the van there, and when we've finished in the lighthouse we'll go over. I suspect we'll get more from them than this bloke.'

In the lighthouse, the young man sat in the far corner from the cashier's desk and gift shop area, under a large map showing all the shipwrecks on the Goodwin Sands since medieval times. It was black with tiny figures of ships and dates. Three burly officers towered over the shrunken figure, carbines held across their chests.

Nolan and Moore walked over.

Nolan squatted down in front of the man. 'I'm Detective Chief Inspector Nolan. Who are you?'

The man stared ahead, not focusing, not making eye contact.

'Do you understand me? You're in very serious trouble. You'd help yourself a lot if you answered my questions. What were you doing at the top of the lighthouse? Where did you come from? Who sent you?'

The man continued staring. Nolan repeated some questions and added some others, cajoling one moment and threatening another. The man sat as still as the map above him.

Nolan got up. 'Have him taken to Fenningstone, Sergeant,' he said, deliberately loud enough for the man to hear. 'I don't think he knows anything important. He's just a dupe. Anyway, we don't want the monkey. We want the organ-grinder.'

The man's expression changed – a mixture of resentment and shame – but he still stayed silent. Nolan waited a few moments. 'OK, take him,' he said eventually. 'He may not be talking now, but he will. We don't have any shortage of offences to charge him with.'

Nolan knew from the first few minutes of meeting him that Sergeant Moore was quick and bright – a man he could bounce ideas off. 'It's ludicrous, isn't it?' he said. 'Really, you could hardly make it up. A man takes over a lighthouse by himself to shoot a rocket at a power station but doesn't have any live ammunition. And anyway, what damage can a handheld rocket launcher actually do to a power station? What conclusions do we draw from all that?'

'It wastes our time and ties up our resources.'

'I agree. But it doesn't just tie them up; it diverts them. It could have diverted them for hours, but I think things went off at half-cock for the organisers. Come on, let's go over to the café and see what the Stranges and Angela Wilson have got to say for themselves.'

'You know them too, sir,' said Moore.

'Amazing, isn't it? Anyone would think I am some sort of genius copper, knowing everyone and having them come and see me, when in fact they are also friends of Frank Sterling. As per usual, the same as a private investigator as when he was a plod like us, he's got himself mixed up in something, and somehow the rest of us get drawn in as well.'

The wooden duckboards from the Old Lighthouse to the station café clanked under their shoes and boots. On the way, Nolan's phone pinged. Moore went on a few paces and waited. *He's discreet as well as quick on the uptake*, thought Nolan. He said his name into his phone and listened. As expected, initiation of a disaster plan meant that a superintendent had to take control as soon as possible. Nolan knew Elsworthy, and knew that he was sound and without ego. He gave a situation report and waited.

'Any point in me coming over to Drangeness, Mr Nolan?'

'I don't think so, sir. Not at the moment. I'm sending the man who staged the attack, if that's what you can call it, over to Fenningstone now. The man who apparently stopped it, Frank Sterling, seems to have disappeared. We're thinking that he slipped past the roadblock with people he met, and we're trying to trace him through ANPR.'

'Not *the* Frank Sterling.'

'Yes, sir, I'm afraid so.'

'Still a thorn in our sides, even now. We'll leave it there for now, Nolan. Keep me posted, and tell me how you get on with these friends of Sterling's. If you're right, and Drangeness is a diversion, we must be ready for the real thing.'

In the L-shaped café, Moore's colleagues had sectioned off the bottom part, and seated around a table with a plastic red-and-white-checked table cloth were Mike and Becky Strange, and Angela Wilson. The last time Nolan had seen them was after Sterling's case at Earlsey Tech. In fact, thinking about it, that was when he did tend to see them – after roller coaster rides of crime, hazard and often death instigated, or at least latched onto, by Frank Sterling.

He sat down at the fourth chair, and motioned Moore to bring over a fifth. He saw the three coffee cups on the table. He turned to a nearby police officer, the one who seemed to have prepared the meeting area, and asked for more coffee and two more cups and saucers.

From outside the little cordon, the café was full of noisy people made hungry and thirsty by all the drama and frisson of danger and incident. The staff behind the counter running up the long arm of the 'L' were harried but cheerful. Takings would be high, and with luck, so would tips. The young girl at the till totting up the cost of the food and drinks on the self-service trays had a ruddy face, and wisps of perspiration-dampened strands of hair stuck to her face.

'This is Sergeant Moore of our Armed Response

Unit,' said Nolan. 'He's my number two here in Drangeness. This is Angela Wilson, librarian at Sandley library, and Mike and Becky Strange, who run the Cinque Port Arms pub in Sandley.'

The group exchanged cautious nods. Nolan could tell that Moore was pleased at his de facto promotion and that he was trusted as an investigator as well as in an operational capacity.

'I'm glad it's you here, Andy,' said Angela. 'We'll get a good hearing.'

'Well, I need an update,' said Nolan.

'What about Frank?' said Angela.

'Frank is all right as far as we know.'

'As far as you know? What does that mean?'

'He was here, but he managed to get out for whatever reason.'

Angela shook her head. Mike and Becky remained still and quiet.

'Tell me what you know,' said Nolan. 'This is not just about Frank. Other things are going on.'

The others nodded at Angela. She had been appointed as designated spokesperson.

It was like a three-quarters-completed jigsaw. That was Nolan's conclusion when Angela had finished her account, and a jigsaw for which, until now, only he had most of the pieces. It wasn't standard procedure to involve civilians in an operation, but times were exceptional, and he trusted all the people round the table.

He summarised. Mike had been kidnapped by a gang, but just beforehand had handed a memory stick to Frank and set him off on the run. Becky and Angela had rescued Mike and they'd all gone into hiding. Frank had been chased to Deeping and then to Dovethorpe, where he'd met the intelligence officer, Husain. Frank and Husain had got to Fenningstone, where it looked as if they'd stayed with Joey Miller. They'd found out what was on the memory stick, split up, and then Frank had travelled down to Drangeness, on the South Kent Light Railway, to thwart the attack on the power station.

Frank had disappeared, and so had Husain. The role of the man with the prosthetic leg was largely unexplained. He was at Fenningstone, awaiting further questioning. Miller was sedated in hospital after his beating up, and the gang chasing Sterling had not been far away when that had happened. The attack here in Drangeness had turned out to be just a stunt, a feint of some kind, and not even that well organised.

The whole thing was a mess. To describe Moore as flabbergasted, a man who'd seen and heard much in a short career, would have been exaggerating, but he shook his head a fraction as the steam from his coffee wisped up around his face.

'I don't know why I don't have you all arrested,' said Nolan, only half-joking. 'We've wasted so much time, and we still are. If nothing is happening here, the odds are that it's planned for somewhere else in our catchment area while our resources are fully deployed.'

Angela was indignant. 'My experience of you lot is that we'd have been wading through your bureaucratic treacle for ages before anything happened.' She wound herself up for a rant.

Mike Strange, who'd sat in characteristic silence during the information exchange, straightened up. 'So, if not here, then somewhere else. I've just remembered something about Mohamed Husain.' Those around the table fell silent and looked across at him. In the rest of the café there was also a sudden, eerie silence, as at a dinner party when everyone takes a sip of wine or a mouthful of food at the same time. 'He's a talented intelligence officer,' mused Strange in the stillness, 'and I imagine he's always known more about this affair he's let on, but some things he's had to do have become… distasteful.' Strange paused. 'Including involvement in extraordinary rendition. I don't think that's changed.' The hubbub in the café resumed. 'Perhaps, having seen this as a diversion,' he continued over the swell of noise, 'it's an airfield you should be looking at.'

'Lydcote,' said Moore.

Chapter 39

Even with his earphones on, even with the blustery
April wind gusting over the scrub and the lakes, even
inside the silver Mercedes, Asif could hear Kurjak's
screams – rising to a crescendo and fading, then rising to
a new crescendo. In that respect, they were like babies'
wailings when they are distressed. But Kurjak's suffering
was far beyond distress and into another terrible,
unimaginable dimension, and in him there was no
wellspring of courageous defiance as in Joey Miller.

Once so discontented, so angry, so radicalised, Asif
felt a heart-wrenching nostalgia for his semi-detached
home and family in the small town on the outskirts of
Manchester. He searched for some music that might
drown out the awful noise.

In the kitchen of the house, Zahra looked on his
efforts. Sometimes he delegated the wetwork, as he had
with Mike Strange near Sandley. Sometimes he took
pleasure, as now, in doing it himself. The man passed out
on the chair in front of him was hideously disfigured.
Blood and urine mingled and pooled on the worn lino
of the floor. Zahra motioned for Hamid's gun.

Asif flinched again when he heard the sharp crack of
the weapon's discharge. At least the screams had stopped.

Zahra and Hamid emerged from the cottage. Hamid
gestured for all the members of the cell to gather around

Zahra in the shelter of the copse. Generally, Zahra commanded and expected everyone to follow without question. But his training and experience made him realise that blind obedience, fuelled by fear and promise of reward, was no longer enough. Even those at the periphery would know that something had gone wrong, that things were falling apart. He was told he had charisma. Now was the time to exercise it.

He stood in front of his twelve-man cell, clasping his hands in front of him, his feet apart and slightly splayed. He'd known Hamid and Rashad, next to him, for decades. He looked over the faces of the others – those he'd known only for a few months. There were a couple of Bosnian Serbs, like Kurjak. They might be difficult. Nevin was Scottish, from one of the satellite towns round Glasgow. Four men, including Asif, were from the Manchester region. There were the two Poles who had helped with the Mike Strange interrogation and a man from Ulster.

Zahra didn't dwell on what might have motivated a less motley and more ideologically committed group. The men in front of him were not interested in his story of oppression as a marsh Arab. They had stories and grievances of their own. They weren't interested in religion or ideology. Except for Asif, who had joined by mistake, money was the motivation.

Zahra began with praise. 'You have all done well and showed commitment. You have been loyal and effective.' He continued in that vein for a few sentences.

Hamid stared glassily ahead. He knew Zahra's real views about the incompetence and amateurishness within the group.

Zahra scanned his audience, making eye contact with

each of the men. 'All this makes what I say now even worse. This is what has happened. Kurjak and our other so-called bosses have betrayed us. Our alleged role was to support a power station attack from the lighthouse at Drangeness. But there was never meant to be any real attack. The plan was for us to be caught within the cordon that we have just avoided. In one way we owe the men we hunted – Husain, Strange and Sterling – a debt. In the end they drew us away from pointless failure as worthless decoys. Now we know the real objectives of our so-called leaders. We have become a troublesome group and must be destroyed.

'How? Our organisation has captured a drug cartel accountant. A deal has been done with the British security services to send this man abroad, outside British jurisdiction, for torture and interrogation. The lighthouse fiasco was to distract the local emergency services, while the man is taken by aeroplane from an airport only four kilometres from here.

'Now we have a choice. We can melt back into our former lives and give up the promises of money that were made to us. Or we can be bold, seize this man for ourselves, and take all the profit from his ransom. I choose boldness, revenge and money that will transform our lives. Are you with me?'

The effect of Zahra's personality was predictable. The men before him gave out a ragged, multilingual cheer and shook their fists. On the fringes, Asif closed his eyes. 'Oh shit,' he whispered.

Chapter 40

Jess parked her car on the pavement of a new estate on the northeast outskirts of the small marshland town of Lydcote, the nearside wheels over the kerb. In the early evening, the gusty wind had dropped and light was leaching out of the cloudless early evening sky. The sun's dying rays tinged the fading blue with streaks of orange. At the end of the road, houses to the left and playground to the right, there was a large farm gate and next to it a smaller one for walkers and dogs. The end dwelling, with a black BMW in the driveway, looked inviting and cosy set against the abrupt desolation of the open country.

Sterling had met Jess's grandfather Eddy in their neat council house and admired his record collection, an eclectic mixture spanning the decades but principally comprising American country, including Johnny Cash of course, rhythm and blues and folk. Now the old man was looking after the boys as Jess did her final favour. Sterling was curious about the set-up, but Jess had not been forthcoming. All that would have to wait till the end of his current adventure.

'It was all fields here when I was a kid,' said Jess. 'I used to tag along with my brother and his mates. We went everywhere in those days. Out in the morning, back for lunch, out in the afternoon. If you didn't know the town, you'd be hard pushed to know how to get to the footpath.' Words gushed from her as they approached the gates. 'Right. I've got your bag safe at home. You've got the wire cutters and the torch. Very wise to turn down the gun. Highly dangerous. You're sure about the phone?'

'Yep.' Sterling had turned down Eddy's World War II service revolver, encouraged at the time by Jess's surreptitious roll of her eyes and waggle of warning forefinger, and a spare mobile for fear of his location being traced.

Jess pointed diagonally across the field. 'Remember what I showed you on the map. You can see the track. Basically, you go diagonal until you come to the drainage ditch. Then you follow the ditch up until there's a board to cross it over. Then diagonal again to the next ditch and follow that. I think there's a proper wooden bridge over that, for cattle as well as walkers. Diagonal up to the old railway line and follow that. You'll see a stile on each side. The trains stopped years ago. I can't remember what's after that, but you'll see the airport buildings somewhere in front of you. The footpath goes around the bottom of the runway. There was no fencing when I was last around there, but that was years ago.'

They reached the gate. 'Thanks, Jess. I really appreciate your help.'

The young woman ran her hand distractedly through her fine hair, sweeping strands that had escaped her ponytail from her face. 'I must be mad myself, aiding and abetting a madman. You men. You're like children, all the thrill-seeking.' Her face was flushed and angry.

'What's your problem, Jess?' Sterling let his irritation come out. 'You've been having a go at me, on and off, since Drangeness.'

She looked into his face for a long moment, as if

committing everything to memory. 'My husband, the boys' father, was like you...'.

'Was...?'

'Exactly, Frank.'

Sterling touched her shoulder and she flinched. 'He'd have told you,' Sterling said. 'It's not thrill-seeking, or maybe not just thrill-seeking. If I start something, I want to finish it. Something dangerous is happening, and I've got a chance to stop it.'

'Yeah,' mocked Jess, 'with your torch and wire cutters. Good luck with that.'

Sterling shrugged. 'I've done all right so far, and something's always possible in any situation. Anyway, this is a long shot. As we said, it could just be a wild goose chase. I could be back here in an hour looking for a phone box and asking you for a lift to Appledore station. I'd better go before it gets really dark. We'll catch up about your husband... and everything. Thanks again, Jess.'

She nodded, still too angry to speak. She turned abruptly on her heels and strode off back to her car. Sterling watched her go, and then turned back to the task in hand.

The earth was soft and spongy on the diagonal track bisecting the early-growing cereal, and the sponginess continued over the next field, which seemed to have been left fallow. Sterling did as Jess instructed, going diagonally northwards and then right along whatever barrier presented itself. On each occasion he came to a crossing, first, as Jess described, the mere board across a ditch, then the wooden bridge with rails over a more substantial, rush-clogged stream, and then, along the railway track, a crossing with a stile on either side. Out in the country, the temperature had dropped a notch or two, and it was eerily quiet, but Sterling was reassured by the accuracy of his friend's directions. Standing on the stile on the other side of the track, he could see the airport buildings about a quarter of a mile away. He calculated that he was about half a mile from the gate where Jess had left him. Sticking to the railway line, he came upon a wide livestock crossing over another stream, or perhaps the same one as before as it meandered through the district, picking his way across over rotten planks and gaps through which he could see dark, still water. He eased around the metal gate, and used his torch for the first time to check the sign attached – a large red 'S' on a white background. It wasn't clear now where the footpath went next, except that he could see the lit-up end of the runway and assumed the path curved around that.

More interesting was the heavily grassed track from the 'S'-marked gate that seemed to follow the sluggish stream down towards the airport buildings, obviously some kind of emergency access. Though he could not see the stream, he knew it was there from the ghostly-pale, tall, densely packed seed heads of the rushes winding into the distance. Jess had said that there had been no fences around the airport when she was a child and nothing seemed to have changed in the meantime. It was likely it was flanked and protected by other means – streams, sewage channels and the railway line. But the wire cutters were reassuringly solid as he took them from the small backpack he'd borrowed and hefted them in his hand. They might be no use for cutting wires, but they'd be useful in a fight. He'd timed his walk perfectly. Just as darkness fell he'd found the track, and the lights from the airport buildings and the runway were bright enough to guide him in to his target.

Sterling kept to the left of the track as he got nearer, keeping in the shelter of the tall rushes. He calculated that he was coming sideways onto the terminal building because there was a large car park at the back and the runway was on his right at the front. Next to the building, on a small apron attached to the runway, was a small passenger jet with canopied air-stairs attached. From the building to the stream further down there was a heavy-duty palisade fence for which his wire cutters were completely unsuitable. Coming the way he'd come, Sterling was on the departure side of the airport. If he wanted to get into the car park and into the back, he'd need either to clamber down into the stream and around the palisade or go towards the jet and through security and passport control. He didn't think he'd get far with that.

The whole airport was quiet. Apart from the jet, no other planes were visible. In the car park, there was a Range Rover and a couple of saloons. Sterling edged as closely to the buildings as possible, choosing a depressed, relatively dry spot in a gap in the rushes close to the turbid water that gave him a view of both the car park and the area on which the jet was stationary. He needed to decide what to do next. He whistled softly – 'Wanted Man' came naturally – and thought of the cosy little house next to the field three quarters of a mile away. Not long ago, he'd seen a spy programme where a recruiter had presented her target with the age-old choice – to have excitement, adventure, the chance to do good, or to fade back into the old, conformist, boring, 'nothing' life. In his damp hidey-hole, the 'nothing' life was infinitely more attractive.

After ten minutes, it was still completely quiet. No one appeared in the car park or anywhere on the perimeter. The jet remained stationary. Apart from one or two lights over the car park and on the runway side, it looked as though the airfield was closed for the night. Sterling decided he'd just get closer in – perhaps as far as the jet – and if everything was really shut, he'd backtrack to Lydcote and phone Jess. He'd done his bit. In fact, he'd done his best. He'd phone Andy Nolan and check if it was safe to go back to Sandley. But just as he emerged from his reedy den, he sensed and then saw headlights winding around what must be the airport access road, coming in the opposite direction from his own approach.

He slipped back into his hideout and waited. Moments later, another Range Rover pulled slowly and quietly into the car park behind a sleek saloon, followed by another, more nondescript car. Sterling counted twelve men emerging from the vehicles. In the gloomy light he recognised the bearded man with the hooked nose, Zahra, and his sturdy henchman. The group spread out each side of what Sterling was certain was the rear entrance to the terminal. From his vantage point, Sterling could not see the actual doors, and the whole group disappeared from view, but then he heard pounding and bustle, a crash and then silence. Then the shooting began, sharp, staccato reports and then more sustained fire, muffled because they were clearly coming from within the building.

In the far distance, Sterling saw flashing blue lights, at least five sets, and willed them to turn from the main Lydcote–Drangeness road onto the access road. A trick of the light, or dips in the terrain, or bends in the road, made them seem to get closer and then recede, until it was certain that they were on their way. In the car park, four armed response vehicles lined up, and behind that an ordinary saloon. Armed police officers poured from the vans, responding immediately to shots from the terminal from defenders that Sterling could not see.

Sterling shrank back in his hideout. The sudden, savage escalation from somnolent, silent, marshland Monday evening to intense firefight, or, if he was thinking straight, two firefights, disoriented him and muddied his plans. He certainly wasn't going to mosey up to the building to have a nose around now. Jess had talked about rumours in Lydcote of dodgy goings-on at the airport, illegal or at the boundaries of legality. The car park and the building were at the moment clearly suicidally dangerous areas for armed men, let alone someone like himself. Any new action, or action he might influence, was on the runway side, perhaps around the jet, and connected to the Lydcote rumours.

There were at least a hundred metres to the side of the terminal that were both beyond the view of police marksmen and out of sight of the tall, bearded man and his gang within the building. A stand-off appeared to have developed on the car park side. Sterling squinted and focused on the area around the jet. Instinct and experience told him that if action stalled in one place, it erupted in another. He wasn't disappointed. While the deadlock continued around the car park, the police being confined for cover behind their vehicles, and prevented by the palisades from gaining access to the restricted area, a huddle of three men edged backwards out of the terminal and towards the jet. Two of the men were armed with guns or pistols, and one was speaking into a walkie-talkie. To Sterling's eye, the third man, the one in the middle, was both a shield and a prisoner, and once they reached the shelter of the canopy, any opportunity for rescue was gone. Sterling stayed where he was. Realistically, he had no choice.

The shots on the runway side seemed to galvanise the police in the car park. A heavily kitted-out officer in a black helmet took up a loudhailer, repeating the 'armed police' mantra that had been shouted at the beginning. Again he was met with a ragged volley of gunfire, and ducked back behind his van. But now his men fanned out each side of the entrance. There were muffled explosions and a whiff of tear gas in the air. Sterling could not see, but was sure that the police had stormed the back of the terminal.

By the air-stairs near the runway, one of the armed men had been hit in the leg. Releasing the man in the middle, the other armed man took his wounded colleague and dragged him up the stairs and beyond range under the canopy. The man left in front of the jet, slight and small in a coat that was too long in the sleeves, looked around short-sightedly, confused by his sudden freedom. Almost immediately, the bearded man and his henchman emerged from the terminal, and just behind them a smaller, younger figure with a backpack.

Brief introductions took place on the tarmac. The small, myopic man's confusion continued, but he appeared to be convinced by Zahra's urgent sales pitch – better than the other fate that had been lined up for him. The younger figure's telephone screen flared and he gestured down the grassy track, as if pointing directly at Sterling, who shrank back into the darkness of his reedy nest. The quartet set off at a brisk pace, the new addition clearly struggling with the unevenness of the ground and the need for haste. After fifty metres, another figure burst, or, more accurately, shambled from the terminal building, looking wildly around and spotting the escapees. He set off in pursuit, half lurching, half stumbling. Even if he'd been fifty metres further away, Sterling would have recognised Husain's roly-poly physique and unique rolling gait.

There was little time to think, and nothing was clear-cut. Sterling didn't entirely trust Husain, but Zahra and his buddy, as well as chasing Husain and himself around east and south Kent, had threatened Stacey and her family and assaulted Joey Miller. So, given that Zahra was certainly his enemy, and Husain probably his friend, this was Sterling's only chance to make any kind of difference at all. When the fugitives had shuffled past, he sprang out from the side of the stream and sprinted to the henchman who was bringing up the rear. Because Hamid was looking back towards the jet, he only sensed movement to his side and in his peripheral vision at the moment Sterling cannoned into him. Sterling reached with his left hand for the gun that Hamid was straining to aim, and with his right hand bashed the side of Hamid's head with the wire cutters.

Having got the advantage, Sterling used rage, festering over two days, and adrenaline, to keep the upper hand once he had seized the gun. Hamid was strong and wiry, but too slow and surprised to be able to stop the second blow. The other three had walked on another ten metres next to the reeds before they realised what was happening, and in that time Husain had reached Sterling. Zahra stepped forward, gun in hand, in front of Asif and the small bespectacled man. Zahra stared coldly at Sterling, crouched over the still body of Hamid, and the wheezing, doubled-up figure of Husain.

Even in the gloomy light that drifted over from the airfield and terminal, Zahra looked tired and diminished, almost as if he simply couldn't be bothered anymore. Although he had the upper hand, he wasn't one for gloating, or summarising, or complaining about the inconvenience Sterling and Husain had put him to – in all his life no one more awkward and irritating – and how he was going to enjoy despatching them. He simply steadied himself and raised his gun, pointing it directly at Sterling. Sterling swallowed and his stomach churned. Why hadn't he done things differently? Why hadn't he been a bit more cautious? Why hadn't he used his head? He closed his eyes, awaiting oblivion.

Instead, there was a soft clunk, a loud crack and the sound of a bullet humming off into the darkness. When Sterling opened his eyes he saw Zahra reeling from a blow from the young man's backpack. Husain was wheezing, but that wasn't the only reason why he was bent over. As he straightened he held up his own gun and shot three rounds rapidly into Zahra's flailing body. Propelled by the bullets, Zahra lurched into the reeds and fell with a splash on his back in the slimy water, Ma'dan returning to marsh. Sterling rose shakily to his feet. He'd consistently underestimated his former travelling companion. He walked over to the stream. Zahra lay amongst the crushed and crumpled rushes, blood gushing from a chest wound, his eyes staring sightlessly into the night sky. Sterling knelt down and reached for the neck that had no pulse.

The small man looked dazed and confused, the

consequence of long internment, the young man Asif defiant and relieved. The commotion on the grassy track had caught the attention of armed police in the car park.

'Frank,' said Husain, 'we can't stay here. This man was going to be illegally rendered, for torture and interrogation.'

'Not my problem, Mohamed. Anyway, mixing with those blokes,' – Sterling nodded at the unconscious form of Hamid, and Zahra, half in and half out of the stream – 'he probably deserves it.'

Husain shook his head. 'That's not how we do things here, or not how we should do things. I really believe that. Otherwise we're like any rogue state. If we go back to the terminal, the other spooks will pull rank on the police and he'll be gone – no habeas corpus, no legal process, no rule of law. Frank…'. Husain was pleading.

Sterling looked back towards the terminal and over to the runway. Husain hadn't turned out very reliable, but he wasn't a bad bloke, and hadn't actually done Sterling any harm. 'Come on, then. I'm not planning to go back there either. Who wants to get arrested and be detained all night? I got here across the fields. I'll get you to Lydcote and then you'll have to sort yourself out. You've got your wad of cash, I expect.' Sterling turned to the young man. 'You saved our bacon. Do you want to tag along? Same terms – sort yourself out in Lydcote.'

Asif nodded and slung his backpack over his shoulders. He held up his phone. 'I can probably help if we get lost.'

The newly formed quartet walked off into the enveloping darkness just as two armed policemen emerged on the runway side of the terminal building. By the time Sergeant Moore had secured the airfield, exchanged harsh words about jurisdiction with the shadowy agents who had emerged from the plane, established the body count, including Zahra, set up an emergency dressing station for the wounded, including Hamid, and updated a shell-shocked CS Elsworthy and a more sanguine DCI Nolan, Sterling and co. were long gone.

Chapter 41

Getting back to Lydcote should have been as straightforward as coming, just by reversing the directions – right and down after each barrier, diagonal left till the next one. The first part was easy enough, along the grassy track to the 'S' gate, across the cattle bridge and almost immediately over the stiles of the railway line, but finding the diagonal at the side of the railway track was difficult in the dark.

When Sterling had found it, they paused for the small man they had rescued, who was finding the obstacles and the spongy earth difficult. He and Husain spoke occasionally in a foreign language, possibly Spanish. His long incarceration had given him a passive, sheep-like quality. Sterling and Husain moved away from the others as they rested.

'You're not the slouch I had you down as, Mohamed. I never thought you'd use the gun.'

'You knew about that? Well, we get training, obviously. Anyway, you've sprung a surprise or two of your own, Frank. I didn't expect you to turn up here.'

'You were careless. I found something about extraordinary rendition in your coat pocket the same time as I found the gun. Then I had a hunch about the airfield, and I got a bit of help.'

'I thought you might have. In the short time I've

known you, I've come to know how skilfully you enlist help.'

'Whatever,' said Sterling. 'When did you know Drangeness was a red herring? It was when you translated the last message in the ice cream van, wasn't it? You weren't that bothered when I gave you and Chambers the slip at Hykewood Station.'

Husain looked away.

'Come on, Mohamed, tell me. I'm doing you a favour here.'

'No, not then. I phoned my handler in the early hours this morning and he told me the extraordinary rendition plan for Lydcote.'

Sterling remembered the phone cradle that was askew on the breakfast counter. 'That's what did for Joey.'

Husain looked down. 'I'm very sorry. I'd no idea it would work out like that. I didn't plan for you to be my fifth column either, Frank, but you going like that at Hykewood Station solved my problem. To be honest, you leaving me in the lurch salved my conscience for my earlier… fibs.'

'Easy to say about Joey,' said Sterling. 'And as far as I can see, I may have done a couple of sneaky things to you, but you totally bamboozled me – it's hardly… proportionate.' He was angry about Joey and Husain's role leading up to the assault, but there were still things he needed to know. 'How did you get to the airport?'

'Taxi. And when I got there I befriended the chef and hid in the kitchen until the firefight started and I saw my chance. The chef and I had… shared interests, and I made it worth his while.'

Sterling nodded. 'Who's the kid?'

'The cell's little intelligence wizard, with his laptop

and phone, keeping them on our heels. I'm afraid he was probably the one who tracked us in Fenningstone, though he didn't do any of the operational stuff. He got radicalised, then he joined the wrong group, and now I reckon he just wants to go home to Manchester. He's played a clever hand if you think about it, bashing Zahra and helping us. He hopped off the wrong horse and onto the right one.'

'What about this other bloke?'

'He's a drug cartel accountant. What he doesn't know about the organisation isn't worth knowing. His strategic importance and insights into the global illegal narcotics trade are priceless to the anti-drugs agencies. He fell into the wrong hands – well, a new set of wrong hands – and was actually getting sold for extraordinary rendition by the very people who were meant to be protecting him. The whole deal is all about money. Sold to our lot for £2 million – for interrogation and torture in some friendly country not so keen on human rights.'

'What are you going to do with him, Mohamed?'

'It's all politics, Frank. There's no rogue in my section. That was just another convenient misdirection. He's going to face the music, but we're going to shield him from the section doing extraordinary rendition, and make sure everything is done the right way. We've still got a bit of conscience. We'd better get moving.'

After false starts and tracking back, the group eventually found its way to the gate and the little semi-detached house on the edge of the countryside.

They walked through the estate to the cemetery on the other side of the main road. Sterling had fulfilled his side of the bargain. 'They'll come for you eventually,' he said, addressing Asif.

'I expect so,' said the young man. 'If it comes to it, can I say how I helped you back there?'

'Let's cross that bridge when we come to it. There's a lot on the debit side of the ledger.' Sterling pointed out the essentials. 'Unless you've got something else in mind, buses to Fenningstone at that stop. Buses to Hastings here, via the town centre. Mohamed, you'd better give him some cash.'

The young man picked Hastings. Sterling could see him texting the bus stop code for the next bus.

'What about you, Mohamed?'

'We'll be making our own arrangements, Frank. This man won't run. He may be a financial wizard, but he's a stranger in a strange land. Besides, I'm the devil he knows.'

'This is it, then.'

'This is it, Frank. You won't see me again. I'm sorry about how I treated you. I regret that I didn't trust you more. I'm sorry about Joey.' He fished in his pocket, pulled out his cash and handed over a bundle of notes. 'For both of you – for services rendered.'

'Don't mind if I do, Mohamed. I can't afford to be proud, and this is language that Joey understands.'

'Thank you for your help. It's been… an experience. Take care.'

The two men shook hands, and Sterling strode off down the street, past Asif at the bus stop, and into town.

Outside a pub next to the church, he found a phone. Inside, he closed his eyes and leaned against the metal-framed glass, the universal phone box smell of stale air and cigarettes assailing his nostrils. Mind and body were flooded with a sense of extreme tiredness that overwhelmed all other feelings. Rallying, he dialled the number and waited for the pick-up. 'Can I order a taxi to Appledore station? I'm just outside the Red Lion in Lydcote.'

'Certainly, sir,' said Jess, entering into the spirit of it. 'It'll be five minutes. I'll bring your bag. Have you got the torch and the wire cutters?'

'The torch, yes. But I'm afraid I dropped the wire cutters in a sewage drain on the way back.'

'Never mind. The police have been round. They tracked my number plate.'

'Yeah?'

'The boys were in bed. The officers have gone now. I didn't tell them anything. There was nothing to tell really – just said I dropped you in Lydcote. But you've got a story, I bet, haven't you?'

'Yup. I tell you what, before you put me on the train at Appledore, what about a cup of tea? I'll tell you and Eddie all about it.'

'You're on,' said Jess.

Chapter 42

'If we go through the whole thing again, Angie, as far as we all understand it to date, you're not going to run off to old Mamujee and spill the beans, are you?'

Sterling and Angela were sitting in the snug of the Cinque Port Arms with Mike and Becky Strange, a few evenings after the Drangeness incident and the shoot-out at Lydcote Airport. Pandit Mamujee, an Assistant Chief Constable in the Kent force, and Angela had been seeing each other since Sterling's Earlsey Tech case.

Angela gave Sterling the dreaded Wilson stare. He sat up straight and shuffled awkwardly.

'I don't think I really need to dignify that with a response, Frank, but I will anyway. You are my dear friend, and I am very fond of you. I'm very fond of Pandit too, and have high hopes for the relationship with him, but I would never "run off" and tell tales out of school, and he would know full well not to take advantage of our friendship for professional purposes, and the consequences if he tried to. In short, if you tell me something in confidence, it stays confidential. Does that address your query, both from my angle and his?'

Mike inspected a beer mat. Becky hid a smile by sipping her wine.

'Yes, completely… Sorry, I wasn't thinking properly. Mike, I reckon you can start us off, with your contacts.'

Mike sipped his water. 'There are a few interwoven strands to it – Zahra's cell, the larger network that the cell was part of, and two branches of the intelligence services that were at odds with each other – we might as well call them SI5 and SI6.

'Zahra and his friends were always problematic to the network. Zahra was a kind of guerrilla-for-hire around the world. His family got him out of Iraq and he received a higher education in Florida. It's not clear when he was started along the route he chose, but he popped up in various spots, fomenting trouble and sometimes masterminding atrocities. In a way, he'd gone rogue and was beyond managing when he came to England to lead a home-grown cell here – the cell that Mohamed Husain managed to infiltrate.

'The network he was part of doesn't have any kind of religious or ideological orientation. Everything is about money. Its leadership looked globally for money-making opportunities, and getting hold of a drugs cartel accountant – we still don't know how – was an excellent one. So they negotiated to "sell" the man you said you escorted from Lydcote Airport, Frank, to one British intelligence branch – SI6 – for extraordinary rendition. They obviously came up with the idea of a dummy attack on Drangeness power station, ordering it to be supported by Zahra's cell, firstly to ensure that the cell was destroyed and its members captured, and secondly as a diversion from the handover at Lydcote Airport while the police and other agencies were otherwise occupied.

'Husain and his branch – SI5 – were and are against extraordinary rendition.' Mike looked through the window of the snug and into the street. 'Mohamed's a funny one. He'd been involved in extraordinary rendition and had come to find it distasteful – states exporting torture to more compliant states. So part of this whole episode, for him, is about redemption, even if that's in a more Christian than Muslim tradition.

'Anyway, Husain's role was to find out what was going on and disrupt the plans of the network and SI6. Husain's talented. You can't penetrate a cell like Zahra's for a few months and not be good. The trouble was that in the end you can't avoid mistakes, and that's when he made a run for it and involved me, knowing that I share his and SI5's views on extraordinary rendition. So I was happy to help.

'He got away. I didn't. So that's why I handed my memory stick to you, Frank. I think we know most of the rest of it. Zahra and co. captured me. Becky and Angie did the rescue. You went on your journey around the coast to Lydcote, picking up with Husain in Dovethorpe. The Drangeness thing – Kurjak and his organisation must have arranged the fiasco at the lighthouse. Zahra, having been betrayed but having escaped, tortured Kurjak, the network leader, and switched his attention to rescuing the accountant at Lydcote, presumably for a mixture of revenge on his network and a money-making opportunity of his own. If it had come off, he could have struck his own deal with SI6 or sold the accountant back to the cartel.

'If Zahra hadn't escalated things – attacking Joey Miller in Fenningstone, and then torturing and killing Kurjak – maybe the police wouldn't have acted so quickly. Andy Nolan is excellent – quick to work things out at Drangeness, quick to track how you got to Lydcote, quick when the cottage-owner found his wife tied up in his shed and a body on his kitchen floor, and quick to get armed police to the airport.'

'Yeah. Andy. He's good, but he's not best pleased with me,' said Sterling. 'He said I should have got him in sooner. I expect he's said the same thing to all of us.'

'Don't leave town,' said Becky.

'Exactly. There'll be more questions. We get all the hassle, and basically we're the innocent parties. Husain was slippery. He went along with me when it suited him, but he never told me everything, and sometimes he just told lies – all that stuff about his section being compromised.'

'He's a spy, Frank,' said Mike. 'That's what spies do. Anyway, he wasn't completely wrong – SI5 and SI6 being at loggerheads is not far off. People underestimate him. I wondered how he managed to hide himself in the airport before it all kicked off, for example, but he did.'

'Some things we'll never know,' said Angela. 'I'm thinking about us, and our legal position, and whether we should be getting in touch with that solicitor of yours – what was his name? – John Evanston, from your case in Southwood.'

'We shouldn't really have things like stun grenades in the van,' said Becky, 'and maybe we broke the law rescuing Mike. Frank stole a boat and bashed a man over the head with wire cutters at Lydcote, but that's got to be self-defence. The man Zahra attacked Joey and killed the network chief, Kurjak. Husain did for Zahra and then disappeared. What else is there?'

'Surely, something like perverting the course of justice and obstructing police enquiries – applicable in varying degrees to all of us,' said Angela, '– and anything else that can be dredged up.'

Sterling sipped his pint. 'Andy doesn't like loose ends. But if he knows what happened, and so long as no one has got away with anything really evil, he can live with that. We did a bit of law-breaking, technically, but the right people have copped it or are going to cop it. Husain killed Zahra, saving me in the process, and the cell members will be put away for a long time. The other thing is the politics, and Andy is good there as well. Husain and the narco-accountant will be protected by SI5, and negotiations will be conducted between them and the police – in the interests of national security, I expect. Andy can live with the politics as well, if the result is satisfactory. I'll have a chat with him off the record.'

'So we won't contact Evanston for the moment,' said Angela. 'How is Joey, Frank?'

'He's good. He's back home. The attack apparently looked worse than it was, but obviously he's still shaken up. He told me to fuck off when I went down, which, if you know him, is a good sign. We had a pint together and he took Husain's extra wad of money. He accepted my apology and we've fixed up another get-together. I'm really relieved. He's a decent bloke and a good friend. And it'll save you having a go at me for trampling over people when I'm on a case, Ange.'

'At least you're getting aware of it yourself, Frank. Big step forward.'

'I went and saw the ice cream man as well, and squared things with him. The Heselthwaites were all right about their boat, after a bit of chuntering.' He looked down at the table. 'And I'm seeing Stacey.'

'What,' said Angela, 'as in "dating"?'

Sterling nodded and drained his pint. He didn't want to go into it. 'Right, I think I'll go down to the Strand and try The Admiral Benbow. You coming, Ange?'

Angela raised an eyebrow, barely containing her surprise. 'Sure,' she said loyally.

A frown appeared in Becky's forehead, shock mixed with incomprehension. 'You never go down there, Frank. This is your local.'

'It's probably safer down there. Things won't get dumped on me.'

'We help you, Frank. Lots of times.' Hurt and anger tussled in Becky's face.

'By choice,' said Sterling. 'And you love the action.'

Mike put his hand on Becky's arm. He turned to Sterling. 'You're right, Frank,' he repeated. 'It's been bothering me. I did land you in it, and by extension everyone else. I'm profoundly sorry. I owe you, and I'll make it up to you, I promise.' He turned back to his wife. 'Didn't we get some Dover sole delivered earlier this evening?'

'Yep,' said Becky, with a smile. She'd picked up the direction of travel.

'What about Dover sole for you and Ange, Frank, nice and quiet here in the snug, with those chunky chips you like, and some mushy peas?' said Mike. 'I think Jerry's still got some homemade tartare sauce. I'll open a bottle of Prosecco to celebrate another successful case. All on the house.'

'This is not where "making it up" to me begins and ends, Mike, is it?'

'Of course not. This is just for starters. A small goodwill gesture.'

Sterling had been half-standing and half-sitting. He eased back into his chair. 'All right,' he said.